A
DIVIDED
MIND.

December 2019

Pat !
Merry Christmas !
It was so amazing to see you walk through the door!

A

DIVIDED

MIND.

I am so proud of you and your published work.

M. BILLITER

So... my best work to date — and all due to my son's creative imagination

I ♥ U —
Mary xo

TANGLED TREE
PUBLISHING
tangledtreepublishing.com

For information, contact the publisher, Tangled Tree Publishing.
WWW.TANGLEDTREEPUBLISHING.COM

EDITING: HOT TREE EDITING
COVER DESIGNER: CLAIRE SMITH
FORMATTING: RMGRAPHX

ISBN: 978-1-925853-26-1

DEDICATION

I love these pictures because they capture my beautiful boy. Kyle is never without a smile. And he's always game for fun.

Kyle was the younger, smaller twin, who suffered the most from my premature labor. But from the moment the doctor placed him beside me in the operating room, he stole my heart. I saw determination in his captivating hazel eyes that never left mine. He was my survivor, my brave heart.

And this story wouldn't have been possible if it weren't for him.

When Kyle was in his senior year of high school and confessed he was "hearing voices," my maternal instinct was to make them go away. Kyle's reaction was to discover what was going on. My son and I navigated the world of mental health together without any clue of what was ahead.

And again, I saw that drive to live and thrive in his eyes.

And once again, I felt powerless to help. In those times, I often found that the journalist in me surfaced. As a career journalist, I ask a lot of questions. My teenage son wasn't too talkative. I asked questions I wasn't sure I wanted to know the answers to. But what started as a search for answers grew into a fictionalized story of what could happen if a divided mind is left untreated.

Kyle let me into a world I never knew he had endured. But instead of resigning himself to this life, I saw a young man choosing to have a different path. He worked tirelessly with counselors and mental health experts until he found someone in the field who understood and knew how to treat him. There was never an "easy" solution, but Kyle's determination to be more than his disease was heroic. And once again, my son stole my heart.

There were many times when we were writing this story that I wanted to take his hand and steal him away to a time when mental illness never touched his life. But Kyle stayed the course. I've never been more proud or in awe of someone. My son taught me what it means to live life on life's terms and not our own.

So sweet, beautiful boy, this story is for you. By answering all my questions and delving into the darkness, *you co-authored this and gave us a story that was unlike any I've written*.

Kyle, you are my sunshine and bring me more happiness than is humanly possible. It is such an honor to be your mom. I will love you forever.

Mom

***

A note to our readers: While there are similarities to our journey through mental illness, this book is a work of fiction. In writing this story, Kyle and I imagined "What if...?" and let our imaginations run free. The gift of fiction is that it allows the what-ifs in life to live, if even for a moment in time.

If you struggle with depression or another mental illness, you're not alone. Please reach out to someone. Help can be found at the National Institute of Mental Health (NIMH) or by calling their helpline: 866-415-8051

CHAPTER 1

TARA

"WHEN Branson was little, he always did everything first." I glanced at the silver-haired man dressed in black slacks and a white shirt. He sat with his long legs crossed and a legal pad on his lap. His attire, like his demeanor, was monotone. He acknowledged me with a slight nod, the same gesture I gave when I interviewed a college applicant to indicate I was, indeed, actually listening.

"He had just turned a year old, and it was the anniversary of my father's death. I remember because my dad died right after the twins were born, and all these firsts happened together. I was in the kitchen baking something for my mom." I shrugged. "It's just what I did. Anyway, we lived in a condo, and the kitchen was super small. But suddenly Branson appeared in the doorway." I managed a smile and the man nodded again.

"I remember looking over the kitchen counter for Branson's twin brother, but Aaron was still on the blanket where I left him, gumming some toy. Even though they're identical, they're nothing alike." I paused, the awareness of that truth feeling as hollow as it sounded.

"Anyway." I shook my head. "Branson must have crawled to the kitchen, because there he was. And then he stood up." My hand went to my chest. "It was amazing. He was so proud of himself. Then he moved toward me. I dropped the kitchen towel and held out my arms because he had never walked. But I knew...." Tears flooded my eyes, and the only thing I could see was the sixteen-year-old memory.

"I knew he was going to fall, so I reached out for him." My voice shook. "And now...." I bit my lip to stop it from trembling, but I couldn't quell the inferno that threatened to erupt, drown me and wipe out my family. "I see him falling and I want to catch him. But I don't know how."

I lowered my head. My throat burned, raw from mourning every dream I had for my child that vanished with one phone call.

"Mom, when you get home, I need to talk to you about something."

"What?" Even now I can hear my exasperation, the agitation from being bothered at work.

"It's nothing. We can talk about it when you get home."

"Branson." My tone became more parental, more authoritative. It didn't evoke a response from my teenager. "Bran, you have to tell me. You can't do this, can't leave me to wonder. I have a class to teach, and I won't be home for a few hours. What's going on?" I exhaled loudly enough for

him to hear.

What I heard in reply reawakened a maternal instinct that had gone dormant once my sons outgrew the dangers of electrical outlets and choking hazards.

"It's nothing." His voice was flat, emotionless. "We can talk about it later."

"No, tell me. What's going on? Are you in trouble?" I held my breath while my heart beat so loudly I heard it in my ear.

"Mom, it's just that…."

"What?" My mind raced: pregnant girlfriend, drugs, failing a class, fight at school? "Branson?"

There was a moment when the life I had envisioned for my child was still intact.

"I'm hearing voices."

And then it was gone.

CHAPTER 2

BRANSON

"*SO,* Branson, tell me why you're here."

What do you mean, why am I here? You know why I'm here. Because I'm fucked up. I blacked out in school and came to with bloody knuckles.

I rested my left foot over my right thigh, leaned back in my chair, and said, "I'm just going through some stuff right now."

"You want to be more specific?"

This therapist had to be in his fifties. No hair. Overweight. Heart attack waiting to happen. And his clothes weren't right for a high school counselor. Way too formal. Along with his name. *Clive? Oh brother.*

I pulled on a loose thread on my frayed, faded jeans and looked at him without emotion. "I don't feel what other people do."

"Can you give me an example?"

"I don't feel happiness, excitement. Basic emotions that

make you happy. They're gone." His office was surrounded by white-painted bricks, like everything in the high school. But even if they dismantled the school brick by brick, as the construction crews outside were loudly and disruptively doing daily in the school's grand remodeling scheme, it wouldn't change the structure. Some institutions couldn't be updated because they'd always be filled with memories of the people who have come through the hallways.

"Well—" Clive paused like he was carefully considering something. "The emergency intake counselor had it spot-on with depression." This time he leaned forward and the confusion on his face was there before he said, "I'm just surprised she diagnosed you with post-traumatic stress disorder."

Fucking awesome. I shifted in the uncomfortable side chair in his office and glanced at the framed picture of some Asian girl on his desk. *Probably his daughter. Adopted? Or maybe his wife's Asian?*

"Is there any reason why you think you have post-traumatic stress disorder?"

"At a very young age, I was exposed to violence in my house by my father." The response was instinctive. My past was part of my identity. I wore it the same way I wore number eighteen on my track speed suit, had for as long as I can remember. "But," I broke script, "since it happened so long ago, I doubt that's the case. I don't think it's PTSD."

"Then what do you think it is?"

I hate questions. You're the therapist. You should already know the answer. "I'm not sure."

Clive leaned back in his chair and glanced at his computer like there was something on it, but I couldn't see it to be sure. Then he wrote something on his notepad, flipped back through the pages, and I waited. *I'm always fucking waiting.*

"I can see where she got the PTSD, but I don't think it's that."

Didn't we just cover this? For Christ's sake, I just want to leave. I'm hot. Angry. And this guy is fucking irritating.

"Treating the depression is key, because it's like a train on its tracks. Once it falls off the tracks, it never quite gets back up. It'll just continue to get worse as the tracks get older and are left unattended."

Okay, dude, I understand it can get worse. That's why I'm here, so it won't. Still, as annoying as he was, there was something about him that I liked. Maybe it was the dragon posters in his office. And there was no doubt my mind was off the rails.

"Besides the depression, let's talk about what happened at school last week."

I put both feet on the ground, rested my elbows on my knees, leaned forward and stared at him. "I don't remember what happened. I just remember coming to in the bathroom with bloody knuckles."

"Do you remember anything before that?"

My stare intensified. "Not at all."

Clive typed something on his computer and then sat back in his chair. It looked more comfortable than mine, but the guy was seriously pushing the suspension. He had to be like two-fifty plus. "I read that you had a disagreement with a classmate?"

"Yeah, some girl in my poli sci class was using some language I didn't agree with toward one of our foreign exchange students."

"What did she say?"

"This girl was bugging this kid because he was saying 'negro' and she's partially black, I guess. I dunno. She looks white to me, but..." I shrugged. "She flipped a bitch on this kid and said, 'You need to fuck off and quit saying that word.' But he's from Spain and they use 'negro' to refer to the color black. He didn't mean to be offensive. It's a cultural thing. But she flipped out, and that's the last thing I remember."

Clive's round face made one of his blackish brown eyes look bigger than the other. He was like an Escher painting. "When this girl in your class got upset with the foreign exchange student, do you remember what you felt?"

"Anger."

Clive nodded. "And when you get angry, what happens?"

"I black out."

"What was it about this girl or this situation that angered you?"

"Just the way she was speaking to him." I leaned back and gripped the armrest of the chair until whatever fingernails I had left dug into the fake leather. "She was being mean."

"That could be said of many situations in high school. What was different about this one?"

"It was just...."

I tightened my hold on the chair and looked at Clive.

He leaned forward and his gut hung over his pants. The lines on his forehead crinkled like he was genuinely interested in what I had to say—like it really mattered.

"Look," I said, ready for him to change his position about me. Ready for him to lose interest. But the sincerity on his face never wavered. I loosened my grip and spoke directly to him. "She was being really mean. And this kid…." I paused and my voice lost its anger. "He couldn't defend himself."

Clive seemed to chill and slightly smiled. "Understood." He steadied me with his eyes. "And the bloodied knuckles?"

I relaxed against the back of the chair and shrugged. "I guess I punched the bathroom wall."

A full smile broke on Clive's face. "Better the wall than…."

"I would never hurt someone." I couldn't seem to get across to anyone who would listen to me or actually hear me that, while I may have been losing my grip on reality, I wasn't going to lose my shit on someone else. "I took my anger out on the bathroom wall."

"And hurt yourself in the meantime."

I rolled my eyes. "It's kind of like that saying 'If a tree falls in the forest and no one's there to hear it, did it still make a sound?'"

Clive shook his head. "If you don't remember punching cinder block, does your hand still hurt afterward?"

"And the answer would be?"

"It hurt like hell."

When Clive laughed, his whole belly shook. That made

me smile, but then as if on cue, my blistered and scabbed-over knuckles began to sting. "They itch real bad," I said, glancing at my bruised fist. "But my mom told me to leave them alone or it would stop the healing process. How is that even possible?" I looked at my therapist. "Sometimes she makes up the craziest shit just so we won't do something."

"You've got a great sense of humor," he said with a chuckle.

I shrugged. "Sometimes you gotta laugh at this shit or it'll drive you crazy."

He nodded. "So let's talk about your other symptoms. How long have you had these voices?"

"Since around eighth grade, but I never said anything to anyone because I thought maybe they'd go away. But they've never been this bad before."

He scribbled something on his notepad.

Yeah, do the math. It's going on five years now. Five years of suffering. It's been a slow build, so actually five long years of slowly suffering.

"Do they tell you to hurt yourself? To hurt others?"

"No." My tone was sharp and piercing, like one of the many knives I collected. Knives I had to give my mom when I told her about the "static" in my head. I stared at him. "I would never intentionally hurt myself or someone else."

"How often do these voices occur?"

"Most every day." It didn't quite feel like a punch to the gut when I admitted it that time. When I told my mom about the static, it hurt like a pain I'd never felt. I never wanted to have to tell anyone. I could see the sadness in her green eyes, but I just couldn't live with it anymore.

"Now about these intrusive thoughts. Can you tell me about them?"

"I wouldn't like to."

"You don't have to go into detail, but every little bit helps."

"They're very violent, and it happens at least twice a day, at any time." The fear came back that I'd be judged, locked up even. That I'd be alone.

"The Paxil will help with the depression, but sometimes once that's treated, the other symptoms become more pronounced."

Fucking awesome.

"So if that happens, if you start to hear more voices or have more intrusive thoughts, come see me."

I nodded.

"Dr. Cordova will be overseeing your psychiatric care, but it's a dual-prong approach with medication and counseling."

I stared at him.

"It can be tricky, especially in the beginning when they're trying to figure out the best dosage and medication, but we'll work together with Dr. Cordova to determine a course of treatment that works for you. How does that sound?"

Like I wish I hadn't said anything. If there's not a pill to shut off the static, then why the fuck am I here? "Sure. Thanks."

"All right then. This was a good start. Is there anything else I should know?" He glanced at the wall clock, and I knew our time was up.

"It was nice to meet you." I stood and so did he. At 6'1", I was taller than him by maybe an inch, but he easily outweighed me. "Thanks for your help and walking me through this." I actually meant what I said, and I think he saw it in my eyes.

"You're very welcome." He firmly shook my hand. "I'll see you very soon. If you ever need anything, just come to my office."

I opened the door and was thrust into the hallway of my high school, surrounded by the chaos of people running around, trying to get to their next class.

The noise was a welcome relief, because for a minute, it shut out the static.

CHAPTER 3

TARA

"IT'S Wyoming. It's not like there're a plethora of choices for child psychiatry."

"Tara, he's not a child. Branson's seventeen."

I looked at the ceiling of my car and wanted to punch through it. Instead, I gripped my cell phone until it felt like my knuckles would bleed. "Ed, I know how old our son is. My point is that there aren't a lot of psychiatrists who treat *adolescents,* especially in Wyoming."

"In Sheridan there are. We could have Branson in with the best shrink in town."

My jaw tightened. "Well, the children and I live in Casper. Sheridan's a bit too far to travel."

I was pretty sure he grunted over the phone. *Asshole.*

"Well, in Casper, Dr. Cordova's supposed to be the best," he said.

I blew out a mouthful of hot air. "And he normally has a two-month wait list. I *only* got in with him because the school called after Branson blacked out and he was hurt when they found him in the boys' restroom." I closed my eyes, but my son's mangled, bloodied and bruised fist remained. I had held his hand up to my lips and kissed it, something I had done so many times when Branson was a toddler and hurt himself. But he wasn't little anymore, and there was no salve to take away the pain in his eyes.

"Yeah, Branson told me he was sticking up for someone?"

I opened my eyes. The parking lot to Wyoming State University was empty and the sky was beginning to darken. The aspens had lost their leaves, and their naked branches looked like spindly fingers poking through the starless night. The clock on the dashboard read five, but it was getting darker earlier and it felt later. Carson and Jack, my younger children, were home alone.

What the hell am I doing here?

"Tara? Who was Branson sticking up for?"

And then I remembered. I was alone in the car in the college parking lot at work because I didn't want Carson to hear me on the phone with her father, and then for Jack to miss his, who never called. What a train wreck.

Four children from two different fathers. How did I end up with this life?

"Tara? Hello?"

"Uh, Branson thought a foreign-exchange student was being ridiculed, so he spoke up and then…." I shrugged because I didn't really know the end of the story. I only knew Branson left the classroom, and then the vice principal found him in the bathroom. "Branson thinks he punched the bathroom wall. I guess there was blood...." I couldn't finish the sentence. Nor could I break down to the one man who was the least safe for me to be vulnerable around.

Oh my God. Tears poured out of me like rain. I couldn't stop or predict when it would happen; I only knew that since my son told me he was hearing voices, I hadn't been able to get a handle on my emotions. I couldn't control my feelings, and my son feared he didn't have any. Though when he told me about the static, his face grew ashen and his broad shoulders seemed to fold in on him like the weight of the world was bearing down. He looked like a wounded bird, and the pain on his face was something I would never forget.

"He looked so haunted." The thought escaped my lips before I could stop it.

"Branson's not haunted. That's a little extreme."

And as suddenly as my heart had opened, it closed just as quickly. I nodded and swallowed hard. "Dr. Cordova scheduled Branson to visit with the high school counselor so he has someone on campus he can talk to. And the emergency intake counselor put him on Paxil."

"Paxil? What's that?"

"It's an antidepressant, and according to the doctor who was on call—Dr. Valenti? I can't remember her name—Paxil is the only FDA-approved drug to treat post-traumatic stress disorder."

"Branson does not have PTSD." Ed's voice was terse.

Of course not, because that would mean you'd have to actually acknowledge the hell you put us through. "Well, it'd be a lot better of a diagnosis than…."

"Than what?"

"After we went to the counseling center, this Dr. Valenti got us in right away with Dr. Cordova. He didn't come out and say it, but with the voices Branson is talking about, I mean isn't that…?" *I'm not going to be the one to say it. Besides, my son is fine. He's just going through a tough time.* I sat in my car, silently crying—again.

"Tara, what did Dr. Cordova say?" I understood the edge to his plea. The same fear gripped me when Branson told me about the static. I had more questions than answers, and the one person who could fill in the blanks wasn't able to, or didn't want to. I wasn't sure which. My son looked shell-shocked and had retreated from the conversation when I pressed him for more information, just shook his head and walked away.

"Tara?"

I swallowed hard. "Well, Dr. Cordova didn't say anything exactly. He said he still needed to assess Branson and distinguish the voices, like if it's one or more and what they say. I don't know. But voices?"

"Jesus, Tara, it's probably just his conscience freaking him out."

I nodded. That made sense. *I talk to myself. Doesn't everybody?*

"I need to speak with this Cordova guy," Ed said.

"They squeezed us in next week. And Branson will be talking to the school counselor, some Clive Turina."

"Talking to a high school counselor? Are you kidding me?

That's not enough."

"I know!" I hit the steering wheel with my palm. It stung but I didn't care. "I know it's not enough, but I'm doing what I can. I got him into the emergency intake, and because of that, they got us in with Dr. Cordova. I don't know what else to do."

"What time is the appointment?"

My mind blanked. I didn't even know what day it was anymore. "Uh."

"Tara."

"It's next week. It's written on a card. I'll text it to you when I get home."

"Yeah, do that."

"Ed, I think we need to discuss the Navy."

"What about the Navy?" His tone had enough of a bite that I flinched.

"I just don't think Branson should continue his application with the naval academy."

"He's worked too damn hard to just give up, Tara."

"I know that, but with everything going on—"

"Tara, it's final. Branson is going into the naval academy."

"They think he has PTSD. The Navy isn't going to accept someone with PTSD."

"He doesn't have any reason to have PTSD, Tara."

No matter how often it happened, it still leveled me. His denial was mind-blowing. Ed refused to acknowledge the abuse, and therefore it didn't exist. While it aligned with what my domestic violence counselor told me, that an abuser only accepts their reality, it never made his blatant denial easier to grasp. In Ed's twisted version of our life together, my career broke up our family, not his fits of fury. In Ed's world, there was no reason why our son wouldn't be navy-bound.

"What if they don't accept him?" I knew I was pushing the limits with my ex, but I was 150 miles away and didn't have to face the negative consequences of his disapproval.

"Then he doesn't get accepted. I've got to go." The call disconnected.

A thirteen-minute call that seemed like thirty, and I still wasn't any closer to knowing how to help my son. I stared at my phone until the slideshow with individual pictures of my four children surfaced. Branson's picture was the first that popped up.

Branson's head was shorn courtesy of the Navy's summer institute, but even the barber's shears couldn't cut away the hint of golden blond that shone in the sun. Branson always looked like the California-born boy he was, beautiful and strong with a noble look that reminded me of the Bible stories I grew up hearing of King David, the young warrior who battled the giant. Branson was made for greatness, and this picture proved it.

His hazel eyes were wide and alive, his energy palpable, his posture perfect as he stood at parade rest in a red T-shirt and navy shorts, marked with the blue-and-gold Navy insignia. He wore the colors well. A midshipman in dress whites stood between the groups of high school juniors who had been selected to attend the naval academy's summer seminar institute.

Branson had been selected to represent Wyoming. He was one of the tallest young men and the only one smiling in the picture. He stood as proud as Bancroft Hall, which rose majestically in the foreground.

God, he looks so happy.

Pride swelled in my chest and then just as quickly made it shake. I touched the screen, traced his face from just a few months ago. *What happened? Were you okay then? I don't understand. Branson, come back to me. Please. I need you to be okay. Please.*

Sorrow touched deep and spread wide. It felt like it would swallow me whole, but if it meant my son would be okay, then I didn't care. I cried out to a God I had long questioned and wondered if He even existed in our lives.

"Take everything from me." I tapped my chest hard with my forefinger. "Put your wrath on me." But no matter how much I tried to physically hurt, the internal pain was greater. I placed my hand against my chest. "Don't punish my son for the sins of his parents. Just let him be okay. I'll do anything You want. I'll give You anything, just don't take my son. Do. Not. Take. Branson."

I clasped my other hand over my chest and prayed with everything I once believed. *If You are this merciful God, then show mercy on my son. Heal him. Restore him. Make him better.*

Sadness engulfed me, but anger welled outside me like a tornado that touched down on the one person I knew could handle my fury. I hit the steering wheel and raised my fist to the heavens.

I will never forgive You if anything happens to my son. Never.

CHAPTER 4

BRANSON

"SONUVABITCH!" I slammed my locker door shut, but my running shoes and gym clothes still fell to the floor. "Great."

Aaron looked over at me. "What are you freaking out about?"

"My damn clothes fell out of my useless locker." The locker room floor smelled like armpits and assholes, not something I wanted attaching itself to my clothes. I grabbed my shit off the bright blue painted cement floor that practically blinded me.

"Calm the fuck down."

I looked at my twin, who was dressed in cargo shorts, flip-flops, and a gray Hollister T-shirt. "Shut the fuck up."

"Settle down, guys." Coach Walker strutted into the locker room. "Bring that energy to the track." He brushed past me and patted me on the back. The guy was built like a Marine, but with a haircut that contradicted his muscle tone. With long, feathery hair, he looked like a dark-haired Hulk Hogan.

"Sorry, Coach." I stuffed my crap back into my locker, putting my workout bag in front of the clothes to create a wall so nothing would slide out. I quickly shut the door and it locked into place. *Thank God.*

"Come on, Aaron. It's late. I want to go home and eat dinner." *I'm tired of waiting.*

"Yeah, yeah. Just let me fix my hair." Aaron walked past the lockers and toward the double-door exit, then turned right at the blue-and-gold arrow on the wall that led into the bathroom.

I followed behind him. "Why you fixing your hair? There're no girls to impress. Unless you consider Chelsea a girl."

"She's *my* girl. And I'm gonna keep this one around."

Aaron stepped in front of the mirror, tilted his head sideways and combed his fingers through his hair. I didn't know how it worked, but it magically fell into place every time. *Lucky bastard.*

"*Dude,* are you ready yet?"

"If you cared more about your appearance, you'd get girls."

I glanced at myself. I had acne on my chin and forehead, bags under my eyes, and my hair was no longer high and tight like the military preferred. It was shaggy and unwashed, and I sort of looked like I'd been doing drugs. Combined with my turquoise and black striped hoodie that everyone called a "stoner rug" and low-riding jeans, I looked more like a dealer than a decent athlete who'd made the top ten in the state last year.

I shrugged. "Why do I need to worry about how I look when I've already got a girlfriend?"

"My point exactly," Aaron said. "Have you seen Dakota?"

I punched him square in the arm.

He rubbed the spot tenderly. "I'm just stating the truth."

"Wow. You're a dick." I shook my head. "I'm going home. I have way too much homework to wait around for your shit." I turned to grab my backpack when my cell phone vibrated in my jeans. *What now?* I grabbed it and saw "Ed Kovac" flash on the screen. *What does he want?* I held the phone out to Aaron.

"You can't ignore him forever. You know he's calling about what happened at school. He's persistent."

I slid my finger across the screen. "Hey, Dad, what's up?"

"Hey, fella. I was calling to see how you were doing."

I nodded. "Been better. How are you?" I looked at Aaron and rolled my eyes, putting two fingers to my head like a gun and pretending to shoot myself. Aaron stifled a chuckle.

"Yeah, well I heard about the incident."

The incident? It's like Voldemort, the thing that shall not be named.

"I just wanted to make sure you were okay."

"I'm fine, Dad. I just want to get home."

"Oh. Okay, Branson." He sounded wounded, like I'd let him down, which wasn't uncommon.

I glanced at Aaron and cocked my head toward the exit. My brother grabbed his backpack and we headed toward the parking lot, the setting sun bleeding into the sky like a rotten tomato.

"So how're you doing, Dad?" I tried to mask my tone and sound interested when really I just wanted to get home so I could relax in my room and text Dakota.

"I'm good. Just worried about you."

"Well there's no need to be. Everything's been taken care of."

"Yeah, I spoke to your mom."

"I'm guessing that wasn't fun for you guys." I walked beside Aaron. We passed construction workers packing up their tools, finishing their day. *Great, they'll probably be home before I will.*

"We're just worried about you," my dad said in my ear. "Your mom said some intake counselor put you on some medication."

"Yeah." I nodded. "They did it for my own *safety*." My sarcasm seemed to please my dad, because he laughed.

"Fella, there's no reason for you to be on that. You know how I feel about medication."

"I know, but it's just temporary." *Because every teenager has blackouts, Dad. No big deal at all.* I saw my car in the distance. "Well, I'm about to drive. Can I call you later?"

"Sounds good. Talk to you soon."

I pocketed my phone and unlocked my fading dark green '96 Saab. It was supposed to be both Aaron's and mine, but in reality, I paid for everything. And by everything, I meant gas, oil, and the constant maintenance of this death trap we used for transportation.

"Get in." I looked across the peeling hood at Aaron, who was flirting with Heidi, a fellow pole vaulter.

He held up a finger.

I swear to God, if he doesn't get in the car in the next two minutes. I slid into the driver seat and the strawberry-scented air freshener that hung from the rearview was not working. The inside of the car actually smelled worse than the locker room, if that were even possible. I looked over my shoulder to the back seat, Aaron's extra pair of track shoes and socks lying on the floor. *Yep, that'd do it.*

As I observed his mess, I began to hear a scramble of noises. The sound grew inherently louder, like it was coming from the back of my head, but it was unclear, jumbled like the static on a radio.

I turned my head, trying to find the source, but it just grew louder. I looked at the ignition, but my keys weren't in it. I glanced at the radio, but the dial wasn't turned. I pulled out my cell phone, but the screen was dark. The static came in waves crashing against my skull. I pressed my hands against my ears, but it only magnified the volume.

"Aaron!" I yelled, and even with the windows rolled up, my brother looked at me.

I dropped my hands from my ears.

"Bro, you all right?"

I shook my head, then reached over and unlocked his door. He tossed his backpack behind the seat and sat down beside me. "What's going on?"

For a moment, I thought about telling my brother about the constant noise, the unending anger I felt every day for no reason, and the lack of happiness that made me feel empty and utterly alone. But as I stared into his hazel eyes, I saw his concern, and I couldn't burden my twin with my problems.

"I'm just dehydrated."

"Okay." Aaron's eyes were a reflection of my own before I began to lose my mind. He gripped my shoulder, and for a minute it seemed like he knew what was happening, like our twin thing was working.

But then he laughed. "Bro, no need to lose your shit. Let's go home."

CHAPTER 5

TARA

WHEN your child confesses that they've been hearing voices and they can no longer keep the "static" quiet, there's not really anyone with whom to share this revelation. *Who would understand this and not judge? Who won't look at my son differently?* My sister, Serena, wouldn't judge, but she lived in Paris, and the time difference alone made it more of a headache than it was worth. *Nope. Some things are best left unsaid. Besides, I don't even know what these voices say. Maybe it's nothing more than a headful of negative self-talk.* I set my leather briefcase beside my glass desk in my home office and placed my double-shot espresso on its appointed leather coaster. French doors with beveled windows and smoke-tinted glass led into this glorious space that I customized after I bought the house. The walls were painted sage, and thin strips of stained pine molding accentuated the perfectly square shaped room. I inched up my Hugo Boss ankle-length slacks and unbuckled my

Christian Louboutin platform sandals that wrapped around my legs, carefully positioning my red-soled shoes beside one of the upholstered side chairs. I wiggled my bare feet on the thick vanilla-colored area rug that protected the hardwood floors. The rug served a two-fold purpose, keeping my feet warm in the winter and allowing my high-back, deep-seated ergonomic chair to stay in place and not roll away from me anytime I moved.

I lit one of the wicks on the aromatic candle that was perched on the ledge of the bay window and looked out into our backyard. The half-acre had been ambushed by leaves in varying shades of autumn. It was beautiful. The aspen trees were shedding, and their leafy colors lit up our backyard like Times Square at midnight. Part of me wanted to grab Branson's hand and go run through the foliage, but I didn't. I had dinner to prepare, homework with Jack, college applications to either accept or reject, and at some point I had to sit down with Carson and Jack and explain to them what was going on with their older brother. I hoped I could make sense to a twelve- and six-year-old regarding something their forty-five-year-old mom hadn't been able to even grasp.

The list was endless, and it always kept me in a constant state of catch-up. Besides, those days of frolic and fun were gone. My life was a series of calculated actions to ensure the best possible outcome for my family and staying on top in my career was pivotal to that end.

I turned my attention away from the leaf pile and back to the candle, moving it closer to the ledge and lighting the last of the three wicks. It infused the air with eucalyptus and spearmint. Supposedly the combination cut stress and brought serenity. If only a candle could live up to its packaging.

I took a quick sip of my espresso and returned it to its leather coaster before pulling a stack of applications out of my briefcase. I carefully set the crisp, unfettered manila folders beside my laptop. In this room, I had the semblance of control. Everything had a place, and there was a place for everything.

I flipped up the lid to my silver laptop and continued to stand while I typed in my password: Sunshine. Every thirty days my password required to be changed, so I rotated words associated with each of my children. Sunshine was a reference to Branson.

I couldn't dive into that well again, not now. I had too much work to do, and the dean of my department was on my ass to finish the first round of early submissions. Glancing at the stack of applicants, I exhaled slowly. Bad moods did not make for good decisions.

Later.

I sat down and turned my attention to the screen on my laptop. A long list of "friends" was parked on the right side of the screen, and photos and posted comments took up the rest. A stream of new comments and updates continually fed forward. All these "friends" looked happy, their children sane. Then again, almost no one posted their crappy day on Facebook. And those who did annoyed the shit out of me.

I didn't use the word "hate" often, but I hated Facebook,

Twitter, LinkedIn, Instagram, and Flickr. But I was contractually obligated, by both my publisher and the university, to have an active presence on social media. So I posted on Facebook, I tweeted on Twitter, I linked in on LinkedIn, and I snapped pictures and chatted on Instagram and Flickr.

And despite my misgivings about the online society we had become, I was good at connecting in that environment. Next to my profile picture on Facebook were my statistics and a very flattering photo that highlighted the strength of any fair-faced redhead—my green eyes. If my photo didn't impress a viewer, my stats would: Tara Louise Lafontisee, age 45, Director of Admissions at Wyoming State University at Casper, Master of Arts in Educational Leadership from University of Kentucky, Published Author of *Unlocking the Mystery of College Admissions: The Five-Step Plan for Pursuing Higher Education*. My work and education were front and center. To the naked eye, they looked great, even impressive, because that's what I did for a living. I packaged people to look amazing. As the director of college admissions, I knew at a glance whose résumé and transcripts would move forward and whose wouldn't. I knew what students I could market and promote, and what students wouldn't rise above their own GPA.

To someone like me, I knew from glancing at my online profile what was missing: family and relationships. And what was missing on someone's profile was more telling than what was on it. I purposefully sidestepped the two failed marriages and four kids. Those were future relationship killers. And I certainly wouldn't post a comment about my son's recent happenings.

I could only imagine the update: `Hey, everyone, here's some news. My son may be crazy. LOL!`

I couldn't even muster a fake laugh. There wasn't anything funny about mental illness, or thinking that my Branson suffered from anything other than the occasional teenage cold, cough, heartache, or acne. I could not, would not allow myself to see him as anything other than depressed.

Instead of posting about Branson or anything real happening in my life, I posted what high school seniors and their parents coveted at this time of the year: tips on how to succeed with their college application.

`Happy September! The last date to submit an application for early admission with Wyoming State University is fast approaching. Wyoming State University is home to the Posse. We ride for the brand! So what does it take to be a part of our Posse? While a near-perfect ACT score and straight A's certainly make strong candidates, an applicant's admissions essay is often the deciding factor from moving their submission forward. So who are you? What sets you apart? Are you a nontraditional student? Have you had to overcome obstacles to obtain your education? Or perhaps you're the first person in your family who's seeking higher education. Whatever sets you apart,`

whatever makes you stand above the fold, at
WSU, we want to know, so tell us your story!
The Posse's in town—look out!

I added a link to the university's admission page and hit
post. All the university's social media outlets were linked
together, so when I posted on one, it posted on the others.
Later I'd add a fun picture of campus life, and Instagram
would buzz with Posse chatter.

I sat back and stared at the screen.

Who are you? What sets you apart?

It would give parents and students something to chew
on until my next designated feed. It would drive traffic to
our site, create interest, and increase admissions. And more
admissions dollars meant a bigger year-end bonus for me.
Brilliant.

I stared at my questions, wondering how my son would
answer. What would he say? Did he even know who he was
anymore? I flicked away a tear that threatened to spoil the
one thing I was good at. *Keep it together. You're no good to
anyone if you're a crying mess.*

My attitude had taken a serious nosedive after my
conversation with Ed. I didn't know why I always expected
a different outcome when I spoke with him. I married a man
who over time showed me and our children who he really
was: an angry, bitter, abusive man. While I was brilliant at
navigating my career, my compass in my personal life was
seriously misdirected.

When I finally left Ed, I ran right into the open arms

of a cowboy, seeking refuge and safety for my children and me—and for a moment, I thought I had. I got pregnant on our honeymoon, and Jack was born in our first year of marriage. Jeff seemed to embrace the idea of a son, but the reality of parenthood was more than he could handle. My cowboy preferred to spend his time on horseback rather than with his family. It didn't take me as long to leave that time.

Now I was alone, and that was how it was going to be.

"Momma?"

I turned in my chair. Jack stood in the doorway to my office, his hands interlaced and a pensive look on his six-year-old face.

"Hey, little man." I walked toward him.

He looked up at me and his brown eyes filled with tears. Immediately I knelt down. "Oh no. What's wrong?"

"Branson said I'm an asshole and that he hates me."

I pulled my first grader into me and held him, closing my eyes as I felt his heart beat against my chest. For a moment, it was the only sound that mattered.

Jack pulled away. "That's a time-out word. I'm not an asshole."

I nodded. "You're not, and I'm so sorry that happened. Branson's just…." Dread pulled at my heart. I had put off this conversation long enough. "Can you go get Carson for me?"

Jack nodded. "She's in her room."

"Okay, can you run lava fast and go get her?"

A smile surfaced on his chubby face. "Only if you time me."

"Of course." I pulled out my cell phone from my blazer pocket. "Okay." I held my thumb over the timer screen and looked up at Jack. "Ready… set… go!"

I pressed start, and my little man's feet pounded against the hardwood floors as he darted away. I sat back on my legs and watched the timer. How long would it take before I had to detonate my family with the news about their brother? Then Carson stood in the doorway to my in-home office. Sixty seconds.

How long was my call with Branson when he first told me about the static? It had to be longer than sixty seconds, right? Or can a life truly change in a minute?

Maybe it was karma. How long did it take a student to open the envelope I sent either accepting or rejecting them? Sixty seconds? Thirty? How long did they think about that envelope afterward? I already knew the answer to the last question. My email inbox was full of letters from angry parents, distraught students, and high school counselors all making their last-ditch effort for the university to reconsider what was ultimately my decision. I never did. The hard truth about the college selection process was that it boiled down to five admission requirements, and applicants either hit all five or they didn't. It's why my book was a success and landed me in the position I was in. The college screening process I had created was foolproof. It wasn't just an inflated ego talking—my five-step process had been adopted by universities across the globe.

I had shaped Aaron and Branson's academic careers, starting from the kindergarten they attended to their high school enrollment, with my screening process in mind. Every step of their academic lives was calculated on what I knew worked. But there wasn't any chapter in my *New York Times* bestselling book to address the issue of a kid coping with mental illness. Not one. I had chapters devoted to kids in trouble, kids on probation, even kids with drug felony possession charges—every single walk of life was addressed because every single one of those applications had crossed my desk at some point in my twenty-year career. But not once had I been confronted with a Branson-like candidate. Maybe this was some kind of karmic payback for the candidates I rejected.

Carson breezed past me with a feigned air of conceit. "Hello, Mummy. How are you?" She plunked down on the couch beneath the bay window, her long legs splayed out and draped over the arm of the couch. "Good day, was it?"

Her makeshift British accent was a knockoff from watching *Sherlock* or maybe *Dr. Who*—it was hard to keep up with Carson. She was a force all of her own, and she instantly lowered my resolve.

"Hello, darling," I played along. "Marvelous day. And you?"

She shrugged, and her long, strawberry-blonde wavy locks bounced. In the genetic gene pool of life, Carson hit a home run. She had her father's Croatian coloring, which made her skin look suntanned and vibrant year-round, and she had inherited a softer shade of my red hair and emerald green eyes that made for a striking combination. But more than just her physical beauty, Carson possessed joie de vivre, the joy of living spirit of her French great-grandmother, Louise, whom I was partially named after. When my French-born father, Jacques Lafontisee, married my Irish-born mother, Molly O'Brien, they had to integrate both countries into their firstborn child's name. Tara Louise represented Ireland and France at its best.

I wasn't as diplomatic with the naming of my children. With the exception of my youngest, who was named after my father, they were named after locations my ex and I had traveled. Ed's father was an engineer for the railroad, so his family moved frequently. Ed had been named after Edinburg, Texas, and his sister, Brooklyn Rose, was named after the city of her birth and New York's state flower. A beautiful name for an ugly person. She preferred to be called Rose, which fit her thorny personality.

It was my ex's brilliant idea to carry on his family's naming tradition. In retrospect, it was lame, though the names of my children thankfully weren't. Aaron, Kentucky, Branson, Missouri, and Carson, Nevada—each held a special place in my heart because they gave birth to each of my children. Ed's career as a golf pro led us to scout many golf locations and assist in the development of new ones. So when it came time to pick names for not one but two babies, we each chose a location where we had traveled. Ed chose Aaron because I vetoed Lexington or even Lex for a boy. And I chose Branson.

Now any time I said one of my children's names, I remembered a point in time when life was actually good between their father and me. I only wished my parents were alive to see their only granddaughter, who seemed to blossom before me.

"School's quite a bore lately," she lamented. "But little Jack beckoned me to your study to discuss something. Might I be in trouble?"

I laughed. "No, you're not in trouble. But where's Jack?" I looked through the open french doors, but my little man wasn't in sight.

"Oh yes, Branson came up and mumbled something to Jack, and then they disappeared into the basement."

I exhaled. "Swell. Well, hopefully Branson apologized to Jack and is making things better. What were they doing?"

"Branson got a new Pokémon game, and he wanted to show Jack how to play it."

I faintly smiled. "I don't know if I should be mad at Branson or pleased."

"What's troubling you?"

I rose off the rug, walked over to the couch and sat beside her. "I've been meaning to talk to you about Branson."

"His trouble at school?"

I shook my head. "What do you know about it?" I asked, then quickly added, "And he's not in trouble."

"Okay." Her voice shifted, and in that subtle change, I knew my daughter was aware of more than I realized.

"He's not in trouble with school," I clarified, even though it was unnecessary. "He's... did your father say something to you about this?" The heaviness in my chest thickened.

"Dad said something about depression, but you know Dad." Carson leaned toward me. "It's okay. Branson's going to be fine."

I tilted my head against her. "Baby girl, I don't know that. None of us knows that."

"Everyone gets depressed."

I slowly nodded. "That's true. But Branson...." The unfinished sentence dangled like a noose ready to hang me. "He's hearing voices."

"Oh, Mommy." Her voice dropped and she wrapped her arms around me. "I'm so sorry.'"

I leaned my head against hers, my eyes brimming with tears.

Emotion bubbled in her voice. "Is Branson going to be all right?"

My mind instantly wanted to respond with the right answer, the safe answer, the one I had subconsciously conditioned myself to say should anybody ask about my son. But this was my daughter, not someone who expected me to be perfect or polished. What she did expect, what she deserved, was for my heart and not my head to answer.

"I don't know. I don't know if Branson's going to be okay. I'm going to do everything I can, but I don't know if it'll be enough." For all the corporate spinning I did, that was the most honest statement I'd made in years.

And beneath that honesty was the question I most feared.

Am I enough? Am I enough to fix my son?

CHAPTER 6

TARA

THE faint sound of CNN filtered through my open bedroom window. Five in the morning, just like clockwork. I wasn't sure why I even set an alarm; with neighbors like Lance and Jan, I knew I'd never be late.

I turned on my side toward the bay window in my bedroom and listened to their morning routine. I knew it by heart. The white noise of CNN played while Jan made some concoction in the blender. She usually talked to her toddler, Camden, who wasn't as much of a morning person as his mother.

As soon as Camden started to fuss, Lance entered the scene. I couldn't always make out what he said, only that it always made Camden giggle.

I smiled. Camden's giggle was the best start to my day.

I closed my eyes and saw Branson and Aaron when they were Camden's age. Toe-headed blonds with blue-green eyes that still favored blue; their eyes didn't turn hazel until their second birthday. In the memory, they were fair-faced and bright, blue-eyed little boys. *My God, they're beautiful.* My chest swelled.

Beneath the warmth of my blankets, I took a long, deep breath, hoping the smell of Cheerios and baby shampoo would find me. Hoping the familiar scent of my twins' childhood would return. Instead, Camden giggled, I grinned, and again I returned to my little boys in the morning as I prepared to go to work.

"More?" I said to Branson and Aaron, who held their Scooby-Doo bowls toward me for cereal. "You want more?"

"Yes, Momma!" they said in tandem. "More, peas, more!"

I dropped to the kitchen floor beside them, and four little arms wrapped around my neck. "Squeezy hugs," I said as they tickled my neck with kisses. I was enveloped by twin love, and I was over the moon. I was kissing them all over and my boys were giggling and happy. We were enraptured with love.

"Enough!"

His voice startled all three of us. Immediately the morning shifted and we all froze.

Ed walked into the kitchen in his suit and tie. Angry eyes. Irritated tone. Frustrated stare.

I popped to my feet and tucked my boys behind me.

"Tara, you can't rile them up like this in the morning. It makes the job at the daycare center more difficult."

I nodded.

"More, peas?" Branson stepped out from behind me,

holding up his Scooby-Doo bowl.

I curtly shook my head and tried to shield him from his father.

"Goddamn it, Tara. If you keep feeding them every time they're hungry, they'll end up overweight. America already has an obesity problem. We don't need to add to it."

He snatched the bowl away from Branson and sternly pointed his finger at him. "Listen, fella, I'm just looking out for you. You don't know what's good for you." He pointed to himself. "But I do."

Branson nodded because he was too young to understand, but he was already old enough to know better than to cross his father.

Tears streamed down my face as I jumped out of bed and started to close the side window in my bedroom. I knew how Lance and Pam's morning ended. Their routine would seem monotonous, possibly mundane and downright boring to many, but to me, it represented something I never had in either of my marriages—normalcy. It was daily proof that it existed.

With the blinds drawn, I stood in the shadows with the window still open. No matter how often I listened to their morning unfold—and I listened religiously—I never heard cupboards slam, raised voices, or harsh words exchanged. I never saw Jan leave her house lowering her head, avoiding eye contact out of shame, or to mask a bruise on the side of her face from being pressed too hard against the refrigerator by the palm of a man's hand.

Every morning I woke to CNN and toddler Camden

talking and saying, "No," to his oatmeal or fried eggs or whatever Lance cooked. I never once heard Lance humiliate his son or create fear in him. What I heard was what I imagined happened when two working executives seemed to balance their work life with their home life.

I slipped away from the window and my neighbors, out of my pajamas and into my workout gear. When winter hit, I'd be at the gym, but until that happened, I hit the pavement.

I placed three boxes of cereal on the kitchen table beside cereal bowls my boys had long outgrown, texted my kids that I was running, and locked the door behind me. I'd be home before they ever knew I had left, but I always let them know just in case.

The wind was strong, but I was stronger. I had to be. I tucked my head and braved the Wyoming wind that pushed against me. The pressure was familiar. *Ed. Work. Finances.*

I looked at the hills on Fifteenth Street. Instead of one long, slow, steady incline, it was a series of rolling hills that dipped, curved, and varied in size. In a word, it was torture.

You got this.

Every morning it felt like these hills would kill me, and my shinbones would probably agree. They ached, throbbed and called out in agony for me to stop, but I never did. Each morning when I crested the first hill and burst over the other side, I felt like Rocky. By the time I hit the peak of the next hill, I felt like a Rocky sequel. And when I reached the third hill, hell, I was ready to tackle anything. Or anyone.

Gonna fly now.

It didn't hurt that by the time the fourth and final hill

was in my sights, so too was a fire station. The firemen were usually buffing the engine or whatever the heck they did, and no matter how tired I was, I would kick it up a notch until I was out of their line of sight. Motivation took many forms, and something about saving face was mine.

Then I'd fall back into my slow, steady pace. My morning routine wasn't nearly as idealistic as my neighbors'—hell, my life wasn't anywhere near theirs—but it worked. I was feeling good about the day and my run, a strong kick and stride to my step when I turned the corner to my street.

In the distance, I saw him, and suddenly I couldn't breathe. Lance was heading toward me, pushing a baby stroller with Camden tucked inside. Rocket, his red corgi, trotted beside them. In a pair of khakis, denim shirt, and loafers, Lance seemed like he belonged in a lecture hall, not on an oil field surveying the soil. He hardly looked like a geologist, but I knew better than anyone how looks were deceiving. Camden had on a little navy windbreaker and a baseball cap, his feet bouncing against the bottom of the stroller.

"Daddy, Daddy, Daddy."

His voice echoed toward me. My eyes stung and my throat tightened.

Branson.

I no longer felt like Rocky. My feet were stuck in cement. I couldn't find my rhythm, couldn't catch my breath. I could barely see.

I wiped my eyes aggressively. *My boys never had that. They never had a chance.*

Rocket ambled along, his white collar of fur a startling contrast to his red coat. His bobbed tail wagged when he spotted me, but I didn't call his name, or Lance's, or even Camden's.

I just waved goodbye.

CHAPTER 7

BRANSON

FIFTH block. Last class of the day. Biology. I was exhausted from staying up late to beat my new Pokémon game and text Dakota, but it was worth it. *One more block and I'm outta here.*

I concealed my cell phone under my desk, carefully looking between it and my teacher. All signs go. I scrolled through my phone and her name popped up.

`Hey, Dakota. Had my appt yesterday w/ Clive.` I hit Send, and within seconds my phone vibrated with her incoming text.

`How was it?`

`Well, I'm still crazy.`

My girlfriend wasn't convinced. `You're not crazy.` A winky-face emoticon made me smile.

I immediately texted in return. `Want to hang out after school? So we can talk about it?`

`Sounds good. sys`

The sudden spark of what resembled happiness made the rest of dissecting frogs manageable. For everyone's concern about me hurting myself or someone, cutting into a frozen frog didn't prompt any crazed thoughts. Now the kid next to me who kept tapping me on the shoulder like he had a nervous tick, he deserved a beatdown just for annoying me.

"Branson, help me out. What is this?" He pointed to a part of the frog.

"For the hundredth time, it's the liver."

"Oh, that makes sense."

No shit.

I was identifying the other parts of Kermit's anatomy when tick boy tapped me again on the shoulder.

"What?" I glared at him and he backed away. That sudden jolt of anger triggered the shadow people. I shook my head, but it was still there. I saw a shadow of a person pick up the scalpel and attack tick boy with exact precision, cutting him across the throat. The only color I could see was red.

I scanned the room and made eye contact with the teacher. "May I use the restroom?"

Mrs. Markentelle was the only teacher who didn't question someone when they had to take a leak. She handed me a hall pass, and I quickly ran to the bathroom, needing to make it stop before I hurt someone. The bathroom was vacant. Alone, I realized it wasn't going to be that easy. I hadn't told anyone about the shadow people. I knew they weren't real, but the sight of them scared me.

What the fuck's wrong with me?

I grabbed my phone and texted my mom. `Can you excuse me from 5`^th^ `block?` I paced the filthy, disgusting boys' room and waited. *Come on, Mom. Pick up the fucking phone.*

`What? Why do I need to excuse you?`
I shouldn't have to explain this shit.

`Just hurry up and excuse me.`

Her response was instant. `Why?`

`I'm just going through some stuff right now.` I'd gotten good at avoiding the conversation. If I didn't want to talk about it, I didn't. It'd been my secret, my shame. They didn't need to understand because they wouldn't. *Just excuse me from class before something bad happens. Why can't anyone get it?*

`Okay.`

Her text was all I needed.

I went back to the classroom and grabbed my backpack before the teacher even noticed I had returned. I hefted it over my shoulder, the weight of too many AP textbooks digging into me. The pain was a welcome relief, and for a moment my mind wasn't trying to kill everything it saw.

I texted Aaron. `I'm going home. Taking the car. Get Chelsea to drive you.`

`Dude, you have to pick me up later. Chelsea has basketball practice.`

I wanted to text back that my lazy identical twin could walk home—we only lived two blocks from the high school—but I knew he'd say the same thing about me. And I wasn't in the mood to fight, too busy trying to avoid what the shadow people did daily in my mind.

I drove the short distance from school to my house in record time. Cookie-cutter houses blurred past me. We had the ugliest one on the block. A white ranch-style home with one sad tree in the front yard, our house stuck out among all the log-built homes with green-tiled roofs. Despite its lack of "curb appeal," as my father the douchebag had commented when he first saw our house, I liked it. I liked that we didn't look like everyone else. Fuck 'em.

I opened the front door and Bandit, our black-and-white boxer, greeted me.

"Hey, girl." I patted the top of her head.

Other than Bandit, the house was empty. Just the way I liked it. No one to bother me or ask stupid questions.

I texted Dakota. Outta school. Come over.

While I waited for her, I opened the freezer and palmed four frozen waffles, dropping them into our four-slice toaster and tapping my foot on the kitchen floor. It was also a relic from owning an older house, but the linoleum made a cool sound against the heel of my boot. I tapped some random tune and increased my speed as the coils on the toaster reddened, snapping my fingers to the beat when the waffles popped up golden crispy. Reaching into the refrigerator for the tub of butter, I grabbed a knife out of the drawer, slathered the waffles in butter and then flipped the lid to the syrup, filling every deep pocket and causing the butter to slide off the stack.

"Hells yes." I grabbed a fork out of the kitchen drawer and pierced the top waffle, sinking my teeth into the fluffy deliciousness.

Lately food had become more important to me. There was something about chasing the next good snack. The anticipation, the excitement, the mystery of what new treat would become my next favorite indulgence had sparked something that wasn't macabre.

I glanced down at my stomach and lifted my shirt. My stomach was still flat, my six-pack visible without flexing. Thanks to P90X and Coach Walker's workouts, I could eat anything and not gain a pound. I had a sick body, and this stack of waffles was my reward.

I glanced out the large front window in the living room, seeing Dakota's silver Jetta in front of our house. She was on her way up the walk, and another momentary surge of happiness helped me forget that I was insane.

I choked down the rest of the waffles, tossed the paper plate into the trash, and put the fork in the dishwasher. *Don't need Mom bitching about the dishes.* I wiped off my mouth and opened the front door just as Dakota reached it.

She gently kissed me. Her touch was the only thing that could calm me down.

Our kissing intensified until I looked at her and asked, "Do you want to have sex?"

"Duh." Her brown eyes and dimpled smile reflected an assurance that I was wanted.

I took her hand and led her downstairs.

My bedroom was a windowless mess of ski gear, track shoes, and clothes. Kinda embarrassing, but then Dakota's room wasn't any better. And her mom was always home. Mine wasn't.

I kissed her again, harder and with more passion. Our clothes were off within minutes, and I was on top of her. I reached for the box of condoms I hid on the side of my bed and slipped one on.

"I'm always afraid I'm going to crush you," I said as she guided me into her.

"You won't, don't worry."

Dakota had been my first, but I wasn't hers. Still, we seemed to fit. She was tall and I was tall. We both liked sex because of the relief it provided, and we had fun doing it. Better yet, the shadow people never appeared when I was having sex. They were a guaranteed no-show. If only I could fuck all day long.

It always seemed to end too quickly, putting me back in the real world once more. I rolled off her and we laid in bed without any clothes.

"So, how was school?" My tone was meant to be as sarcastic as it sounded. Dakota whacked me on the shoulder and laughed. "Same old thing."

"How many classes do you have at Kennedy?" The advantage of dating someone who went to our rival high school was that I really didn't know much about her day or what a typical day was like, so my interest was genuine. It wasn't just after-sex talk to be polite.

"Only one, so I get to spend a little bit more time with you," she said with a wink.

The thing I liked about Dakota was that she was a flirt. It was one of the first things I noticed about her when I met her during a round of night games, our version of hide-and-seek played late at night and in a park.

The other thing I noticed that night was that Dakota was hot. She wore a white tank top without a bra, and her brown nipples showed right through. She looked like her native ancestors from the tribe she was named after. The Dakota Indians were as rare in Wyoming as my Dakota. I knew when I first saw her that she was one of a kind and I was hooked, so I asked her out. I also knew she had dated other guys, some of them my friends, but she always made it seem like I was her first and only boyfriend.

"How is it that you only have one class?" I asked.

"Most of my courses are at college. I only have to endure one last high school class before they release me."

"Lucky."

She shrugged, and her long dark hair fell over her naked shoulder.

"I'm sorry we couldn't talk yesterday. I had soccer practice, and then I came home and fell asleep. How'd your appointment go?" she asked.

"It went all right. I think they're going to start asking me to take more medication. What are you on?"

"They always change my dosage and medication. Right now I'm on Prozac." '

"And that's for your depression," I stated rather than asked. I knew Dakota had suffered from depression and had turned to self-harm. Scars from cutting her hip riddled her athletically toned body.

"Yeah, the Prozac's supposed to help with my mood, but I think a Butterfinger and a Mountain Dew do a better job."

I laughed. "We should go hit the Loaf 'n' Jug. I just got paid, my treat."

"What about your mom? Won't she be home soon?"

I rolled my eyes. "She won't care."

"Your mom cares."

"I know she cares. I just meant she won't be home anytime soon, so we can go get our treats, come back and go to sleep."

Dakota leaned over and kissed my cheek. "Sounds like a plan."

The world stopped. Being with Dakota calmed me, but sleeping beside her relieved me. It felt good to know I had someone there. And Dakota was the only person who made the static, the shadow people, everything that was wrong with me go away.

When we were together, I felt normal.

CHAPTER 8

TARA

"WHAT are we doing about this?"

My back was turned, but I knew from the sound of his voice that it was Aaron. The weekend had finally arrived, and I was actually making dinner, not nuking leftover takeout. I stirred the unnaturally orange-tinted chunk of cheese, which was slowly melting in the pot, and looked over my shoulder at him.

The only physical difference between Aaron and Branson was the shapes of their heads, or so Aaron believed. According to my firstborn, his head was coconut-shaped while his identical half was more elongated, "like a horse," as he once described. It was an awful comparison, but it made me look at Aaron's head differently. If anything, Aaron's head was more ball-shaped like the volleyball named Wilson that Tom Hanks hung onto in the movie *Cast Away*. Now anytime I looked at Aaron, I noticed his rounder, ball-shaped noggin and wanted to yell out, "Wilson!" I never saw the horse shape on Branson, but lately I questioned everything I thought I knew about my son.

"Did you see this?" Aaron gripped a white piece of paper with the blue-and-gold United States Naval Academy insignia. The paper was so crisp, the creases where the letter had been folded for the envelope were perfectly pleated. "What are we going to do about this?"

I took a deep breath. "*We* aren't going to do anything about this. *I* will handle it."

"Mom, the Navy is still pursuing Branson."

I nodded.

"They don't accept kids who are basket cases."

"Hey!" I startled both of us. "That's not fair." I lowered the heat on the stove and set the spatula on the spoon rest. "And it's not nice. Branson isn't...." Familiar sorrow settled into my heart. "Don't say that about him." My eyes brimmed with tears. "Don't."

"Mom." Aaron's voice softened, his hazel eyes overshadowed by his eyebrows that arched in concern. "People come out of the war with mental problems. They don't go into it with them."

"Mental problems?" I flicked away a tear. "Branson's just going through a tough time right now." *God, I sound just like Ed. Maybe denial is easier than reality.*

"Tough time? You don't just black out when you're having a tough time."

I had talked to Carson, but I had never spoken to Aaron, figuring he already knew. Something about twins, they knew what the other did before they did it. "Did you hear about that at school?"

"Branson told me himself."

"What did he say?"

"He just remembers being in the bathroom, his fist all bloodied, and he was afraid he had hurt someone."

"Oh no." I didn't think my chest could ache any more, but each time I learned a new piece to this puzzle, my stomach dropped and my heart felt like it sank with it. "What did you say?"

"I was just like 'What the fuck?'"

"I know it's…." I shook my head. "I don't know what's going on. One doctor thinks it's post-traumatic stress disorder, and another thinks it may be… something else."

"Like I said, people leave the war with PTSD, not go in with it."

"I know." The sarcasm was evident to both of us. "I said something similar to your father, but—"

"Dad didn't want to hear it," Aaron cut me off with cold hard facts.

"It's your dad's dream for Branson to serve in the Navy."

"But Branson wants it too. He's been dreaming about being in the Army or some military branch since, like, the third grade."

I tilted my head. "I don't remember that dream the way you do. Branson never spoke about the military until his father planted the seed and then had him apply for their summer seminar program."

Aaron placed his hands on his hips, ready to take his stance against me.

I held up my hand. "Let me finish. After Branson attended the Navy's summer program, *then* his sights were set on applying to the academy. I don't think it's been this lifelong dream as you remember it."

"Mom, the kid's been playing *Call of Duty* since, like, fifth grade, and he's always wanted to fight the bad guys."

My stomach flip-flopped. *Maybe you just haven't known what bad guys Branson was referring to.* I didn't say anything, just reached for the recent letter from the Navy.

"I'm trying to put the brakes on this." I carefully brushed the embossed insignia with my thumb. It was raised, the linen paper smooth to the touch. "But your dad seems to think we should just let Branson go through the process and wait and see if the Navy rejects him."

Aaron raised an eyebrow. "Well, I guess it's better than us rejecting him. We just won't let him go too far enough into the process."

"Why is it that if your dad suggests something, you're more open to it, but you come in here fully loaded and ready to argue with any suggestions I have?"

"Mom, I'm just trying to make the best decision for Branson, not you or Dad. It's not about you guys."

Shame crept into my stomach with a heat that spread to my face. "You're right. I'm being petty. But it's still not your responsibility nor place to make any decisions for your brother. You've got to trust that I'm on this. I'm the parent, not you." I paused for a beat. "I get that you're concerned, but this whole thing just...."

"Sucks?"

I chuckled. "Yeah, it sucks, but I'm the mom and I've got this." I folded the letter and handed it to Aaron. "Put this back on the entry hall table."

Aaron set it on the counter. "Branson's already seen it."

"I'm sure he was the one who opened it. It's addressed to him, after all." I glanced at the kitchen table. There was only one backpack strewn about. "Where is he?"

"He took the car. He had to work tonight."

"Oh. Is that his backpack or yours?"

"It's Branson's. I left mine in Chelsea's car. Can I do homework at her house tonight?"

My head pounded with a headache that refused to release its vise grip.

"Mom?"

I pressed my thumb into the side of my head, but the throbbing wouldn't stop.

Aaron looked over my shoulder. "You making homemade mac and cheese?"

I nodded.

"Branson's favorite," he said without a trace of envy or jealousy or whatever emotion identical twins shared when one was shown favoritism over the other. Branson loved mac and cheese and Aaron loathed it. Probably my fault. It'd been a staple in their diet when I first divorced because it was inexpensive. Then after my second divorce, cheesy elbow macaroni became a means of survival—not for cost, but effectiveness. It was quick, easy to make, and better yet, it didn't require any thought.

I resumed stirring the block of cheese that had melted

to a small chunk. The bottom of the pot was coated with a thick, creamy texture. Super cheesy, just the way Branson liked it. Or used to. *Who knows anymore?*

Aaron towered over me, his large hands cupping my shoulders. He tried to massage away the tension, but there wasn't anything that would remove the strain. "Mom, it's really sweet that you're doing that, but I don't think mac and cheese is going to fix it." His laughter tickled my ear and made me giggle.

"I know. I get it. Stupid mom move." I tilted my head back on my son's chest. It was solid, firm and defined. Aaron always felt different to me than Branson, even as a child. When I picked Aaron up, it was like hefting a bag of potatoes, but Branson was always so much lighter, thinner, like air.

"You can save it for him when he gets off work," Aaron said.

"At this point, I'd do anything if it meant Branson would be okay."

He kissed the top of my head and I smiled.

"Don't worry about Branson. He'll be okay," he said.

I wanted to believe it, but I knew from the empty tone in his voice that it was wishful thinking.

CHAPTER 9

BRANSON

REFEREEING games had to be the best and worst part of my job at the parks and recreation center. It was the best because I got paid to watch league sporting events, but the worst because when these assholes and idiots started to fight, I had to be the one to break it up. And if that wasn't bad enough, this fucking woman kept spouting off behind me.

"I think that's a foul."

I nodded and kept my focus on the basketball court.

"Didn't you see that? That player just charged him."

I bent over and cupped my knees, trying to look like an official. As if I were actually watching the game for traveling and personal fouls. As if.

"Okay, that right there is blocking. He just blocked the other player. Aren't you going to do something about it?"

I hit my absolute breaking point and spun on the soles of my new Nikes. "Listen," I started through gritted teeth, but no one was there.

What the fuck? Where'd she go?

I glanced around the gym, but the only people sitting in the bleachers were the next team waiting their turn up in the nosebleed section. My focus darted to the double doors leading in to the gym, seeing no one. I looked at the emergency exit, but the door remained locked.

There wasn't one woman in the entire motherfucking gym. My body drained of anger and fear settled into the pit of my stomach as a chill crept up my spine and tingled my scalp like someone had just run their fingers through my hair.

I signaled to the other referee and thumbed toward the men's locker room as if I had to take a leak, then quickly left the gym and walked past the locker rooms to the maintenance room. I opened the door and shut it behind me, sealing myself in where no one could find me.

I started pacing. "Okay, Branson, get a grip." Mops, buckets, and cleaning fluid surrounded me. I grabbed a mop and cracked the wood handle over my knee. Splinters flew through the air, and the release gave my mind something else to focus on.

I grabbed another one, snapped it over my right knee. Then another. Soon the mops were scattered on the ground like matchsticks. The stringy, yarn-like ends looked like decapitated women's heads.

Not helping.

"I've got to get out of here."

I peeked into the hallway. I didn't have the money to

replace the mops I damaged. Nor did I want to. Seeing no one there, I returned to the gym where the shift supervisor, Dan, had covered for me.

"Hey," I said when I approached him. "I'm not feeling so great." I touched my stomach for good measure.

"Yeah, when you didn't come back right away, Pete came and got me."

"Oh man, Dan, I'm sorry. I think it's the shitty cafeteria food at school."

He smiled. "It's either that or all the vending machine food you eat."

I grinned. "True that. But something's tearing up my gut."

"Go on and head home. This game's almost over, and the next one got canceled."

"Why was it canceled?" *Was there some woman who complained about my refereeing? Please tell me some woman complained about me.*

"The other team was a no-show."

Disappointment settled in my skin. *So no woman? I'm just fucking crazy. Great.*

"Okay then, I'll see you Saturday."

"Is that your next shift?"

I nodded. *If I don't lose my mind before then.*

"Feel better."

Not likely.

I raised my chin with a "Thanks" and headed straight toward my car. The moon was hidden, if it was even out, and the night air had the bite of fall with winter closing in.

Ski season. I just need the slopes and solitude of the mountain.

The parking lot lights weren't working, making it nearly impossible to see, but I wasn't afraid of the dark. Most people were afraid of what they couldn't see—I was afraid of what I could.

The old Saab started right up, and the Red Hot Chili Peppers' "Under the Bridge" blared from my stereo. The dark and melodic melody, the strumming of guitar strings, and the opening line began to settle my mind.

The city was my only friend.

It was a song about drug abuse. Loneliness. Despondency. I didn't do drugs, but the feelings fit. I cranked up the volume, but the dial was already turned as far as it would allow. Rolling down the window, I drove toward my exit. It was nearing eleven, so there wasn't much traffic, but any ambient sound was better than the static.

I flipped on the turn signal, the old car sounding like a lawn mower dying as I rounded the corner. My house was less than three blocks away, but it was dark and the roads weren't well-lit. I was in a school zone, and even though school wasn't in session, I didn't speed; I knew a cop was always parked on a corner street, waiting to write a ticket.

Still, as steady as I was driving, I didn't see it until something thudded against the side of my car. Adrenaline rushed through me and I tightened my grip on the steering wheel. *What the...?* The car felt like it was dragging something along with it.

Oh my God, was that a child?

I quickly pulled over and jumped out. In the stream of the headlights, I saw a black cat lying in the road, its face caved in and blood running out of its mouth. *Oh no.* I glanced back at my car and saw blood on my driver-side tire. *What the fuck? How did I not see it?*

The music from my open car door hung in the air and reminded me just how alone I was. I grabbed my cell phone out of my left jean pocket and called 911.

"This is 911. What's your emergency?"

"I just hit a cat. Can I get someone to help?" My voice was racing along with my heart.

"What's your location?"

I looked over my shoulder at the streetlight in the distance. "I'm on Beverly between Second and Twelfth."

"Animal control is closed for the night. We'll send Metro down right away."

The call disconnected as quickly as it had commenced, my cell phone screen glowing in the dark night. I stuffed it back into my jeans and walked toward the cat, staying by its side.

You're not alone. Emotions caught in my throat. *I am, but you're not.* The cat made this little noise like it was running out of air. For a moment I wished I were the cat. I shook my head to dislodge the thought, but death was always on my mind.

The Red Hot Chili Peppers echoed in the darkness. I pulled out my cell phone and called my mom.

CHAPTER 10

TARA

MY cell phone rang and I jumped. A textbook was on my lap, and a rerun of *Full House* was blaring on the television. Jack was curled up beside me on my bed, a blanket sprawled across him, and Bandit lay on the corner of the bed. She looked up at me as I quickly grabbed my phone. The screen flashed eleven thirty.

"Branson? Are you all right?"

"Mom?"

"Yes? Branson, what's wrong?"

"I may be late coming home tonight."

"Okay, what's going on? What happened?" I sat up, Jack's head rolling off my lap and landing softly onto the bed.

"I hit a cat."

"Oh." I exhaled. "I'm sorry. Are you okay?" I pressed the cell phone into my ear. Nothing. I reached for the remote and turned off the television. "Branson? Are you okay?"

"I'm good."

His words didn't match his tone. "Bran?"

"Yeah. I'm okay, Mom."

I shook my head. "No, I don't think you are. Where are you? I'll come get you."

"No! I don't need you to come get me."

I slowly nodded. "Okay, so what do you need?"

"Leave me alone."

All the air left my lungs, a tightness filling my throat that didn't allow me to respond, even when there were so many things I wanted to say. *Please, Branson, don't shut me out. Let me help. What do you need?*

Instead, I just sat on my bed, overtaken by the all-too-familiar sting of tears and the hollowness in my gut where certainty once resided. I used to know how to make everything okay for him. How to speak his language. Better than any of my other children, I used to understand Branson. Now I just seemed to annoy him.

"I called 911, so they should be here soon."

I nodded. "That was smart." I cleared my throat. "I can still come get you, so if you change your mind or if you need me, just call."

"I will."

And then my phone went dark.

I held it and wanted to throw it across the room, smash it against the wall. I wanted to hear something, anything other than my soul, shatter. Instead, I carefully slid off the bed and tucked the blanket around Jack, sweeping the hair off his face and kissing his rosy cheek. *Please don't grow up. Just stay little. I can do little.*

I walked barefoot against the hardwood floors to the kitchen. A nightlight shone softly against the cocoa-colored walls and bounced my reflection against the kitchen floor. The cream linoleum was old, but it added to the country charm of the kitchen. Or at least that was what I told myself when the estimate to replace the floor was more than my budget allowed. Ironically, the disadvantage to having more degrees than both my ex-husbands was that either of the two bastards could have asked *me* for alimony. Thankfully their male egos kept that money grab at bay. But since both were lower income earners than me, it meant they paid less in child support, so I supported a family of five on just my salary alone.

I grabbed a mug out of the cupboard and poured day-old coffee into it, placed it in the microwave and watched the timer count down the seconds.

My son was somewhere out in the dark, on the side of the road with an injured, possibly dead cat. *Branson, I'll wait. I'll wait until you're ready to let me in.* The emotions lodged in my throat. The sadness that was ever-present in my life. This sorrow that was now second skin.

I opened the microwave before the timer woke the rest of the family and reached for the cup. Wrapping my hands around its warmth, I imagined a man's hands wrapped around me—protecting me, insulating me, holding me.

I sat alone at the kitchen table in the dark. There was no one I could talk to, and I so desperately wanted to talk to someone about this.

How do I help him? How do I make sense of this? Is my son going to be okay? Will he ever be the Branson I knew, or will I only see what he wants me to?

His black backpack was still on the kitchen table, because since this started, I hadn't held Branson accountable for anything. Instead, I gave him absolution for everything: calling his little brother an asshole, texting me to get out of class early, and now shutting me out. It didn't matter what it was, I didn't hold my son responsible. I granted his every whim.

I did it because of one emotion that overrode all others: fear. It held me as its captor with a litany of what-if scenarios that haunted my every thought and subsequently dictated my actions. *What if I'm too hard on Branson and he snaps? What if he loses his mind completely? Will he ever return to me, or will he be lost to me forever?*

I placed my hand on my chest to slow my breathing. To comfort me. To be there when no one else was.

I sat alone in the kitchen, backpack in front of me and a myriad of questions that remained unanswered. By not keeping Branson in check, was I giving in to the disease? Was it a disease, or an illness? I had no idea because I hadn't asked those questions. I hadn't wanted to know the answers. I didn't want a diagnosis, because then it would make this nightmare real, and that was not what I wanted for my child. It was not who Branson was or the future I'd planned for him.

I pulled his backpack toward me, and a blue composition notebook fell forward. Since they were born, I dressed Aaron in red and Branson in blue. Now I was pretty sure their favorite colors were based on my need to color-coordinate my identical twins.

I reached behind me and flipped the light switch to the chandelier that hung above the kitchen table—another relic that was so old it was now, thankfully, retro again.

As I thumbed through the blue notebook, journal entries streamed past me. I glanced at the cover, and Branson's perfect left-handed penmanship noted **English 1010**. Beneath the course title in black ink, barely visible, he had written, **A Casual Stranger**.

What? I shook my head. Branson was enrolled in a college-level English class that high school seniors could take and earn college credit. By the time Branson entered the naval academy—if he did—or any top-rated college, he would have enough college credits to place him on the honor track. Again, all part of my five-step process and the path I'd placed my boys on since kindergarten.

If anything, I should have been mad at my son—Branson was messing up my plan—but I half-heartedly smiled. I had to; I had no more tears left.

I touched the pages in his journal. Branson's penmanship was flawless. He held the pen so hard against the page, his writing left behind ridges and bumps. I fingered his entries, each one deeper on the page, creating another wave of words that rose off the paper like a buoy in a choppy sea.

Then I read a passage and realized maybe his words were meant as a signal in a tide before the storm.

SEPTEMBER 3

WELL, MY FAMILY IS COMPLETELY AND UTTERLY INSANE. EVERY DAY THERE IS CONSTANT FIGHTING. TO STOP THIS FIGHTING AND TO GET JACK OUT OF IT, I BROUGHT HIM TO MCDONALD'S. I FOUND MYSELF NEAR TEARS BECAUSE HE'S TOO YOUNG TO BE GOING THROUGH THIS STUFF. I JUST HOPE IT ALL ENDS SOON AND WE ALL START ACTING LIKE A FAMILY AGAIN. THE ONLY REASON I BROUGHT JACK TO MCDONALD'S IS BECAUSE IT'S A DELICACY FOR US SINCE WE RARELY GO OUT DUE TO OUR FAMILY'S "WEALTH." WE AREN'T VERY WEALTHY, BUT WE TRY.

I stared at the top of the page where he had dated the entry, then got up and looked at the calendar on the refrigerator, flipping back to August. The boys began their senior year in high school August 25. September third was just the second week into the semester. *What fighting? What is he talking about?* I vaguely remembered him taking Jack to McDonald's, but what fighting?

I sat back down at the table and turned to the very first entry in the composition book.

AUGUST 25

WHENEVER I THINK ABOUT THE FIRST DAY OF SCHOOL, IT REMINDS ME OF THE BOOK THE PERKS OF BEING A WALLFLOWER. THIS HAPPENS EVERY YEAR AND IT EXCITES ME, BECAUSE I IMAGINE MY HIGH SCHOOL YEAR BEING AS FUN. I ALSO SET GOALS FOR MYSELF TO GET THE BEST EXPERIENCES OUT OF THE YEAR. THIS YEAR MY GOALS ARE SIMPLE: GET A 4.0 GPA, RECEIVE A MINIMUM OF 3 OR HIGHER ON MY AP TEST, ENJOY SCHOOL EVENTS AND ACTIVITIES, AND THE LAST AND MOST IMPORTANT IS BRING THIS GIRL I MET AT THE

HIGH SCHOOL SUMMER INSTITUTE PROGRAM TO ONE OF THE WILSON HIGH SCHOOL DANCES UP HERE. THIS GIRL IS AMAZING IN EVERY WAY, AND I PROMISED I WOULD.

I smiled. Goals. Girls. He must have been talking about Dakota. It sounded like a great start to the year. *So what happened?*

The edge of the paper looked recently burnt, like it had been held against an open flame or lit by a match. I knew Branson liked the look of old books, but now only half of his first name was visible. I thumbed past "son Kovac" to the next page.

AUGUST 28

IT'S ONLY THE THIRD DAY AND SO FAR MY GOALS ARE THINNING. SOMEHOW MOST OF THE SCHOOL DESPISES MY EXISTENCE. THIS IS VERY FUN AND EVENTFUL, BY THE WAY. AND THE GAY RUMOR'S UP AND RUNNING AGAIN. MAYBE THEY JUST SAY THIS STUFF ABOUT ME TO MAKE THEMSELVES FEEL POWERFUL. IT'S NOT LIKE I HAVEN'T DATED A GIRL OR ANYTHING, BECAUSE I HAVE, BUT IT DOESN'T HELP.

I knew Branson had been called "gay" his freshman year. And Aaron had been called "Tubs." But I honestly thought it was part of being a freshman on the football team. I told the boys to ignore it. Branson wasn't gay, and Aaron wasn't fat, but even if they were, it was moronic to engage in the stupidity. But now the anger that pulsed through my veins made me want to hurt someone, anyone who had ever called my son "gay" or made him question his worth or identity as a man. As if being gay was some crime?

Three days into the semester and my son had already lost hope. I didn't know he was still being called names. *Has this been going on since freshman year?* I tightened my jaw. I would not only find out who had said what, who bullied my son, but I would ensure their future college careers ended up as pathetic and limited as they were. *Bastards.*

I returned to Branson's English journal and continued reading.

BESIDES, ALL DATING CAUSES IS UNNEEDED DRAMA AND JUDGMENT. YOU COULD BE DATING THE PRETTIEST GIRL IN SCHOOL, BUT SOMEHOW PEOPLE FIND A WAY TO MAKE THEM LOOK HORRIBLE. I ACT LIKE THE GAY RUMOR DOESN'T BOTHER ME, BUT IN REALITY, IT HURTS.

I felt sucker-punched. All the air left my lungs and I found it hard to breathe as I stared at that last sentence: I ACT LIKE THE GAY RUMOR DOESN'T BOTHER ME, BUT IN REALITY, IT HURTS.

I knew the onslaught of grief was about to erupt. *I didn't know it was this bad. I thought it was just a freshman phase. I can't believe it's been going on this whole time. Where have I been? Why didn't he tell me? Why didn't the school tell me?*

My sadness suddenly turned to anger. *Why* didn't *the school tell me?*

I knew the dynamics of an academic arena better than anyone. The administrators weren't as clueless as they appeared. The drug dealers and addicts were no longer the main focus of a school administration—their radar was honed on the loners and the bullies. They focused their sights on the outcasts and their tormentors because they were likely to be the school shooters and their intended targets. They knew who bullied who and which kids teetered on the edge of the fray.

I gripped my cell phone that contained the personal phone number for every high school principal in Wyoming. The perks of my job would come in handy when I reached out to a few of them. *Someone will pay.* I knew what principal to hold accountable at Wilson High School, but the bigger question was who was he protecting?

Principals sought me out. As the admissions director for the only four-year university in the state, they needed my endorsement of their students. I had clout, but someone held more if they hadn't safeguarded *my* son.

So who's Branson's tormentor? Who's the bully the high school knows but hasn't done anything about?

I turned to my son's journal for answers.

THE MAIN CONTRIBUTOR IS ASHLEY BAILEY. THEN I MAKE A COMMENT ABOUT HER DRIVING, WHICH ISN'T EVEN A BAD COMMENT, AND SURE ENOUGH, I'M THE BAD GUY AND I GET IN TROUBLE.

My jaw clenched. *Oh my God. This is why Branson served detention?* It happened at the beginning of the school year, a couple weeks ago. Branson told me it was his fault, that he had said something about someone he knew was off-limits. *She's off-limits but Branson isn't?* Rage coursed through my body, sparking every primal instinct to protect my child against those who hadn't.

"So because of Ashley, a detention is now on my son's

permanent record as a derogatory mark against him, which tarnishes his academic résumé for college applications. Not to mention the fact that he had to forfeit participating in an indoor track meet because he made some comment, spoke up against this bitch, had to miss a required practice because he was serving detention, and then couldn't compete in the one thing that actually makes high school tolerable for him?" My voice rose. *"Are you fucking kidding me?"* I slapped the kitchen table. My hand stung, but the pain was welcomed; it felt better than crying and feeling powerless.

"Momma?"

I jumped and a startled cry escaped my lips.

Jack was dragging the large tan throw blanket from my bed and rubbing his eyes. "Are you okay?"

I pushed my chair back and went to him. "Did I wake you up?"

Bleary brown eyes looked up at me. "Uh-huh."

"Oh, buddy, I'm so sorry." I scooped him up in my arms, blanket and all, and carried him back to my bedroom. "It's still nighttime." I tucked him back into my bed and pulled the blanket around him, his radiating warmth like a heating pad against my skin. It had the same effect too, my tense muscles relaxing. I just wanted to crawl into bed with him. But Branson was still out, and I wouldn't rest until he was home.

"Go back to sleep." I kissed his forehead.

Jack smiled. "I was having good dreams too."

"Really?"

He nodded. "We were at the fair!"

I put my finger to my lips. "Shhh. Carson and Aaron are still asleep."

Jack giggled. "And Bandit too."

I nodded. "Yes, Bandit's sleeping too. So go back to sleep and dream about the fair, and all the fun rides we go on."

"Even the roller coaster?" His brown eyes twinkled in the moonlight coming through my window, lighting up my son's face.

"Yes," I said, playing to his challenge. "Even the roller coaster."

He pumped his fist in the air. "Yes!"

My whole body basked in his delight. *I miss it when it was this easy.* My son needed me, and I could provide everything to meet those needs. This was the best age in a child's life. Innocence and wonder hadn't been replaced by hard edges and disappointment.

I thought of Branson being bullied, being abused, and my pulse quickened.

"Momma's gotta go back to work. I'm sorry I woke you up. I'll be quiet," I said and kissed Jack. I lifted my laptop off the bed and tiptoed quietly out of the room, partially closing my bedroom door before returning to the kitchen table.

Ashley Bailey. Why do I know that name?

I fired up my computer and immediately conducted a Google search. A perky white-blonde with iridescent blue eyes and caramel-colored skin surfaced on the screen. I scrolled through the available images: Ashley cheering on the Wilson varsity squad, Ashley washing cars with other barely clad cheerleaders, and Ashley taking a seductive lick of a sucker.

Seriously? Lolita much? Come on, get an original idea.

I hit the arrow key on the images, sending them streaming past me until one made me grab my mouse and stop the roll.

"Oh my hell." His trademark lacquered blond hair, piercing green eyes, and devil-may-care smile won elections. Senator William Scott Bailey, Jr. "Holy fuck. She's the senator's daughter?" I quickly lowered my voice. "That's why Branson gets bullied and detention and she gets off scot-free."

When he arrived for a site tour of the university, I got stuck taking him around campus. He was charming, but arrogant. He did have good handlers though. Mere minutes after he ended up with me as his tour guide following an agenda switch, he had the lowdown on who I was, what I had studied in college and in grad school, everything I had ever written, and my dismal marital status.

"Marriage is overrated," he said playfully.

I remember laughing despite myself.

"Actually it is. A person's marital status isn't as big a polling issue as it used to be. More voters come from single-parent households, so being a divorced single dad is actually more relatable for voters."

I rolled my eyes, then remembered this guy knew how to play politics and was serving his second term as Wyoming's only democratic senator—a first in decades. Many proponents criticized his first win into office, claiming he "pulled a Jeb Bush" and relied on his marriage to a foreign-born wife to pull in the minority vote. In Bailey's case, his ex-wife was Ecuadorian-born, but when she left him for his chief of staff, Scott became the broken-hearted hottie from the Cowboy State, calling Casper his home when he wasn't on the hill.

Still, no matter who he was, where he lived, or his voting practices—which I actually favored—his bitch of a daughter had been bullying my son and that wasn't going to happen.

I snuck back into my bedroom and grabbed my stack of applicant files, thumbing through the manila folders. They weren't alphabetized or placed in ACT or SAT rank order, just randomly arranged by my college admissions team. Rachel and Ben didn't sift out any candidate, and early admissions were usually comprised of two separate groups.

There were those candidates who applied early because their income status qualified them for a discounted application fee, which was all part of the university's affirmative action plan. The policies of the admission process had to provide equal access to education for everyone.

But let's get real. Those applicants who didn't make the final cut weren't singled out because of their income status, gender, race, creed, nationality, or sexual preference. When those applicants were excluded, it was because they lacked consistent attendance at school, their grades and personal essays were dismal, and their overall application packets were pathetic. Those candidates didn't have a chance in hell of attending junior college, let alone a four-year university. We'd still send them a polite "Thanks, but no thanks" letter and a WSU decal. They'd get something for their sixty-dollar application fee, which the state paid for, but they wouldn't get the chance to call themselves part of the Posse.

Where is she? I knew her file had to be in my stack.

She was part of the other half of early admission candidates, those students who didn't need the discounted application fee but whose currency was measured by something even greater—status. Those applicants were children whose parents were either legacy alumni or power players in our state who wouldn't allow their children to attend any other school than Wyoming's only four-year university.

I skimmed the white labels that adorned the tab of each file until "Bailey" caught my eye. I smiled.

"Ah, there you are. Bailey, Ashley Michelle, Wilson High School," I exhaled. "Oh, this is going to be fun." I didn't bother to even open her file. Just knowing it was there was enough.

I opened my email inbox and clicked to compose a new message.

I typed "Wilson High School" into the recipient field and "Principal Fred Stanley" popped up.

Fred,

Hello! I'm burning the midnight oil working on the early submissions list. I realized Wilson has quite a few candidates to be considered for the freshman class of 2016. I also recently read that Natrona County will

remain a "school of choice" district. That
must be very exciting news for you and your
administrators.

I drew a deep breath. To the average reader, my email
was innocuous, but what the average reader didn't realize
was that when the top-seated county in Wyoming reclaimed
their "school of choice" status, it greatly impacted the two
high schools in the district. "School of choice" meant high
schools in Natrona County weren't guaranteed enrollment
based on where students lived; a student could choose to
go to a high school across town versus down the street.
And since a school was funded based upon its enrollment,
maintaining a positive public image was vital to a high
school principal. More students meant more funding. I
knew that, and so did Fred.

I returned to my email.

So it is with a heavy heart that I write
this email. As you know, the selection
process is calibrated to the expectations
Wyoming State University has for its incoming
students. We want our student body to be
lifelong learners. As such, we are often
faced with the difficult task of reducing the
list of our early submissions.

I quickly grabbed every folder that had Wilson High
School beside an applicant's name, then shifted through
the folders and placed those applicants with Kennedy High
School beside their name in a separate pile. The stack for

Wilson was thick. I closed my eyes and randomly fished a handful from it, then opened my eyes and pushed the remaining Wilson High School folders off the table. They fell on the kitchen floor.

I looked down and dropped Ashley's file on the top of the pile. "Yeah, buh-bye. That's the reject pile. Karma's a bitch. Because of you, Branson has a mark on a school record I have spent *my* entire life perfecting for him. Payback's a bitch." I inhaled deeply and felt my lungs reawaken with purpose. And then it hit me.

"Oh no!"

I reached down to the Wilson pile on the floor and quickly opened a few folders until I found a handful of legacy candidates. Wyatt Arn. Marybeth Sims. Gene Harpy. Sally Grey. *Don't be sloppy.*

I added the four legacy candidates to the pile of randomly chosen acceptances and counted what remained on the kitchen table. "Congratulations!" I said to no one but myself. "You're the lucky dozen who will join the Posse."

I grabbed the Kennedy High School applicants and did the same thing, pulling a handful of legacy files and adding them to the thicker pile of random acceptances until there were thirty-six Kennedy candidates. I then merged the two piles. Forty-eight early admission applicants from Natrona County seemed like a good number to me. *After all, there're twenty-two other counties in Wyoming with other applicants to still consider. I've got to spread the wealth around.* Rationalizing my actions came easy—too easy.

I returned to my email.

I am pleased to announce that twelve applicants from Wilson High School have been accepted for early admission into our program. Kennedy High School had a record thirty-six early admission applicants this year.

Heat coursed through my body, awakening every cell. I then listed the twelve Wilson students I had haphazardly selected. Ashley Bailey's name was purposefully missing from the ranking of early admissions.

Looking forward to your next batch of applicants. Go Posse!

Best,

Tara

I sat back and looked at my message. While rival Kennedy High School was known for its strong athletic program, Wilson High School gained strength for its academics. It was why I had sent my boys to Wilson. But after my office released the early admissions list, the low number of graduating seniors at Wilson selected to attend their home-state university would make even the most die-hard Wilson supporter rethink where they sent their child to high school.

If Principal Fred Stanley wasn't going to protect my son against the senator's bully bitch of a daughter, I would.

And in the corporate world, this was how it was done.

I hit Send, watched my email take flight, closed my laptop, and read the last paragraph of Branson's journal entry.

MY NEW GOAL THIS YEAR IS TO TURN THE GAY RUMOR AROUND. I'M NOT SURE HOW I'LL DO IT, BUT I'M GOING TO TRY. MY REPUTATION WILL NOT GO DOWN AS THE GAY, SMART KID BECAUSE OF ASHLEY. MAYBE THIS IS THE UNIVERSE'S WAY OF SHOWING ME THAT ABUSE TAKES MANY FORMS? OR MAYBE IT'S JUST ASHLEY BEING A BITCH. DOESN'T MATTER. I'M NOT SURE HOW I'LL CHANGE THIS RUMOR, BUT I'M GOING TO TRY. I HAVE TO.

My eyes stung—from lack of sleep, from crying, from reading my son's journal, from the reality that I'd been AWOL in his life.

I looked at the wall clock in the kitchen. It was after one.

Come home, Branson. I'm fighting for you. You're not in this alone. I'm in the game now, and I'm in it to win it. To win you back and give you the life you deserve. Just come home. Give me the chance to be a better mom. I promise I will. I won't let you down, and I won't let anyone hurt you.

I carefully tucked his journal back into his backpack and zipped it inside.

CHAPTER 11

BRANSON

MY cell phone battery died about a half hour ago, maybe longer. I stared at the cat's dead eyes that refused to shut. Dark pools of black reflected in my car's high beams, making them shimmer.

I knelt in front of the animal and lowered my head.

"I haven't prayed in a really long time, but if there's some patron saint for animals, then please forgive me for hitting it." I cleared my throat. "I didn't mean to." I know I sounded pathetic, like some whining kid who did something wrong and then refused to take responsibility for it. "I really didn't mean to do it." I didn't know who I was trying to convince. Maybe God, maybe myself. Maybe I needed to know that the shadow people hadn't done it. That the static hadn't taken over my thinking, the woman I heard tonight wasn't controlling me. That I wasn't insane.

I made a dramatic sweep of my arm over the dead carcass. "This was just an accident." The void in the cat's eyes was all too familiar. "Please, whoever's up there, whoever's listening, just make sure Metro gets here before another animal or bird gets to this cat and devours it. It didn't deserve what happened to it."

I leaned over the cat and thought about closing its eyes, but I just couldn't bring myself to do it. I shuddered. *Way too creepy.*

"I'm sorry." I cupped my knees with my hands and stood, turning away from the lifeless animal and toward my car.

The clock on the radio was an hour behind. Or maybe it was an hour ahead. Neither Aaron nor I knew how to change it when Daylight Saving Time happened, so depending on the time of year, we were either rock stars and super early or no-shows. Right now it was after two or maybe after one in the morning; I was too tired to remember where we were at in the lapsed time of things.

I turned off the radio, aimed my car toward home and prayed nothing got between me and my bedroom.

The porch light was on, and even though the blinds in the front room were drawn, I could see the faint flicker of another light shining inside.

Mom.

My throat tightened. I held my keys tightly and stood outside my house.

I can't do this. I can't tell her about the woman or the cat or how it's getting worse. She doesn't deserve this.

I swallowed hard and placed my key into the lock, barely opening the door before she was in front of me.

"Branson."

Her voice was the sound of home. It was enough to buckle me, but I couldn't. Instead, I cocked my head. "What?"

She shook her head. "I just wanted to make sure you're okay."

"For Christ's sake, I hit a cat. It's not that big a deal."

"Okay."

Now she sounded wounded. "Listen," I said with an edge to my voice, "I'm tired and I just want to go to bed. I can't do this right now."

Her eyes softened, the green reminding me of String Lake in Jackson, a fishing spot where we used to go with my dad. The water was warm and a greenish blue that was impossible not to stare into, let alone want to touch.

I wanted to reach out to her, to be held, for her to tell me everything was going to be okay. That I wasn't alone. That I'd never be alone. That she'd make this all go away.

I just shook my head. "I'm going to bed."

"Okay," she said with a weak attempt at a smile. "Good night."

I brushed past her as she called out my name. I turned and exhaled. "What?"

"Love you."

I nodded and headed toward the basement, not bothering to undress before plunking down on my bed, but my mind was wide awake. The shadow people weren't there, and neither was the static. I was just too wound up to sleep.

I slid off my bed, grabbed the game remote and went into the den that separated my room from Aaron's. Even if

I could sleep, Aaron's snoring would eventually wake me up. I half-smiled. *At least I'm not a heavy breather.* Aaron needed to have his adenoids removed, but he was a pussy about surgery.

Fuck, if there was a surgery that could cut out the diseased part of my mind, I'd do it in a heartbeat.

I clicked on the TV and didn't bother to mute the sound. Aaron could sleep through the ear-piercing sound of an assault rifle. *Lucky bastard.* The disk loaded with a quick summary and inside look of what the game held for the player. I already knew what to expect, ready to embark on a quest to save America from nuclear anarchy.

The hero of the story was missing one arm, but he had a bionic limb covering his handicap. Dressed in green camo fatigues with a full-grown beard and scruffy blond hair, his best feature was the Scar-L assault rifle he held in both arms. With a tap of a button, I made him aim at the enemies approaching.

I was one headshot away from taking down an angry warlord when I heard something come down the stairs. *Fuck.*

"Mom, I'm okay." I pressed down on the right trigger and bullets flew in a fury of motion.

The footsteps grew heavier, and something pounded against the basement wall.

What the fuck?

I glanced at the stairs and this little dark thing on all fours started down them. "What?" It began to pick up speed. "Oh shit!" The dark creature charged toward my chair. As it grew closer, the huge disfigured animal rushed at me, mouth open, fangs bared.

"Fuck!" I dropped the controller and jumped. My heart raced, adrenaline spiking through my veins, and I quickly closed my eyes.

"It's not there." The snapshot of the beast reappeared in my mind and I saw what it was—a mutilated cat. My heartbeat quickened, and I tightened my eyes until all I could see was black. "It's not there." I listened to my voice to steady my breathing. "There's nothing there."

But my mind still saw the beast. My body still felt the fear. *Make it not real. Please make it not real.* I closed my eyes even tighter until blackness surrounded me and nothing could get through. "It's not real. It's just your mind tripping."

I took long, deep breaths until my breathing slowed and my chest no longer felt like it was going to explode. I waited a really long time to open my eyes until I knew it was gone. Until I knew it couldn't get me.

When I did, nothing was there.

I reached down, grabbed the remote off the carpet and demolished the next enemy that approached my camp.

CHAPTER 12

TARA

"CARSON, sweetie, let's go." My voice was soft as I poked my head into my daughter's bedroom.

Her long, lean torso was buried beneath blankets.

"Carson?"

Strawberry-blonde curls barely moved, but enough for me to know my soon-to-be teenager heard me and would soon be joining me in the car.

I grabbed my keys and wallet and headed toward the garage through the door which was at the end of the kitchen. That door was the bane of my existence. It was heavy, yet it seemed to easily slam shut. Or at least any time one of the kids went to get something from the outside refrigerator. It annoyed the shit out of me, but until I could find a handyman or whoever fixed things like that, I just had to deal with it.

Each morning I held the door open for Carson, ensuring Carson wouldn't let it slam shut, which meant Aaron, Branson, and Jack remained asleep while I drove their sister to school. And after Branson's late night, I wanted him to sleep as much as possible.

Carson and I left early each morning. While my daughter wasn't much of a morning person, she liked to get to school before the crowd settled into the junior high. I understood, preferring to arrive at work before my team and my dean myself. My motto was "First person to work is never late." It hadn't failed me yet, and best of all, it allowed me to always stay one step ahead of the curve.

I stood with my back against the door and looked down at my pajamas. The cotton was worn and the black had faded, but they were still my favorite PJs. The button-down front accentuated my cleavage, my best feature, and the slack-like bottoms flattered my less-than-tone legs. *Why can't they make suits out of pajama material?*

"You're rocking those jammies," Carson said as she stepped past me and into the garage.

I smiled. "It's like you read my mind."

She shrugged. "I tell you, it's our thing."

I nodded and carefully closed the door behind us, then clicked the button to activate the garage door and watched the morning rise before me.

The front yard came into view. Frost had settled on the tips of the grass.

I exhaled loudly. "I'm not ready for winter."

When winter arrived, I had to drive the ugly mom-mobile, a four-wheel drive, all-terrain, all types of weather car that had about as much sex appeal as its dull white exterior and bulky wheels. That car remained parked outside our house where it collected leaves, a film of dust covering the windshield until snow dictated that I surrender my freedom and drive the beast.

Until that dismal day beckoned, I got to drive my dream car. I walked around the back of my sleek silver Jaguar F-Coupe and softly slid my hand along the smooth satin finish. In cost, maintenance, and gas, it was a completely unrealistic car for a mom of four, but if I had one vice it was speed, and this bad boy fulfilled my addiction. Besides, I always reasoned, if life really got shitty, I could sell the car and live on its net worth for a year. It was paid for, so that alone made it an asset versus a liability. I could rationalize what I wanted to believe to offset what I already knew—the car was a luxury I didn't need.

Still, every time I slid into the leather, heated, massaging driver seat, it felt like I'd found nirvana. I pressed the ignition, and a thousand horses revved beneath me. No matter how often it happened, it had the same effect, my body waking up and my energy swinging from nighttime mode into daytime charge.

"Let's get you to school." I shifted into Reverse and eased down my driveway. Gently dipping over the curve that led from the driveway into the street, I cautiously made my way to the stop sign at the end of my subdivision, waited for a truck to pass and then hit the gas. I accelerated onto the main road smoothly, effortlessly, and with the finesse of a seasoned driver.

I shifted from first to second and into third within seconds, the engine responding with a burst of power.

God, I love this car.

"Is stick shift hard to drive?" Carson's voice found its way into my fantasy-filled mind that I was Danica Patrick.

"Uh, yeah." I shifted into fourth and pressed the pedal. The needle on my speedometer spiked.

"Then why do you drive it? If it's hard?"

I shook my head. "I meant no. It's not hard to drive a stick shift." I glanced at her. Her cheeks had a hint of pink blush, and her lips had a cherry sheen that made them look fuller. Her hair fell around her shoulders, and black eyeliner made her green eyes turn up like Cleopatra. She had my eyes and knew how to make them the focal point of her face.

I smiled at her. "A manual transmission isn't hard to drive, but you know the rule. No child of mine will pass their driving test until they can do it on a stick shift."

"That was grandpa's rule for you. It doesn't have to be *our* rule."

I raised my eyebrows playfully. "Oh don't be a hater."

The road curved and transitioned from two lanes into one. I swiftly, expertly accelerated into the curve and passed the car in front of me like a pro.

Carson chuckled. "Oh geez. Get me to school in one piece."

"Always," I said and gently patted her leg. "I may like things fast, but I'm always careful when you're in the car."

She shook her head.

I shrugged. "What can I say? If my career in admissions doesn't pan out, I'll join the race car circuit."

The email I sent to Principal Stanley late last night

surfaced in my mind. He would be reading the short list of early admissions within a matter of hours. I didn't care. He didn't protect my son, so I wasn't going to protect his high school program. *Asshole.*

Carson reached into her black floral-covered backpack and pulled out a sheet of paper. "Did you know scientists have discovered that birds descended from dinosaurs?"

I nodded. "Yeah, I think I knew that." I stole another quick glance in her direction. "Is that for a test?"

She shook her head. "No, it's just my notes from science."

"So tell me about it." This was our morning routine. Carson gave me a mini-lecture on what she had read or discovered, and I savored every minute. I usually learned something new in the process.

"Birds have a direct ancestry to dinosaurs. Certain dinosaurs had scales and feathers on them, and they had the same genes as the present-day chickens."

"How did they figure that out?" I turned onto Wyoming Boulevard, and within a hundred yards, the speed limit changed from forty to sixty. *Hells yes. Open road, dinosaurs, and my little girl. Life is good.*

"Well, they've been able to find a genetic link from reptiles to dinosaurs to birds, so they now know that birds are direct descendants from dinosaurs. Scientists are trying to rewind the evolutionary clock. They want to turn on certain genes to prove birds still have ones that can make them into dinosaurs."

"Nuh-uh," I said. "Really?"

"Yeah." Her voice rose with enthusiasm. "What they've

already discovered by studying chicken embryos is that a present-day chicken embryo shows traces of dinosaur genetics. It was only around fourteen days into the embryonic process, and the chickens had tiny teeth and these kind of scale-looking things that are what dinosaurs had."

"And why would teeth be an indication of dinosaurs?" I knew I should know the answer, but I hadn't even had my coffee yet.

"Because chickens don't have teeth, but dinosaurs did."

"Right."

Wyoming Boulevard wrapped around the city of Casper with miles of unobstructed views. Casper Mountain rose to the west, and to the east, open expanses of land where horses pastured and antelope often appeared for a morning snack were just beyond the reach of our windshield. I stared in the distance at four horses that had gathered around a water trough. Noses down, their long necks and brandy-colored manes glistened in the morning light.

I smiled and elbowed Carson. "There're four, just like you and your brothers."

I didn't have to look at my daughter to know she was probably rolling her eyes at my lame comparison. "True," she said. "And at least we're not fighting over the feed bucket. Have you seen how much Branson's been eating lately?"

I chuckled. "He's just a teenager. Okay, so where were we with the dinosaurs and chickens?"

"Well, these chicken embryos were showing teeth and a tail, but then both went away after like a month into the gestation process. It's like the dinosaur gene gets turned off."

"A gene could just turn off?" My foot released its weight on the gas pedal. Suddenly we lost speed. *Could they do that with Branson? Could they just turn off whatever gene went bad?*

"Yeah, the gene for the chicken to have more dinosaur features just goes away or gets turned off."

"But what causes it?" I pressed down on the gas and the car jerked forward. "Sorry." I quickly downshifted to correct my error. "Why do the genes do whatever destructive thing they do?" The clipped tone in my voice alerted me that I had definitely veered off chicken and dinosaurs and onto my son. "Why can't they just stop these genes before the damage happens?"

"Well, actually they can."

I almost forgot to shift back into sixth. "What?" I quickly glanced at her. "How?"

"You could use the Punnett square to determine what an offspring's genetics is going to be."

"A what?" *There was a test I could've taken? I could've avoided this for Branson?* Then my throat tightened and a great loss swept over me. *Then there wouldn't have been a Branson.* I couldn't have terminated his life just because I knew something was wrong genetically. No way. I couldn't do it, *wouldn't* do it.

I quickly flicked away a tear before my daughter saw it.

"The Punnett square is this diagram. I can show you at home tonight, but scientists use it to predict certain genotypes in an offspring. With certain genes, they can determine if it's a dominant gene in the family or recessive."

"I didn't know that even existed." I looked at my daughter. "I mean, I knew about eye color and that green is a recessive gene, but with your dad's blue eyes and my green eyes, it gave us a, like, one-in-four chance of having a green-eyed baby."

Carson nodded. "Yup, that's right. It's so interesting to me that scientists can do that. And now they're experimenting on chickens and their genetic makeup. This one scientist was able to turn genes off and on in this chicken embryo and manipulate the genes of the tail so it would grow. But if they could do that with chickens, it's like you could know what genes your offspring will have and just—"

"Turn them off."

She nodded. "Yeah, that's the idea."

"But it hasn't been used yet? I mean with people?" *Could I have saved your brother? Was there something I could've done for my son?*

"I think you can do a Punnett square before and after a child is born, but I think it's only afterward when the child *is* born that you would know what genes they actually have. Though I guess you may be able to find out the reason why."

For a moment, I felt a sense of peace, as if the "why" this happened to Branson would be solved. *It's probably something genetic that just malfunctioned. But in today's world, we can fix anything.*

"Some people dismiss science because they think it's just a theory, and because it's theory, it's not real. But a theory is something that's an educated guess made over and over and tested over and over. The only reason it remains a theory is because scientists can't go back to the Jurassic age and prove it."

I turned into the school parking lot and slowed down, not wanting our morning drive to end.

"You can't go back in time," she said when I pulled in front of the junior high. "All you can do is accept what is now and work with it."

We'll find a way to fix this mutated gene or whatever it is, and then Branson will be perfect again.

"I like how we're uncovering so many mysteries we didn't know before," she said.

I gently smiled. "There's a lot we didn't know, that's for sure."

She leaned her head toward me and I smiled. Carson rarely kissed me. Even as a toddler, she would lean her forehead toward mine when she wanted a kiss. *What gene makes up that adorable trait?*

I kissed the top of her head. "Thank you," I said into her hair.

She looked up at me and warmth flooded my body. "Love you," she said, then bounded out of the car with more enthusiasm than she had entered it with.

I slowly drove away, keeping Carson in my rearview as she made her way into the junior high. The drive home was always quiet and more subdued.

I turned back onto Wyoming Boulevard and scouted the hillside for the trough. The horses were no longer watering. I glanced out the passenger-side window. Three of the horses were huddled together as if they were bracing against the strong Wyoming wind that had kicked up. I searched for the fourth horse. *Where is he?*

The road dipped and then rose again. When the hillside came back into view, I spotted the fourth horse. He was darker than the other three, perhaps the alpha. All I knew for sure was that he stood on the crest of the hill alone, away from the fold.

A sudden ache pierced my chest. I wanted to pull my car over, run to this horse and bring him back where he belonged.

CHAPTER 13

BRANSON

I felt like I had a hangover, or at least what I imagined a hangover felt like. I wasn't much of a drinker. Now pot, that was the money. Nothing freaky happened when I was stoned. Or at least nothing I could remember. Pot relaxed me, and for once I wasn't stressed out. Sadly, my dad's golfing buddy sold me the best weed, and that was only during the summer when he was in town. But if there was ever a day to get stoned and let go, it was today. I barely slept last night. The fucking deranged cat from hell scared the shit out of me, so I had played video games until Aaron's morning alarm buzzed.

By the time I felt like I was finally waking up, I was thankfully in my third block, during which I was a student aid for the front office. I could doze off and no one would care.

I had the vice principal to thank for this new assignment. He had reassigned my classes after I flipped out on that girl in poli sci. If I knew a meltdown could get me out of core classes, I could've been tripping sooner. My knuckles had already healed from punching the bathroom wall, and better yet, that girl who caused all the shit no longer looked at me, let alone spoke to me or bothered the foreign exchange student. Some battles were worth waging—even if I didn't remember them.

I was almost asleep when Mrs. Tuttle gently tapped me on the shoulder and handed me a hall pass. "Looks like you have an appointment."

I looked up at her and smiled. She was a nice old lady. "Thanks," I said.

She grinned. "Guess we'll see you tomorrow, Branson."

The hall pass notified me that I was to report to Mr. Turina's office. *Clive wants to see me. Great.*

"Yeah, thanks, Mrs. Tuttle. See you tomorrow."

I grabbed my backpack and walked toward Clive's office. It had two doors, one that led to the main hallway and another that opened to the back section of the school library. Weird location for a therapist, but hey, with school shootings, probably not a bad thing.

After our last session, I decided to enter his office from the library. I obeyed the sign on the outside of the door and knocked.

I heard him hustle toward the door. *Why am I here again so soon?*

"Oh, hey, one minute." His face appeared in a slit in the doorway. He looked like a pug. "I'm just finishing up with a client."

I nodded and turned toward the row of fiction books that beckoned, grabbing a copy of *Tuesdays with Morrie* and giving it a quick skim. I had read it and liked it. Not what someone would think for a high school student, but I'm not an ordinary kid. I flipped through the pages until I got to the best line. I knew its location by heart.

"I like myself better *when I'm with you.*" I thought about Dakota and smiled. Mitch Albom sure knew his shit.

The door behind me swung open and a Goth-looking kid exited Clive's office. He was wearing a punk hoodie and had piercings on his face. If he was in there, God only knew what I looked like going in.

"Okay, you're up," Clive said.

I followed him into his office and sat in the swivel chair that was really uncomfortable.

"All right, what's going on?" Clive asked.

I shrugged. "Everything's going okay, I guess." *If you don't count the trippy, deranged cat in my basement last night. Or the talking woman who wasn't there. Or let's see, there's always the cat I killed.*

"How's the depression?"

"Still there."

He flipped through his notepad. "You've been on the Paxil for a few weeks now, so it should be kicking in soon."

Great. What's the point of taking a fucking pill if it won't work right away?

"How are the intrusive thoughts?"

"They're still there." I paused.

Clive stopped writing on his notepad and looked up.

If I'm not honest here, then where? "They're happening more frequently."

"That's common." His voice was reassuring. "How often are they happening?"

"Two or three times a day, every day." At the mere mention of the intrusive thoughts, the shadow people appeared and suddenly hurt my therapist. In great detail, I saw one of them grab a pencil and strike Clive in the throat three times, each thrust deeper and harder into his carotid artery. His jugular vein collapsed, and blood rushed down the folds of his neck.

I shook my head and closed my eyes to make it go away. *It's not real. It's not there.*

"Are you all right?" Clive's voice was filled with concern.

If he only knew. "Yeah, I'm good."

"What just happened?"

"Just more intrusive thoughts."

"Are they thoughts, or are they images?"

"What do you mean?"

"Visual hallucinations, like little movements where you're actually seeing things."

"Yeah, they're more like that."

"How do you know they're hallucinations and not real?"

"Because no one else sees them." *Isn't that obvious?*

"How do you shut them off?"

"I usually get into video games or I read. Anything to focus my mind on something else."

"Do the hallucinations say anything?"

"No, they just do things."

"Do you see movement or images? Like shadows?"

What the fuck? My face must have revealed my shock because Clive continued.

"Do you see dark figures? Or shadows? Movements that eventually turn into full-on visual hallucinations?"

I nervously laughed out of fear I'd throw up. My stomach was a mess of tight nerves. *Tell him.*

I looked directly at Clive. "I call them shadow people."

He smiled. "That's a good term. What do these shadow people look like?"

"I never see them fully. They're just quick little movements out of the corner of my eye, not any real shapes. They're just like taunting me, running around. Trying to take me over when I'm not looking."

Clive nodded.

"I've never told anyone about them, not even my mom."

"It must be scary for you."

I shrugged. "It's just what it is. I've kind of gotten used to it." *I've gotten used to being terrified.*

"How long do these shadow people stay around?"

"Just enough so it's there but not enough to make out a shape."

"What do they do, these shadow people?"

"Violent acts." I paused. *Just say it.* "I actually view myself doing it, but it's not me doing it."

"How do you know it's not you?"

"Because I wouldn't harm someone else. It's not necessary."

"Why is it not necessary?" He leaned forward in his chair.

"Because the shadow people do it for me."

He leaned back. "Shadow people is a good term because that's how they start off."

Start off? "Do they get worse?" If sadness had a feeling, it was the hollowness that dropped in my stomach and made me feel all alone. *Am I ever going to be okay?*

"It depends on the person and on each case."

Clive was never the half-empty glass kind of guy. He always seemed to spin things so this dismantling of my life from the inside out didn't seem as grave as we both knew it was.

Still, I had to know. "What about me? What kind of case am I? What should I expect?"

"Well, with prescribed medication, you should be all right."

"Do they go away? Will the shadow people leave?" *Will I stop seeing these faceless, dark figures that do bad things to the people I love?*

"Once again, it all depends on the case."

So I'll be hearing imaginary women for the rest of my life, and disfigured cats will come chasing me every night? Great. Awesome.

"I still don't agree with Dr. Valenti's diagnosis of PTSD, but I'll send my notes over to Dr. Cordova. When do you see him again?"

"I think sometime next week?"

"You mentioned that when these shadow people appear,

they commit violent acts. Can you be more specific?"

"Sure." *Why not? Welcome to crazy town.* "When I get angry or upset or stressed, I'll start seeing stuff."

Clive nodded. "Can you give me an example?"

"When my mom interviews me when I'm trying to relax."

Clive's eyebrows raised. "Interviews?"

"Yeah, she's this director at the college, and she tries out her interview questions on me or Aaron because we're the same age as most of the incoming freshmen she has to interview."

"Oh, of course. And this bothers you?"

"It doesn't bother me. It frustrates the shit out of me, and then...."

"And then the shadow people appear."

I nodded. "Yup."

"And what do they do?"

"Violent acts."

"You see this?"

"I see something carry out a violent act."

Clive rubbed the stubble on his chin. "Against your mother?"

"Yup."

"Like what?"

"It depends on the location or what's in front of me. It could be a pencil, scissors, kitchen knife...." *You name it and I can think of how to use it against someone.*

"And depending on what's in front of you, these shadow people do what?"

"Hurt others."

"Do they hurt others, Branson? Or do they *kill* others?"

"Kill."

There wasn't any shock or horror on Clive's face.

"Listen," I said, with my hands held in defense in the event he changed his mind about treating me, "it's just a part of my life I've come to live with." There was no bitterness or edge to my voice. It was simply a statement of fact.

"It's a real credit to you." Clive spoke in a way that didn't make me feel judged or ridiculed.

"I don't understand. I just told you I'm basically crazy."

Clive shook his head. "You've lived with this static and the shadow people for a while now, and yet you've functioned well despite these symptoms." He leaned forward in his chair, compassion shining in his blackish brown eyes. "It's a lot to deal with, and you've dealt with it well. You've functioned when most people with these symptoms aren't able to. But now it'll come down to you choosing to either be on medication or live with the voices and hallucinations."

"Those are shitty options."

Clive sat back in his chair with a chuckle. "Yeah, the situation isn't ideal, but medication will allow you to function without the interruptions."

"I could have a life without the shadow people *and* the static?" I held my breath.

"Well, with the right medication, the visual and auditory hallucinations will subside."

"But they won't go away?" That sad, hollow feeling returned.

"With your illness, your symptoms will always be there. Medication relieves you of them, but they won't just go away. What that means is if you stop taking your medication, the visual and auditory hallucinations—the shadow people and the static—will return."

And for them to return, I die. "Medication it is." I cupped my knees with my hands and stood up. "And I guess I get that from Dr. Cordova?"

Clive nodded and stood. "Yes. I'll send my notes over to his office today."

"Thanks." I headed toward the door. A world of books and escapism was just beyond its reach, and I couldn't get there soon enough.

CHAPTER 14

TARA

I *don't even know why he has to be here.*

The mere sight of my first ex-husband, Ed, in the waiting room of Dr. Cordova's office made me shudder. His wavy, white-blond hair was cut short, the only way he could control his hair that grew like a Chia Pet.

As I approached the room that was decorated for the younger patients, complete with kid-size tables and chairs, I stared at the primary colors painted on the wall. They were happy, fun, vibrant colors that formed a rainbow that stretched from one bin of happy toy distractions to another.

I glanced around for a place to sit, but the only chair suited for an adult was beside Ed. I quickly looked at him and then did a double take.

Ed's legs were crossed, but it looked like his gut was hanging over his belt loop. *No way.* He hefted himself out of the chair and I almost gasped. *Holy crap, he's gained a lot of weight.* With his white-blond hair, which sat like a cap on his head, he looked like the Pillsbury Doughboy.

He stood, and I instinctively crossed my arms over my chest, hugging myself so tightly I was practically in a self-imposed straitjacket. Anything was better than having to shake his hand or exchange pleasantries as if we were an ordinary divorced couple who decided to call it quits after a decade-long marriage when things didn't quite work out. There wasn't anything ordinary about our marriage, or the shelter for battered women I'd ended up in when Carson was six months old and Aaron and Branson were barely five. Nope, in the waiting rooms of life, this had to be the worst one I could be stuck in.

"Tara. Ed." Dr. Cordova signaled for us to follow him.

"We're not married," Ed said to the doctor's back.

I shook my head. As if the twenty pages of paperwork I had to fill out detailing every aspect of Branson's life from my pregnancy to his birth up to his seventeenth year hadn't quite given the good doctor that impression. *What an idiot.*

I walked down the hallway toward Dr. Cordova's office. Ed was blathering on about some new golf club he had been sent and was trying out at the pro shop. As if every doctor was a golfer. Dr. Cordova nodded with what seemed like feigned interest, or maybe I just wanted to believe that he found my ex as irritating and arrogant as I did. The backside of Ed's black slacks stretched across his ass so tight the seam looked like it was about to burst.

Good hell, what have you been eating? Or should I ask what haven't *you been eating?*

The doorway to Dr. Cordova's office was at the end of

the corridor. With each step toward it, dread stabbed at me. *I don't want to go inside. I don't want to hear what's wrong with my son.* The last time, the only time I was in that office, I cried—sobbed, actually—as I told Dr. Cordova about my son, my sweet, sweet boy and all his firsts: the first time he walked, the first time he drove.

The first time he told me he was hearing voices.

Dr. Cordova held the door open for me. I paused and looked up into his gray-blue eyes, and he gently grinned. "I don't bite," he said.

I weakly smiled and crossed the threshold. Ed had already parked his oversized ass on the couch. Ed's weight was a good distraction, and yet oddly it made me sad. He'd always prided himself on keeping fit and healthy, but now he looked like a diabetic waiting to happen.

Why should I care? What's wrong with me?

I sat on the couch opposite Ed and practically hugged the armrest. I couldn't put enough distance between us.

"I've received the clinical notes from Clive Turina," Dr. Cordova said with a file folder on his lap and a legal-sized notepad on top of that. A pen was at the ready.

"Clive? Oh yeah, he's the counselor at the high school, right?" Ed asked.

"That's correct. His notes were very thorough and helpful." He paused.

I waited.

"How do *you* think Branson is doing?" Dr. Cordova asked.

"I think he's doing great," I said and felt Ed staring at me.

I quickly regrouped. "I mean, he *is* doing great. He's much happier, and…." I shrugged. *Who am I kidding?* "Branson seems more like himself. He's fine."

Dr. Cordova steadied me with his gray-blue eyes. If no one else heard the hesitancy and uncertainty I tried to mask in my voice, he did. He looked at me and seemed to understand the silences, the unspoken truths I dared not say.

My soul was empty. There was nothing left of me that mattered. I had failed my son. I didn't know how Branson was doing because he didn't tell me, and I didn't ask. Instead, I read his journals to try and find out what was going on in his life. But I didn't know. Hell, I never even knew anything was wrong. I didn't know he was being bullied or called gay, or hearing voices. Anything.

I stared into Dr. Cordova's eyes. *How is my son doing? I don't know. I. Don't. Know.*

"Branson's back on track," Ed said. "I think he was just having a bit of a rough patch, but he's solid now."

Dr. Cordova's stock of silver hair shook when he nodded. He scratched the back of his head or patted down his mane, it was hard to tell. For certain he was contemplating how to proceed.

"Well I completed my evaluation, and after reviewing Clive's notes, I think the next course of treatment for Branson is to add an antipsychotic medication."

"What?" My voice rose and my heart shattered. "An antipsychotic medication? Isn't that a bit extreme?"

"I have to agree with my wife—I mean with Tara. I don't want my kid to be overmedicated. That seems to be the answer to everything these days. Don't feel good, take a pill. Getting anxious at work, swallow this. Eating too much, sprinkle this on your food and your problems are solved. No, doctors are way too free with the prescription pad." Ed held up his hands in mock protest. "No offense to you, Doc, but an antipsychotic medication? Tara's right, that's a bit extreme. The kid's just been a little depressed."

"You've already got him on an antidepressant," I said defensively. I couldn't believe I was siding with Ed, but hell, necessity was the mother of strange bedfellows. Then, for whatever reason, I thought of my conversation with Carson. "What about genetics?"

That seemed to get Dr. Cordova's attention. "I didn't see anything in the file of a family history of mental illness." He was about to skim through the larger-than-life folder on Branson when I cut him short.

"There isn't. Or none that we know of." I wanted to blurt out that I thought Ed's sister, Rose, was one brick shy of a full load, but I didn't think that constituted crazy. She was mean, rude, and a downright bitch, but again those didn't qualify as disabilities. "So no mental illness on either side of the family," Dr. Cordova stated rather than asked.

I thought of my family. Both my parents died in their right mind, and my sister lived in their home in Paris. I hadn't seen her in years, but Serena didn't suffer from anything other than boredom.

"Correct," I said. "No mental illness on either side. So...." I scratched my head. "Maybe it's some other genetic anomaly? You know, like a mutated gene or something?"

Dr. Cordova said nothing in response to my failed attempt to earn a doctorate degree in his office and cure my son.

"If you already have him on an antidepressant," I said when no one else spoke, "I don't see why we have to add anything else."

Dr. Cordova's face remained neutral. "The Paxil was prescribed by the emergency intake doctor. I wouldn't have placed a teenager or young adult on that medication, but since Branson's depression has responded well to it, I don't want to change that course of action."

"So if he's responding well to it, why does he need something else?" The panic in my voice was evident to everyone. I felt like I was drowning, and the one person who could throw me a life vest wasn't helping.

"Branson has symptoms that are unrelated to his depression that an antidepressant won't treat," Dr. Cordova said, pulling away any hope to be saved from this tidal wave that was cresting before me.

"Symptoms? What symptoms?" Ed teetered on the shore, but the tide was rising and his question brought him right into the path of the tsunami.

"Branson has had an increase in auditory and visual hallucinations," Dr. Cordova explained.

The wave crashed down, and its impact was almost immediate. My mind shut down as I tried to remember how to breathe. *Auditory and visual hallucinations. What does that mean?*

"I don't understand." My throat tightened around what

I needed to ask and what answer my soul was willing to hear. I was already adrift with no ground in front of me, and I so desperately needed to come up from this swell that threatened to sink me. "Branson... is he still hearing voices?"

"Yes."

Tears streamed down my face faster than I could contain them. "No." I shook my head. "He's just... it's this girl at school who picks on him, that's all. He's just too sweet to do anything about it. So that's it. He's probably hearing *her* voice."

"A girl?" Ed's tone cut through my grief, startling me. "A girl's been picking on Branson? Are you kidding me?"

"No." My reaction was sharp, like a gust of air had been forced into my lungs. "She's the daughter of... well, it doesn't matter who she is. I'm handling it."

"Really?" Sarcasm dripped from his fat mouth. "First you have him in that high school that only the affluent attend, as if my boys belong there. And now some rich little daddy's girl has been messing with my son, and the fact that he hasn't done something to shut her up is pathetic."

"No, it's not pathetic that our son isn't abusive toward women or violent." I swam as fast as I could against the current that wanted to pull me down. "Branson's a gentleman. That's actually a really great quality." I came up for air.

"Oh, here it comes again, the claims of abuse. How many times are you going to play that card?"

"I don't know, Ed, how many times did you hit me?"

111

It was as if someone else was speaking. I had never crossed that line with my ex because the cost to speak up was too great. In his defense, Ed hit me twice, maybe three times. The beatings I could take—it was the psychological mind games and constant verbal battering that struck me down faster than his fists.

"Okay, I think we're getting a bit off topic," Dr. Cordova said.

"No, I don't think so," I replied, finding my feet again. "The abuse Branson *and* Aaron and, hell, even Carson watched, endured, and was part of our daily life *is* the topic. If, and I'm not saying it's true, but *if* Branson is hearing voices or having these visual hallucinations as you claim, then it's probably everything he witnessed. It's probably just pieces of our past that he's trying to resolve. Isn't it obvious how toxic we are?" I waved between my couch and Ed's. "He's an abusive man, and I was the doormat he wiped his feet on every day for twelve years. And"—I held up my hand to stop Ed from speaking—"I was as much a part of the problem as Ed. I didn't walk away. I stayed for *years* after I knew things were bad, allowing my children to live in an abusive environment. So if Branson is hearing anything, it's not voices—it's his past. It's *our* voices. It's our mess."

Ed crossed his arms over his chest.

"Okay, it's mine. I'll take the hit. I don't care," I said. "I just want what's best for Branson, and I don't think that's more medication." I wasn't going to let my son drift further away from me. "I think what Branson needs is intensive counseling to deal with the loss of his childhood, his family—hell, his dreams. We stole that from him. And I think Dr. Valenti was right that what he's suffering from is PTSD." I glanced at Ed. "PTSD is a far better, more manageable diagnosis than...." I wouldn't say it. I couldn't. It would capsize everything I held dear in my life. It was one thing for me to drown; it was an entirely different matter to allow that to happen to my baby.

The room was quiet. My heart pounded and my hands were sweaty. I brushed them against the couch and tried to regulate my breathing that seemed completely out of control.

"I understand this must be difficult," Dr. Cordova said.

"Difficult?" I opened my hands like I was releasing a time bomb. That wasn't too far off the mark. "This isn't difficult, it's devastating."

Dr. Cordova nodded, and when he spoke again, his voice was unnervingly even and calm. "When Dr. Valenti treated Branson, she focused on the presenting problem at the time," he said. "Branson blacked out at school and came to in the men's restroom with bloodied knuckles. At the time, the only known cause of this event was...." Dr. Cordova quickly lifted the notepad and scanned through the sheets of paper in the file folder. "Oh, here it is. Branson was defending a foreign exchange student from a young woman who was verbally harassing him." He closed the file folder. "Post-traumatic stress disorder can be triggered by an event or witnessing an event that causes a flashback or severe anxiety from a traumatic event that previously happened.

And from the medical notes and police records"—he placed his hand on top of the file as if he were swearing an oath— "there is substantive history that Branson witnessed some form of abuse in his childhood."

It was the first time someone, anyone, had ever acknowledged the abuse that I suffered, that my children watched, at the hands of their father. Whenever I imagined this moment when Ed would be held accountable, I always thought I'd feel relief, validation—hell, maybe even happiness. Instead, shame crept over me like an old familiar blanket that had long lost its warmth. There wasn't any pride in knowing I had been abused, or worse, that I hadn't protected my children from its devastating effects.

"So given Branson's past," Dr. Cordova continued, "it was reasonable that Dr. Valenti diagnosed Branson with PTSD."

"Okay," I said. "Then why isn't it that?"

"People who suffer with PTSD may have symptoms that involve intrusive memories of the traumatic event, or they may relive the event in a flashback, which in either account seems real, as if it were happening again. So this would fit with *some* of the symptoms Branson presented with," Dr. Cordova explained.

"Okay, so it's PTSD," Ed cut in.

Dr. Cordova swayed his head from side to side. "I don't believe it's that because symptoms of PTSD are usually grouped into four categories." He held up his index finger. "First, the individual may have intrusive memories." He popped up another finger. "Two, they have a noticeable change in their thinking and mood." He added a third finger. "Three, they may start avoiding situations." He held up a fourth finger. "And finally they may have a change in their emotional reaction to everyday situations."

I nodded. "That sounds like what Branson has. He was defending someone, and it probably triggered something from his past and it affected his mood. He blacked out, and the whole school probably knows about it, so of course he got depressed. But instead of hurting someone else, he hurt himself. How *isn't* that PTSD?"

"PTSD seems on target to me," Ed said. "His mother and I did argue a lot."

"The symptoms Branson has shared with Clive indicate he's not suffering from PTSD," Dr. Cordova replied.

"Why? Because of the voices?" Fear came out as anger. I leaned forward, as if my stance would change his mind. "You said people with PTSD have intrusive thoughts."

"No." Dr. Cordova shook his head. "Someone suffering with PTSD may have intrusive *memories*."

I shrugged. "What's the difference?"

Dr. Cordova slightly tilted his head. "Intrusive memories don't involve voices that tell someone to harm another person or themselves."

I collapsed against the couch as the air left my lungs. The undertow was too strong. I wanted to save my son, but I didn't know how; I couldn't even save myself from each wave of emotion that built upon the other until I no longer knew which way was up.

"My son would never harm anyone." Ed's voice buoyed

me in the room.

I barely nodded. The collar of my shirt was wet from crying and clung to my chest like a leaded apron.

"At this point, there's no evidence of suicidal or homicidal risks," Dr. Cordova told us without any shock or horror in his voice.

As if homicidal risks were an everyday conversation. I couldn't feel anything anymore. My entire body was numb, and my mind had long ago shut the door on this conversation.

Dr. Cordova lifted his notepad and grabbed something from the file folder, placing a sheet of paper in front of him. "My concern is that Branson has a long history of auditory hallucinations."

"A long history?" My pulse quickened. Maybe I wasn't completely checked out.

"He reports that he's heard voices—or static, as he calls it—since at least the eighth grade."

"Eighth grade?" I covered my mouth with my hand. The shock was leveling.

"He's functioned reasonably well in school considering his symptons."

"He's a senior in high school." I lowered my head and continued to cry. "I didn't know." My chest shook. "Why didn't he tell me?" I looked up at Dr. Cordova. "Why didn't I know? I should've known."

"He masks things well," Dr. Cordova said.

Oh, Branson. That only made the sorrow greater, the shame deeper, the loss irrevocable.

"From my initial evaluation, it's hard to tell whether he's

happy or just very creative in how he hides his symptoms. He looks for things to look forward to."

The pain cut through me until it physically hurt to breathe.

"When Branson came to you and told you about the voices, that was a very big step for him. To your son's credit, he's managed life extremely well considering his symptoms."

"But all I heard was that he was depressed. I mean, I *heard* him tell me about the voices, but I just figured...." Tears stung my eyes. "I just focused on the depression."

"Depressive symptoms are easier to report and identify," Dr. Cordova said. "And Branson's depression seems to have improved on Paxil. So as I said, we'll continue with the Paxil. What I will discuss with Branson are his options for treating the hallucinations."

"What are those options?" Ed chimed in.

"There are many medications out there, from Abilify to Geodon, and each one affects people differently."

"Like how?" I asked.

"The chief complaint is weight gain," Dr. Cordova explained.

I shook my head. "Branson's a runner and he's in great shape. That won't be an issue."

Dr. Cordova nodded. "I'd still like to discuss these options with Branson and give him the choice."

Neither Ed nor I countered our son having a voice in his healthcare, nodding from our respective couches.

"Given Branson's history of the psychosis and some of

the other symptoms, we'll work to find an antipsychotic medication that will treat the hallucinations," Dr. Cordova said.

"What can I do?" It was the only question that seemed to surface when what I really wanted to know was how can I fix him?

"I'd like to schedule an EEG. Given the visual hallucinations, I'd like to be sure there's nothing organic going on," Dr. Cordova responded.

"What the hell does that mean?" Ed asked.

Despite myself, I laughed. *He's such an idiot. He probably thinks it's some organic food thing.*

"An EEG is a test that detects the electrical activity in your brain. I'd like Branson to have a sleep-deprived EEG to rule out that there isn't something organic or preexisting in his brain," Dr. Cordova said.

"Like a tumor?" I asked.

The psychiatrist nodded.

And for a moment, I saw the life vest.

Dear God, please let it be a tumor.

CHAPTER 15

BRANSON

HEY, Trevor's going to hang out w/me after school, I texted my mom.

Okay. Who's Trevor? Her reply wasn't as irritating as normal. *Maybe talking to Clive helped.*

Smart kid going 2 help w/homework.

Okay. What class?

Pre-calc.

Okay, have fun! Dr. Cordova wants you to have a sleep-deprived test to check out your brain. Setting it up.

I exhaled. First off, she didn't send short replies. My mom's texts were fucking novels. Second, why did she have to ruin every good mood with something serious?

Okay, I texted back. *Whatever. Starve me of sleep and then study my brain. Sounds like a regular day at camp crazy to me.*

"Trev, you ready?"

Trevor was taller, bulkier, and threw shot put. Dressed in a tight gray American Eagle T-shirt with longer, baggy jeans that couldn't conceal his muscular legs, he was a beast. He nodded with a shit-eating grin on his face.

We climbed into my car, and thankfully it started up without any problems. *At least I didn't embarrass myself in front of him.*

We drove silently to my house. I bumped open the front door with my hip and turned to him. "Bandit's got a bark, but she won't bite."

He reached down and scratched Bandit behind the ear, and the dog immediately became his best friend. "I've got a pug, Frank, and he snores all the time. I think I'd rather have a dog that barks than snores. I can never get to sleep."

"Man, I barely slept at all last night. Between my brother's snoring and…" *The cat from hell.* I shook my head. "I ended up staying up and finishing my game."

"Yeah, sometimes that just gets me more wound up."

I shrugged and led Trevor into the house. "True, but it gives my mind something to do."

Trevor patted me on the back. "God, you're such a nerd. I can't believe you can do calc in your head."

I grinned. "Yeah, don't tell my mom that or she'll have me bumped up to honors math."

"Is that why you're in pre-calc, because your mom doesn't know you're Rain Man with numbers? You're the smartest kid in class. You should be in regular calculus."

I wiggled my eyebrows. "But all the hot girls are dumb, and they're in pre-calc."

Trevor laughed. "Yeah, they're pretty fucking stupid."

"That's okay. The only numbers I care about in that class are theirs."

Trevor may have been better built than me, but he wasn't as smart. "What the hell?"

"The girls' numbers are the only ones I like."

Trev laughed. "That's good. I wouldn't mind getting Ashley's digits."

"Ashley Bailey?"

Trevor nodded.

"Don't even get me started on that annoying bitch."

"What's your problem with her? She's hot," Trevor said.

"Hot doesn't make up for rude. The girl's a major drama queen."

"I've heard that."

I cocked my head toward the kitchen. "Food's in the refrigerator. Help yourself. I've gotta take a piss."

I went into the coveted upstairs guest bathroom that my mom forbade us from using. It was painted this drab gray with cream-colored hand towels that made it look like I was using the bathroom at Outback. I rolled my eyes and suddenly felt like Jimmy Neutron when all the parents in town are abducted by aliens and the kids run wild. "I'm peeing in the shower!" I wanted to yell, but instead, I left the toilet lid up when I was finished. *What do you think about that shit?*

I used her special antibacterial soap. Our house was full of antibacterial soap, lotion—hell, our shampoo was probably anti-something. For all her fear of germs and us catching something, there was nothing in our house that could wash away what was inside my head.

I dried my hands on the fancy towel she had laid out perfectly on the sink, leaving it in a wad on the counter as I looked in the mirror and fingered down my hair. It was wavy and blond like my dad's, and always out of control. Lucky for Aaron his hair was perfection every morning. How the hell we were identical was beyond me. Looking at our baby pictures, it was impossible to tell us apart, but now? I shook my head and tried to get my hair to settle into place. We were as opposite as we could be, and I liked it that way. It prevented me from being called Aaron when clearly I wasn't my brother.

I found Trevor with his nose in our refrigerator.

"Hey, what'd you tell your mom? I mean about why I'm here?"

"I told her you were helping me with my homework."

Trevor shook his head and laughed. He closed the refrigerator and leaned against the kitchen counter.

"So how're your other classes going?" I asked.

"They're all right. Senior year. I'm just ready to get done."

"I'm with you there." I opened the freezer. "You hungry?"

"I could always eat."

"Okay."

I put four frozen chicken patties into the microwave and grabbed two paper plates. When the microwave dinged, I slapped the patties on buns and doused them with ketchup, then snagged a bag of barbeque chips out of the pantry and sat across the kitchen table from Trevor.

Hmmm, this guy isn't too bad. Someone I can finally tolerate besides Dakota. And she's always so busy lately. It's nice to have someone else to hang around with.

"So, what do you think of Mrs. Tuttle?" he asked.

"The office lady?"

"Yeah, her."

"What about her?" I bit into the sandwich. The fried, breaded patty was delicious.

"She's really pissing me off."

"Why? What did Mrs. Tuttle do to you?"

"I don't know. She was just being a bitch to me today."

I thought back to third block. I didn't remember Mrs. Tuttle even asking for Trevor to come to the office. But then I left to go see Clive, so it could've happened when I was gone.

"She's always nice to me."

"Yeah, I wouldn't trust that—someone who's nice all the time. Something not right with that."

I shook my head. "Man, you need to calm down. Mrs. Tuttle's gotta be pushing seventy. She's harmless."

Trevor waved his chicken burger at me. "Just watch your back, that's all I'm saying."

"Got it." I reached into the bag of chips and put a hefty amount on my plate.

"You eat like a horse."

I grinned. "Lucky that way."

Trevor raised his eyebrows. "I dunno, bro. You're not as thin as you used to be."

"What?" My voice rose. "Shut the fuck up." I looked down at my stomach. It wasn't as taut, but I hadn't worked out yet.

"Listen, we both run indoor track, and we both know you feel every extra ounce. I just don't want Coach Walker to ride your shit this season."

"Coach is a douche. My mom says he's got a million-dollar body and a face to protect it."

That made Trevor burst out laughing.

"Yeah, Coach is pretty fugly."

"It's all his acne. It scarred up his face." I shuddered. "It's disgusting. He's got these pits like a fruit that's gone bad or something. Freaks me out."

"Yeah, it's nasty." Trevor sighed. "I dunno, I just worry about my weight all the time."

"Why?" I grabbed some more chips.

"One of my friends used to be able to eat like us, but then he turned eighteen and it was like he changed. He went from having this lean high school body to like a dad body—you know, like what you see in college. Those guys who have beer guts and everything."

I shook my head. "Yeah, well I work out and run track, so that'll *never* be me."

"What about your medication?"

"What?" It felt like my heart dropped to my stomach. "What medication?"

"I saw it on the counter."

I glanced over Trevor's shoulder to the kitchen counter. My antidepressant was in full view for the world to see.

"What about it?" I asked.

"Did you read the side effects?"

"No. Did you?" *What the fuck is up with this guy?*

"Listen, you don't need to get defensive, but you were in the bathroom for a while, so I googled the medication and read up on it. It can cause weight gain."

I thought Dr. Cordova had said something about that, but I couldn't remember exactly. I shrugged. "It's for depression. I get down sometimes. It's temporary."

"Hey, I'm just looking out for you, that's all."

I was about to grab another handful of chips, but instead, I folded up the bag and stuffed it back in the pantry.

"You want to play video games?" I asked.

"I thought we were gonna finish our math homework."

I shrugged. "Like you said, why bother when I can do it in my head. Besides, we can do it later or before class tomorrow."

Trevor held out his fist and I bumped it. "Hells yes. Let's go play."

CHAPTER 16

TARA

I walked briskly into the foyer that led to my office. After my session with Ed and Dr. Cordova, I wasn't sure how well my concealer would cover up the fact that for the last hour, I'd been crying in my car, and the hour before that, I was sobbing in the good doctor's office. There was never a time in my life when I felt more alone or scared. I wanted to talk to someone, but who?

Add to it that I couldn't seem to shake this heaviness that hung on me like extra weight. It was ironic really, because for the first time in my life, I wasn't battling the bulge. Not even close. The only upside to all of this was that I had long ago lost my appetite. There was only one thing I craved, and it was my son's peace of mind.

I quickly glanced at my staff who sat outside the perimeter of my corner suite and nodded toward them as I headed toward my office.

"Tara," Rachel's voice called out after me.

Crap. I turned on the four-inch heel of my Jimmy Choos and flashed the pointed toe of my snake-embossed pumps at my executive assistant. To be fair, in my smoky, slim-cropped Hugo Boss slacks, it was impossible to ignore my footwear. And besides, being cheeky with Rachel helped elevate my mood.

I looked at her and a long "Yes" followed.

"Nice shoes," she said with a twinkle in her eye.

"Oh, these?" I rolled my shoulders and playfully wagged my foot at her.

My assistant had no idea that my six-hundred-dollar footwear was one of the perks of my job. When the dean of academic affairs informed me that I'd be rubbing shoulders with admission directors across the nation, I negotiated a clothing allowance into my employment package. It was unusual for a university, but I reasoned if they wanted to hire the *New York Times* bestselling author of the top-rated admissions handbook, they'd have to sweeten the pot. They did, and each month I had a fat allowance to spend on clothes.

"Yeah, feeling swaggy," I said, and instantly felt my cheeks ignite with heat. *I should never try to mimic the college kids.*

She shook her head and her long blonde ponytail swayed behind her. "You're getting there, boss, but don't go to a nightclub without me."

I wagged my index finger back and forth. "No worry there. I don't do nightclubs." Rachel knew I was always trying to stay current with the lingo of the college co-eds.

No matter how moronic I sounded, I knew that, as the director of admissions, it was important to be in touch with the trends. And the millennial generation developed Urban Dictionary to define their trend toward creative word choice.

"Dean Bryant stopped by while you were at your appointment."

I nodded. *Clearly he's read the list of early admissions.*

"He'd like to see you when you have a moment," she added.

Maybe I could talk to Rachel about my son. She's young. She knows him. She'd understand.

"He seemed pretty bent," she said.

I tilted my head. "Bent?"

"You know, schizo," Ben jumped in. "One minute he's the nice dean of academic affairs who gives us tickets to the football game on Friday, and the next minute he's ranting at Rachel about the list of early admissions."

I volleyed my head toward Ben, my graphic designer. Even though September had passed, it was still warm outside, yet a blue-and-gold beanie sat low on his head. Combined with his goatee and long hair, he always reminded me of Shaggy from *Scooby-Doo*. Not something I'd ever share with him, of course. Or really anyone.

Ben was usually as good as they came, but his comment completely took me off guard. *Schizo.* It was like a one-two punch to the gut.

I shifted my weight on my stilettos and hoped to hell they'd hold me when I felt like I could fall like a house of cards.

"I've never heard that expression," I said.

"I'm sorry." His fair skin tinged crimson. "It's probably not PC to use. I apologize."

I nodded. "I understand that I've created a more liberal work environment because of the nature of what we do. We're constantly in a pressure cooker with enrollment numbers to meet, applications to accept, deny, or place on hold. Parents and students contacting us, and our dean of academic affairs checking on our every move. I understand the frustration. However...." I steadied myself when I could just as easily have cried and told them, *Don't say that. Don't ever hurt someone I love with those words. It's not his fault.* But instead, I swallowed hard and gently smiled at my young staff.

"I don't think using terms like...." I couldn't say it. "I just don't think it's appropriate workplace language, and besides"—I broadened my smile—"there are ears everywhere, and if it were to get back to Dean Bryant, there's nothing I could do if he decided to go to human resources. The university is pretty clear on affirmative action, and while still a new area, individuals with disabilities, like mental illness, would fall under that class of protection."

"Understood," Ben said. "I wasn't thinking. I'm sorry."

I raised my shoulders. "It happens. I put my foot in my mouth all the time."

They both laughed when I knew I hadn't been funny, but it broke the tension from my little workplace speech. "So"—I clapped my hands together to further rally my troops—"anything new on your front?"

Ben tilted back in his ergonomically crafted chair. "I'm still working on the spring brochure."

I nodded. "Good deal. I'd really like to incorporate those taglines we were spitballing about."

Ben rubbed his chin and glanced at the notepad on his desk. "Round 'em up, head 'em out, the Posse's coming—look out!" He looked up at me and smiled. "Those taglines?"

"Okay, now when you read it like that, it sounds corny." I rolled my eyes for good measure. "But didn't we think we could craft a clever spring enrollment promotion with a cowboy riding the range?"

Ben looked at Rachel and then back to me. "We were thinking about maybe veering away from the cowboy and using a team roper instead."

"Okay." *Now this I can do. Work makes sense when nothing else does. These aren't people I can confide in, but I can lead them.* "What'd you have in mind?" I leaned against the doorframe of my office.

"I know Wyoming's the Cowboy State, but we were thinking of having a series of photos with team ropers. Maybe three shots that capture a moment as the team ropers compete. So they're both coming out of the chutes, and in each frame we capture our brand. As the riders are heading out, it'd flash 'Round 'em up,' and then as they're throwing their ropes toward the steer, we'd flash 'Head 'em out.' Then when they've looped the horns and the heels and have the steer tied up, it'd flash 'The Posse's here—look out!'"

"Oh, I really like that. So why the team ropers versus, say, a calf roper? Or a bull rider?"

"A majority of the freshmen coming to WSU are probably going to feel alone because they're on their own for the first time, so we thought projecting the image of a team might possibly, *subliminally,* make them feel more connected?" Rachel's voice rose with uncertainty at the end.

"You two are my dream team. I love it."

I pumped my fist in the air.

"I think that's a brilliant idea, *and* it'll generate interest from our ranch communities who may be on the fence— every pun intended—about whether to send their cowpoke to college. Excellent job."

"Well, you came up with the taglines," Ben said.

"You flatter me, but I know a bad cheer when I make it up, and you turned something corny into gold." I bowed graciously. "Thank you both for making that a thousand times better. Is there anything I can help with?" I looked at Rachel and then back to Ben.

They collectively shook their heads. "We're good on our end. We'll work with the PR department for the photo shoot."

I chuckled. "Good luck with that. They tend to be a bit hands-off, so if you need me to run interference, let me know." I glanced at the wall clock behind Rachel's head. It was nearing four. The college shut down by five in the fall, but there was one more thing I had to do before I met with my dean.

I went into my office, closed the door, and fired up my computer. Typing in my security password, I proceeded to find Ashley Bailey's online application. With a strike of a key, her status changed from that of an applicant with legacy ties to a standard admission.

I drew a deep breath, shut down my computer, grabbed my Kate Spade-embossed binder, and headed out of my office. I glanced at Rachel and then at Ben. "I'll be in Dean Bryant's office if you need me. If this runs late and I don't see you, have a good night and I'll see you both tomorrow morning."

Walking down the hallway toward his office, I didn't have anything prepared to say in my defense for cutting short Wilson High School's list of early admissions. I did have a lot to say about why I did it, but nothing that wouldn't get me in hot water.

Dean Bryant's office took up the entire north wall of the fourth floor. It was obscenely large, and no matter how often I stepped into his ivory tower, the feeling of envy never waned. What I would do with an office that could double as an apartment replete with a minibar and private bathroom, I had no idea. Still, I wanted what he had, but I wasn't willing to pursue a doctoral degree to get it.

Alas, I'll stay in my modest glass corner office.

"Tara, glad you could make it in to see me." He rose when I walked in, and even his height was supersized at 6'6. A row of Stanford basketball trophies stood on the glass shelves in his office, next to the framed diplomas: an undergraduate degree from Stanford, master's degrees from Pepperdine and USC, a doctoral degree from UCLA. While I kept looking for the partridge in the pear tree, fuck if I could find it.

Dr. Shawn Bryant, Dean of Academic Affairs, was my boss and assigned mentor, though I'd never sought his advice in my career. His blond hair and green eyes were too perfect. And for a man who'd just celebrated his fifty-fifth birthday, he looked like a Greek god. He was tan year-round because of his running regime, and unlike 90 percent of the administrators, his gut didn't hang over his belt loop. He was, in a word, dreamy. And in another word, distracting. I didn't need any more distractions in my life.

"Sorry it's so late, Dean." I purposefully shook my head and let my auburn hair fall around my face. Tucking a wavy strand behind my ear, I let the contrast between my fair skin and vibrant hair work to my advantage. I had my hair highlighted and cut every six weeks to ensure it was always in top shape. My sons may tease that I was a "ginger," but I hadn't found a man yet who wasn't curious about a redhead. "I was wrapping up a project with my staff before they left, and time just got away from me. My apologies."

"Stop with the formalities and take a seat." He extended his hand, which looked like it could palm two basketballs, toward the open chair beside his desk, then pulled his high-back black chair toward me and sat next to me versus across from me. He always did that. I was sure it was some educational leadership class on social ergonomics that he'd learned in his PhD program. All I knew was it made me start to sweat like I was in junior high and the cute kid just sat beside me.

I sat down and placed my binder next to me, smiling tightly until it felt like my cheeks were going to explode.

Anything to keep my mind off him and his cologne, which was a very subtle, spicy, sexy scent.

What the hell? Has it been that long since I've been with a man?

I crossed my legs and started to bounce my foot when I realized it was a giant message to Shawn that I was either anxious or irritated. I quickly stopped the shaking motion and crossed my legs at the ankles. It was the body language equivalent to placing my hands in my lap; it seemed natural, relaxed, and signaled that I was neither attracted to nor afraid of him.

Shawn didn't even seem to notice as he reached behind him and palmed a folder. "I was looking through your list of early admissions for next fall."

"Class of 2020," I said, thinking of my sons and the plan I'd put into place when their college graduation seemed a distant date in the future. Now as they were into their senior year of high school, it would be four short years to the fulfillment of my master plan for their life.

I almost laughed. *Things are so not going as I imagined.*

"As you're aware, Dr. Cummins is having WSU participate in the college survey of student engagement," he said, then handed me the memo I clearly had not read.

I skimmed it for the pertinent details. *National survey. Fall semester.* My eyes roved the page. *Where is it? Ah yes.* Retention in college. *Bingo.*

"Of course." I placed the memo on the corner of his desk between us. "I know the president is concerned about our retention rate and how to improve the entire college experience," I said, almost lifting word-for-word from the memo. If having four children had taught me anything, it was to read quickly for content and be able to multitask. And I was seriously multitasking with what I knew and what I needed to appear to know.

"Exactly. And the student learning and retention rate at WSU falls under our department's purview." Shawn opened the file folder. "So you can imagine my surprise when I read the short list of candidates for early admission. It's hard to retain students when we enter in so few." He glanced up from the folder, and his green eyes looked like the Ciaran Mountains in my mother's home country of Ireland.

I softly smiled. *I wish you were here, Mom.* I swallowed hard.

"Is everything okay?" Shawn asked.

I playfully rolled my eyes. "Yes, just having a melancholy moment thinking of my twin boys graduating and joining the class of 2020." *Nice redirect.* Shawn was nothing if not interested in two potential incoming freshmen.

"That's right!" He slapped the file folder. "Aaron and Branson are seniors this year."

"Yes they are. So I was extremely careful to make sure Rachel excluded their files from my early admissions selection process." It wasn't hard, because neither of them applied to this shitty institution. Neither Rachel nor Shawn knew that, though they would've if they'd bothered to read my book from cover-to-cover and not skim the chapter summaries. WSU did not align with my five-step process for locking down an Ivy League education.

"Tara, no one is questioning your credibility. You're the finest director of admissions in Wyoming."

That's because I'm the only *director of admissions in Wyoming.* Community colleges didn't count. Hell, community colleges were built for the candidates I rejected.

I looked at my Dean and smiled. "Thank you." I was striking the right balance between too much and too little eye contact. Too much and he'd probably move to the other side of his desk; too little and he'd think I wasn't interested in what he had to say. Shawn was always sending me to these seminars on body language that he couldn't attend. Today I was exercising every tactic to appear open and not closed during a potential workplace confrontation. And it was just a matter of time before Shawn stayed on task and addressed why I was in his office.

"Tara, this list seems rather small," he said. "I got a call from Fred early this morning, and he's claiming that a vast majority of legacy candidates didn't make the cut for early admission."

I had two ways to play this: feign stupidity, which Shawn wouldn't buy, or... "That can't be right." I allowed my rapid heart rate to come out through my voice. "Oh my goodness." I reached toward the list of early admissions and stopped midway. "I'm sorry. May I?"

Shawn graciously handed me the memo I had sent Principal Stanley less than forty-eight hours ago.

"Well yes, that's my memo, but I don't remember forgetting any legacy candidates." I purposefully pointed toward Wyatt Arn, Marybeth Sims, Gene Harpy, and Sally Grey. Four legacy candidates whose names I had committed to memory. "These are all legacy candidates from Wilson High School," I said.

Now the thing that worked in my favor was that there was only one person who knew the exact number of legacy candidates who had applied for early admission: Rachel. And after Shawn gave her the verbal beatdown today in my absence, it wasn't likely she was going to rat me out to the man who went all "bent" on her.

As far as Shawn knew, I had followed university protocol and granted early admission to all our legacy applicants from Wilson High School. And if that wasn't a slam dunk, I looked up at him with my own bewitching green eyes and beguiled him with a straight-up lie.

"It's possible that a legacy candidate slipped past me, but—" I slowly shook my head. "—it's hard to imagine that the computer would've missed it."

All applicants registered online, so there was a computer printout of everyone who'd applied. The beauty of having a machine involved was that technology errors happened all the time in academia, especially when I went back into the computer and purposefully changed Ashley's status. Later I would change more Wilson applicants to even out the playing field, but for now, I'd covered my bases. Plus, by doing it from work, it would trace the last IP address to the university and not my home. Or at least that's what I hoped.

"You think maybe some of the applicants got miscoded?" I asked when I clearly already knew the answer.

"That's quite possible," Shawn said. "I'll have the IT department look into it and send Fred an email telling him the same."

"I am so sorry if this has caused unnecessary work for you."

Shawn waved the file folder. "Don't think anything about it. Now that you've pointed out the legacy candidates you did spot, I imagine the rest were miscoded. It's an easy error to amend."

"I agree." I smiled, uncrossed my ankles and stood.

Shawn stood and held out his hand. I placed my hand in his, and he gripped it like it was the prize-winning ball. "Thank you for staying late to work this out," he said.

"Of course."

I walked away with my Kate Spade tucked beneath my arm and a smile across my face.

Maybe insanity is contagious.

CHAPTER 17

BRANSON

"*DUDE,* why are you late? Were you held up?"

I looked at my brother. Aaron had on my naval academy shorts that *I* had earned at the summer seminar institute and a tight black Nike shirt. I was in a mismatched purple Dri-FIT shirt and green Nike shorts. Aaron always said I looked like Barney, but I couldn't care less. "I was just hanging out with Trevor before practice and I lost track of time."

"Who's Trevor?"

"Oh, he's just a buddy I have in pre-calc. He helps me with my homework sometimes."

"Why haven't I met him yet?"

"He's just a buddy in math. I don't hang out with him often."

Coach Walker started the practice by sending us around the indoor track twice.

"If one lap doesn't warm you up, two'll fucking do it," I said to Aaron, who was beside me and then sprinted ahead of me.

"Slow the fuck down. It's not a race!" I yelled to my brother's back. I didn't worry about Coach hearing or even caring. There was only one thing Walker concerned himself with and it was the fitness of his athletes. During indoor season, he didn't let us eat any sort of food that had chemicals you couldn't pronounce or saturated fats anywhere in the ingredients, and sugar was off-limits. He wanted us strictly on a protein diet. My lunch of fried chicken burgers and barbeque chips didn't fit into his pyramid.

I fell farther behind Aaron with the shot putters and discus throwers who couldn't run for shit. They were either really in shape and cut, or they were soft and heavy around the edges. There was no gray area with the throwers.

That's okay. I can hang back until I catch my second wind.

"What's up, Kovac?" one of the shot putters called out.

I cocked my head toward him. "Yeah, looks like I'm slumming it with the throwers."

Aaron was about twenty meters ahead of me, maybe thirty. I wouldn't let him lap me. I was always faster than my brother, plus I had a longer stride and a higher endurance that usually carried me through the season and into state. But lately with this stupid medication, I'd felt sluggish and hadn't been able to get the same rev as I used to. I glanced down at my shirt. It was clinging with sweat to my stomach that extended out a little more than it used to.

Maybe Trev's right. Maybe I have gained weight.

The guys next to me all had loose bellies that jiggled

when they ran. I shook my head. *No fucking way.* If other people wanted to be out of shape, that was their business, but I wouldn't let any medication, no matter what it promised to do, make me soft and weak. *Hell no.*

I kicked up my feet and speed, rounding the corner on Aaron quickly and swiftly. The shocked look on his face was priceless as I sprinted past him toward the finish line of the first lap. I looked ahead of me, and the second lap seemed like it stretched farther than my legs could travel. My side hurt, my lungs burned, and for all of Coach's lectures, I understood the necessity of solid protein before a workout. I had no fuel left—for anything. I pushed and my thighs stung with the awareness that I was carrying too much weight.

I drifted back to my original location with the throwers. My acceleration was slowly depleting, and so was my confidence.

Damn, I guess I need to get back in shape.

When I finally finished the second lap, Aaron was waiting in the circle stretch next to some of his buddies. Usually I liked Aaron's friends, but the guy to his left, Jesse, was unbearably aggressive, and his former wrestler mentality that he had to beat everyone was obnoxious.

"You were going pretty slow on your second lap," Jesse said.

Well fuck, this is going to be interesting.

"You all right there, fat ass?" Jesse was taller and easily outweighed me. Still, he was being a douche.

"Usually I'd take offense to something like that, but

I'm just surprised you actually created a full sentence that quickly and succinctly with your low mentality," I shot back.

Aaron and his other buddy James started snickering.

"You wanna go?" Jesse puffed out his chest and reminded me of a king cobra ready to strike.

"Sorry, I'm gonna leave wrestling for the gay porn industry," I said with as much sarcasm as I could carry. "But maybe next time."

Jesse took a step forward and I did too. *Bring it on, douche. I may not be able to do much damage, but you haven't fucked with the shadow people. And they don't take well to being picked on.*

Aaron intercepted Jesse before he tore my face off. "Okay, let's calm down, guys. Branson's just joking around."

The great thing about being an identical twin was that there was no need for words. Twins could share a look between each other that said everything. And the stern look on Aaron's face said I'd better knock it off before I got a beatdown.

When Jesse stepped back, I relaxed my fist, which I had unconsciously clenched. I glanced at Aaron and gave him a wry grin. He shook his head. If my look had words attached to it, it would've said, "See, brother, I can't be crazy because it's statistically proven that crazy people don't think they're crazy." *And I'd have to be crazy to challenge Jesse.*

CHAPTER 18

TARA

"COME on, Ma, trust me. Let's have some fun."

All my children had different names for me. For whatever reason, Aaron called me Ma and sounded like he was Brooklyn born and bred, not the California native he was.

I held onto the passenger door handle as my teenager barreled down the street in his 1996 Saab. The car was older than my son. "You know this is a twenty-mile-per-hour zone, right?"

"That's a mere suggestion." Aaron flashed me a grin.

I rolled my eyes and laughed. "Just get us there in one piece."

Carson was in the back seat with her nose in a book, and Jack was playing his DS. The Pokémon theme song played in the background.

"What's Branson doing tonight?" I asked.

"He went to Dakota's house, if you can call it that."

I looked at Aaron. "What do you mean?"

"It's not really a house, just a shitty apartment. But it does the trick for the two of them."

"Dakota and her mom?"

Aaron nodded and flipped on his turn signal, which sounded like a fast heartbeat. "So you've been to Dakota's house—I mean apartment?"

"Yeah. It was weird, but I had a girl there so it was all right."

"What girl? Chelsea?"

Aaron shook his head and his honey-colored hair waved back and forth. "Before Chelsea." He gave me a wry smirk. "It was just some girl I didn't plan on sticking around with long."

"Aaron, you can't date girls. You only get guys," Carson said. "I see you hanging out with that wrestling guy all the time."

Aaron tilted his head back against the seat. "Shut the hell up, Carson." His voice was light, whimsical and made us all laugh.

"Aaron doesn't like boys," Jack said. "He likes girls with golden hair, like Goldilocks."

We all laughed.

"Nah," Aaron replied. "Listen, little brother, you can always tell the dumb ones by their hair color."

I wanted to elbow him, but I was afraid to do anything to distract my teenager from his driving, which was already questionable.

"So where are we going?" I asked, redirecting the

conversation to something that wouldn't distract him. *If I'm not putting out fires at work, I'm doing it here.*

"Ma, trust me. Let's have a little fun."

I shook my head. "I'll have more fun if I know where we're going."

"You looked really stressed when you came home from work," he said.

I stared out the passenger window. "I was."

"Everything okay, Mummy?" Carson switched into English mode to lighten the mood.

I glanced over my shoulder and reached behind me to grab her bony knee. "Yes, baby girl. I just had a tense meeting with my dean."

"You're not getting fired, are you?" Aaron asked. The panic was evident in his voice. My children could not financially rely on their father.

I pulled my hand off Carson's knee and gently placed it on Aaron's shoulder. "I'm okay. We're okay. My dean had some questions about a recent list of early admissions that my office released. I think I answered his concerns, but he's going to go through the list, and I'm sure we'll meet again." I exhaled. "Nothing I can't handle. I'm not worried." *I should be, but I have too much other crap to concern myself with.*

"I'm sorry, Ma," Aaron said.

I rubbed his shoulder. "Nothing to apologize for. The nice thing about my position is that I can always turn a rejection into an admission and call it a 'computer error.' Happens all the time." *So if I need to let Ashley, that skanky little bitch who's been bullying your brother, into WSU, I will. And then*

I'll make sure she doesn't get any of her designated classes. I may not win the battle, but I always win the war.

"So what's the surprise?" Again I veered the conversation back to something else.

"I thought you could use a night out so I'm treating us for dinner," Aaron replied.

"Really?"

"Really."

"Thank you." I looked back out the passenger window and watched Casper blur by while my son blared music from his iPhone. An auxiliary cord ran from the cassette player into his phone. I wasn't sure how it worked, only that it did, and hip-hop and rap blared from the back speakers, reawakening my dulled senses.

Aaron pulled into the parking lot of the fifties-themed hamburger stand. "Big A" was plastered on a sign along with a dancing Elvis.

I smiled. "Aren't you sick of eating here?"

Aaron grinned. "Only reason I brought you here is because I get an employee discount."

"Yeah, hamburgers!" Carson exclaimed.

"Can I get a sundae?" Jack asked.

"Yeah, of course, buddy," Aaron said.

I gently touched my son's arm. "You're *not* buying dinner. I don't mind tapping into your discount," I chuckled, "but I'm paying."

We had missed the dinner crowd by at least an hour. Though I didn't think my kids ate dinner sooner than seven or eight each night. And thankfully it seemed they had conditioned their stomachs to stretch out their meals.

We slid into a corner booth with red vinyl padded seats, the tabletop was sparkled Formica with a silver band that wrapped around its base. Old 45s hung from the wall, and a jukebox lit up the corner like Times Square at midnight.

"Can I have a quarter for the juice box?" Jack asked.

Aaron almost spit out the water he had gulped down when we slid into the booth. "Buddy, it's a *juke*box."

Jack shrugged. "Can I still have a quarter to play Mom a song?"

Aaron fished through his jeans pocket and handed Jack and Carson a stack of quarters.

When they were out of earshot, Aaron turned to me.

"So, have you noticed anything different about Branson?"

I was afraid to ask. "Like what?"

"I don't know. He seems off."

"How?" I unwrapped my straw and placed it in the cup of water.

"He seems more depressed and monotone, like no emotion. Or the complete opposite and he'll flip a bitch on someone. He just seems like, I dunno, he acts bipolar."

Well at least he didn't say schizo. I stirred the ice cubes. *How much do I tell him?*

"Do you think it's the PTSD or the medication that's doing this?"

"They don't think it's PTSD," I said.

"What else could it be?" Aaron's hazel eyes filled with sincerity.

I scooted in closer to him and lowered my voice.

"Dr. Cordova wants to start your brother on antipsychotic medication."

"Have they done any tests to know if the medication will work on him? To know if he has the thing they're trying to cure?"

It amazed me how neither Ed, I, nor even Dr. Cordova had ever uttered what we all knew we were trying to cure in my son. Instead, we all seemed to dance around the diagnosis of what we suspected he suffered from.

"Dr. Cordova wants to run a sleep-deprived EEG, which will study his brain and rule out anything organic."

"Like hypnosis? Does that shit ever work?"

I chuckled. "No. An EEG is an electrical test that studies the brain waves to rule out something like a tumor."

"A tumor? Why the hell would they think Branson has a tumor?"

I took a sip of water. "Your brother's been having visual and auditory hallucinations." I repeated the doctor's good words without any emotion or feeling.

"So, like schizophrenia?"

And there it was. The word no one ever said and I dared not utter. Every emotion I tried to keep at bay settled at the base of my throat. My mouth went dry, and it felt like I would puke at any second.

I shook my head. "No one's given him that diagnosis yet."

"Ma, if he's hearing things and seeing things, what else would it be?"

I tried to swallow the pool of saliva that had suddenly

collected in my mouth, but my throat felt like it had closed. *I'm going to be sick.* "I don't know." I tried to swallow. "I'm praying it's a brain tumor."

"You know it's bad when you're praying for a brain tumor."

I nodded and kept my focus on my glass of water. *Why is the room spinning?*

"So what kind of schizophrenia are we talking about? Like voices in the head or *Beautiful Mind* visual things? Or both?"

My stomach roiled and tears poured down my face. I shrugged because I couldn't find my voice.

"Oh, Ma."

I lowered my head and put my hand on my forehead to shield the crying that I couldn't seem to control. "I don't know. I don't know what he hears. He calls it static. I don't know what it's like, if it's male or female or what. He made it sound like it's this static noise. And now he's having visual hallucinations, but I'm not sure what they are."

"Ma, this shit's serious."

I wanted to slam my hand on the table and scream that I knew this shit was serious. Instead, I took an even, steady breath. *Aaron is not my enemy.* "I've lined up the EEG, and I count his pills to make sure he's taking his antidepressant. I don't know what else to do."

A cute dark-haired waitress who wore her hair in a messy bun appeared at our table. I quickly wiped my eyes, then looked up at her and smiled.

She elbowed Aaron. "Let me guess, Shirley Temple with

lots of cherries?"

"Shut the heck up, Lucy," Aaron said in a flirty voice. "It's a good drink."

She grinned and handed us each a menu, leaving two kid menus for Carson and Jack, who were still feeding the jukebox quarters. Carson turned toward the table, and I shook my head for her to stay where she was with Jack.

When Lucy walked away, Aaron leaned toward me. "Ma, it's going to be okay. But I have noticed he has a new friend. This guy Trevor? I've never met him, but I guess he's in Branson's calc class."

"So what does that have to do with anything?" My tone was a bit defensive. "Maybe he's reaching out to new friends."

"Ma, I know almost everyone in the entire school, and I've never even heard of him."

"Aaron, there's no way in a graduating class of four hundred and eighty that you know *everyone.*" My son didn't even challenge me on the numbers of his graduating class, knowing I could recite the stats for every high school graduating class in Wyoming.

Aaron shook his empty water glass and fished an ice cube out with his mouth. "I'm not saying I know everyone, but I have seen or at least heard of everyone in our senior class."

"So maybe this is a new kid and you're jealous that Branson has someone new to hang around."

"Why would I be jealous? I hang out with him all the time. I'm just saying he was late to practice today, and

Branson is *never* late to practice."

"I'll talk to him about this Trevor kid. I'm sure he just lost track of time."

"Ma, why is this so hard for you to accept?"

"Accept? You're basically accusing Branson of, I don't know what, creating a friend? I think you have the movie version of mental illness in your mind and...." The familiar sadness took over as I lowered my voice. "It's hard enough to learn your son is hearing voices and now seeing things. I guess I'm just not ready to question a new friend simply because we haven't met him."

"I just have a bad feeling about this one."

I massaged my forehead, which felt like a vise had gripped down on it.

Aaron reached for my other hand. "We just have to be extra careful and make sure his mind is clear."

"Aaron, I don't know how to do that." I looked up at him. "If I knew how to make Branson's mind clear and get him back on track, I'd do it in a heartbeat. Hell, I'd give up anything and everything I have to make him okay."

"Well, we need to try harder."

"I shouldn't even be having this conversation with you, but now that we are, what do you suggest we do?"

"I don't know. Everything we can. I will not let my brother go crazy on us."

"If he has an imaginary friend as you suggest, I think he's already crossed that line."

"Then we give him that antipsychotic medication the doctor suggested and make that imaginary friend go away."

"*If* he has an imaginary friend. We don't even know that yet."

"I don't think we want to wait until he has an entire squad of friends."

I couldn't help but laugh. "Jesus, how did we get here?"

"Well, we could always blame Dad."

That time I laughed so hard my cheeks hurt. "As much as I'd like to blame your father, there's no genetic link on either side of our families. I already went down that path."

"All I know is Branson's not the twin I knew two years ago."

The purity and honesty of my son's emotion seeped into my soul. He had moved from conjecture to certainty.

"I just want my brother back, Ma." Aaron's eyes brimmed with tears.

"Oh, Aaron." My voice cracked and I pulled him into me. *He feels as alone in this as I do.*

"I'm so sorry." He leaned his head onto my shoulder and I kissed the top of his hair. I didn't think it was possible to feel any more grief than I already did. My stomach was hollow, my throat tightened around a thousand emotions that bubbled at the surface as my eyes stung from crying in the doctor's office and now at my son's favorite diner.

Enough, I said to whoever was listening. I didn't care who helped us, if it was some alien in another dimension or if God would actually listen to my cries and come to our aid. I only knew we had hit our breaking point.

Please. Help us.

"It's sad." Aaron raised his head off me. "I don't have

my brother here anymore." He flicked away a tear. "And I miss him. I really, *really* miss him."

"I miss him too." I pursed my lips together to stop them from trembling.

The waitress reappeared, and Aaron quickly smiled in her direction. "Hey, Lucy. Let's forget dinner and go straight for dessert."

CHAPTER 19

BRANSON

DAKOTA pulled into the three-car parking lot. *Full as usual.* She veered her silver Jetta back onto the street and parallel parked along the curb, almost hitting both cars.

"Jesus Christ, slow it down. You're driving like a bat outta hell," I said.

"Shut the hell up. I'm a great driver. I've only had three tickets."

"Yeah, and one hit car." I shook my head disapprovingly, but when she looked at me, I had a smirk on my face.

A big, warm bag of tasty treats sat on my lap. I inhaled the smell of chicken tenders mixed with double-bacon cheeseburgers and large fries as I balanced a tray with two cups of sugary, ice-cold goodness in my hand. *Blizzards. Yum.*

"You ready?" I looked at Dakota, who was checking her makeup in the rearview mirror. "We're just going inside your house, aren't we?"

"Oh shut up. I'm just checking my makeup to make sure I look great." She tilted the rearview back into position and unlocked the doors. The walk from the car to Dakota's apartment complex was about sixty feet, but it was sixty feet of poverty. It was like a scene from a movie: dogs barking, babies crying, people shouting. The block of apartment complexes in Casper was referred to as "Felony Flats," and it was easy to see why. There wasn't one car in the lot or on the street that wasn't dinged, dented, or broken. Screen doors were ripped, and flies didn't even loiter here. It was depressing, to say the least.

"Half of them keep a hide-a-key under their front wheel well," Dakota said as if reading my mind. "I guess they figure if they're evicted, they can always sleep in their car, especially during the winter."

"Oddly, that makes *perfect* sense."

She giggled again.

I balanced the bag of greasy, cheesy goodness in one hand and the tray of Blizzards in the other. "I'm not opposed to hide-a-keys, because God knows Aaron locks us out of our car often enough, but to put it on a car that's already broken into or has missing windows, that's what I don't get."

"It's a sense of ownership. You know I have one."

I nodded.

"And my friend Scotty has a new car. Well, it's used," she amended, "but it's new to him. He keeps a hide-a-key in case his mom kicks him out of the house or something. Then he always has a way to get to his dad's."

"That makes more sense. Except Scotty? Yeah, you don't have any male friends except me."

That time her laughter was throaty and sexy as hell. I embraced the sound.

Dakota and her mom, Helen, lived upstairs in a two-bedroom apartment. As far as safety went, it had average security: a bolt lock and a metal chain across the door, which Helen peered through before opening her door.

"Is your mom at work?" I asked, taking the stairs two at a time.

"She's always working. Twenty-four hours, five nights a week. Shift work." Dakota tried to shake it off, but I could tell it bothered her. Her mom was never home. She was a nurse at the hospital and took whatever shifts they had available, which often meant doubles, back-to-backs, and weekends.

"Ah, you know she's doing it for good reasons. She's just trying to get money to pay for food and all that," I said.

"I know, and I'm really proud she went back to school to get her degree, but it just sucks that I never see her anymore." She opened the door to the apartment, and I was overwhelmed by the scent of hair spray and perfume. "Damn," I said, waving my hand in front of my nose. "Don't anyone light a match."

Dakota giggled. *I made her laugh when she probably wanted to cry.*

We plopped down on the beaten-up, mustard-colored couch. The stuffing was thin and stuck out of the corner cushions, but for whatever reason, it was comfy and soft.

It was like sinking into a giant burnt-colored marshmallow.

Dakota handed me the remote and I handed her a Blizzard. I turned on Netflix and was scrolling through the list of television shows when she elbowed me.

"Stop there," she said with a mouth full of Butterfinger bites and ice cream.

"*Psych*?" I reached into the bag and grabbed a bacon-cheeseburger.

"This is the best show ever. I'm like addicted to it."

"Well, we'll see about that." I clicked onto the first episode of the first season. The lead character's sarcasm was funny as hell.

"I'm gonna go put on my pajamas." Dakota rose from the couch and kissed my cheek. "Be right back."

I opened another cheeseburger and practically popped the entire thing in my mouth. Washing it down with my Blizzard, I was about to grab my basket of chicken tenders when I heard Dakota crying.

I pushed myself off the couch and found her sitting on the bathroom floor, leaning against the tub.

"Babe, what's wrong?"

She shook her head, and her long, jet-black hair hung around her face. I knelt beside her and gently moved her hair.

"What happened?"

She balled something in her hand. "My pajamas don't fit."

I nodded. "Okay."

She closed her eyes and tears fell down her cheeks.

"You don't understand."

I moved beside her and sat against the tub. "I do understand."

"I've gained too much weight." She gripped the pajamas until her knuckles turned white. I gently reached for them.

"No!" She snapped them away and held them close to her chest. "I'm too fat. I'm too fucking fat to wear pajamas! Who's too fat to wear pajamas?"

I just listened, knowing there wasn't anything I could say when what she needed most was to be heard.

"It's so hard," she said with tears streaming down her face. "In the past, I had issues with my weight." She turned toward me. "You know I had an eating disorder."

I nodded.

"So in addition to recovering from that, which resulted in me *gaining* weight, I finally settled into a size that was healthy and good for me. But now that they're trying to turn around my depression, I'm gaining *more* weight. And this." She twisted the silk pajamas until I thought her hands would bleed. "This is *not* helping me feel better about myself or my appearance. I was a double zero." She looked at me. "A double zero."

I looked into her dark eyes that resembled the darkest depths at String Lake, wanting to throw her a life preserver, but I wasn't sure she'd reach for it.

"It just breaks my heart," she said softly. She released the pajamas and they fell between her long, slender legs. "I hate going shopping. It makes me feel uncomfortable and insecure. I'm on two soccer teams, I try to eat right, but if I don't treat my depression...." She sighed. "My depression is crippling. I can't do anything when it's not in check." She looked over at me. "I guess that's the most upsetting part."

I tilted my head.

"The doctors and my mom say it's not my fault, that I need this medication to treat my symptoms, but I didn't *do* anything to have these symptoms. I don't know why I can't snap out of it and be happy all the time, but I can't. I've tried."

I wanted to pull her into my arms and make the pain on her face that I knew reached deep go away, but I couldn't any more than I could make the shadow people or static go away.

I contemplated my next move. "Okay," I started. "First off, what size pajamas are they?"

Her dark eyes seemed to blacken. "What?"

"What size were those pajamas?"

"A zero. I wear a zero in everything." She kicked the pajamas away from her. "I used to be a double zero, but ever since they put me on that new medication...." She lowered her head, shame creeping into her voice. "I can't wear any of my zeros, and ones don't fit. I think I'm in a size two now. A *two*. That's three sizes bigger than when I met you."

If Dakota wasn't my girlfriend and I didn't understand how much she struggled with body image, then I might've laughed and said something insensitive. But she was my heart. "Listen, Dakota, it's the medication. You haven't been on it long, and didn't you say Dr. Cordova said your body would adjust to it and things like weight would level out?"

As if things weren't weird enough, Dakota and I both went to the same shrink. Hooray for me.

She nodded. "Yeah, something like that."

"Okay then. It's only been a few weeks, so things haven't leveled out yet."

I could lose myself in the look she gave me. I didn't hear static. The shadow people vanished. Everything I wanted in this world, everything that mattered, leaned her head on me and wrapped her arm around my waist. "Thank you."

I shrugged and grabbed my stomach that had now become a belly. "Listen, ever since they started me on my antidepressant, I've noticed my body's changed a bit too."

She giggled softly, and then her tone turned serious. "Does it bother you?"

"Yeah, I hate that I can't fit into my jeans that I've worn since middle school. But I don't think about it much." *I think about it* all *the time.* I lied. I lied because I wasn't about to tell Dakota how much it bothered me that my body was changing. That I couldn't outrun Aaron. That I was heavier and slower.

I didn't tell Dakota for the same reason I didn't tell her about the static or shadow people. I didn't want her to know that part of me. I didn't ever want her to look at me differently or be afraid of me.

"Well you've only gained like, what, five pounds?" Dakota said.

"Five pounds is equivalent to five hundred for a runner. Listen, I was like you and we were both able to eat anything and not see a dent on the scale. I don't know how much I weigh now, and I don't want to know. Scales suck." I looked around the bathroom and found Dakota's scale parked in the corner next to the toilet. "In fact, fuck this shit." I pushed against the bathtub to stand up, then bent over and grabbed the scale.

"What are you doing?" The shock in Dakota's voice made me grin.

"Come with me." I held out my hand. She reached up and grabbed it, and I helped my very tall, still very slender girlfriend to her feet. "You're beautiful." I kissed her sweetly, softly.

She leaned her head on my shoulder. "What are you doing with my scale?"

"Oh, this piece of shit?" I palmed the scale and waved it back and forth like a flag on Independence Day. "Come with me." I marched out of her bathroom, through her living room and out the front door of her apartment.

A group of lowlifes sitting on the bottom stoop of her stairs looked up when we came out. I cocked my head toward them. "Just getting rid of a little trash," I said, then threw the scale like a shot put as far as I could in the alley behind her apartments.

Dakota shrieked, and the guys on the bottom stair hooted and hollered. "Yeah, buddy."

I grinned. "Nothing's gonna make my girl feel bad about herself."

"Hell no," one of the tattooed freaks said.

She waved to him. "Hi, Scotty."

He jutted out his chin, which looked like it belonged

on a bulldog. The guy was seriously built. I grinned in his direction.

Dakota reached her arm around me and pulled me into an embrace. "Are you crazy?"

"That seems to be the diagnosis."

She leaned up, kissed me and then led me back into her apartment. "My mom's not going to be home until morning. Text your mom that you're staying the night at Jimmy's."

I shook my head. "She can check with Jimmy. I'll tell her I'm staying at Trevor's house."

CHAPTER 20

TARA

BRANSON'S journal was propped next to my computer as I waited for the university's slow web advisor to load.

"Come on." I tapped my bare foot on the carpeted floor in my office.

Jack and Carson were asleep, and Aaron left to get ice cream with Chelsea. The dinner and dessert he ate mere hours before wouldn't hold him until morning. *Ah, to be a teen again.* I felt bloated and couldn't drink enough water to drown out the salt the cooks at Big A seemed to shake on all their meals.

Aaron opened his heart, and I wasn't about to close it. So when Branson texted that he was staying overnight at Trevor's, I didn't alert Aaron. He needed to be seventeen and carefree, not carrying the burden for his identical half.

While I waited for my computer to load the university

software, I thumbed through my son's English journal. I hadn't read it in a few weeks, but I imagined it still contained the answers to questions I wasn't asking.

SEPTEMBER 8

LIFE IS GOING WELL. I MET A NEW FRIEND TODAY IN PRE-CALCULUS, TREVOR. I'M ALSO STARTING TO SLOWLY GET MY REPUTATION BACK. TODAY I ACTUALLY TALKED TO TWO PEOPLE WHO HATE ME MORE THAN ANYONE, AND IT WENT SURPRISINGLY WELL. MY NEW FAVORITE CLASSES ARE ENGLISH AND PRE-CALCULUS, NOT BECAUSE OF THE STUDENTS BUT THE TEACHERS. IT'S NOT THE SUBJECT THEY MAKE EXCITING, IT'S MAKING THEMSELVES MORE FUN AND HAVING MORE THAN JUST THE AVERAGE TEACHER PERSONALITY.

The journal entry ended with classroom notes about some woman named Mary Rowlandson who was abducted by Native Americans and held hostage for nearly three months, but survived. She published her journal to reveal God's purpose to colonial America.

Trevor. *So that's when he met him. But who are the two people who hate him more than anyone? Ashley? Did the little bitch get her rejection letter and decide to suddenly stop terrorizing my son?*

I shook my head, knowing the letters just went out. That couldn't be the reason.

I inhaled a deep breath. The air was stale in my office, so I pushed out of my chair and walked to the bay window, lighting the eucalyptus candle. I waited for the mixture of eucalyptus and spearmint to fuse the air, then sat back down and scratched my head. "What two people did he talk to? Is there someone else who's bullying him?"

I glanced at my computer, the spinning wheel signifying it was still loading the university software. I rolled my eyes and returned to his journal.

SEPTEMBER 9

YESTERDAY I SWITCHED INTO AP GOVERNMENT. I NOW HAVE TWO AP CLASSES AND I'M THRILLED. BY THRILLED I ACTUALLY MEAN HORRIFIED. I BARELY PASSED IT LAST YEAR WITH A B, AND I'M NOT QUITE SURE WHAT'LL HAPPEN THIS YEAR, BUT I SET A GOAL TO GET A 4.0 GPA AND THAT'S WHAT I'M GOING TO DO. WHETHER I HAVE A SOCIAL LIFE OR NOT IS ALL BASED ON THE EXTENT OF HOMEWORK AND ACTIVITIES I HAVE THIS YEAR. BELIEVE IT OR NOT, HAVING TO STUDY FOR A TEST IS MORE IMPORTANT TO ME THAN GOING TO SCREW OFF WITH MY FRIENDS. MY BOXING IS GETTING INCREASINGLY BETTER, WHICH IS AWESOME. EACH DAY I WORK OUT, I HOPE TO GET MY JABS AND HOOKS FASTER AND MORE POWERFUL. LET'S JUST SAY I WON'T BE AN EASY OPPONENT TO WIN AGAINST.

The journal concluded with bibliography notes on Jonathan Edwards, who delivered some sermons to backsliding puritan congregations that were "falling out of Christ."

I'm sure Branson loved learning about him. I may not know my son well, but we both shared a disdain for religious fanatics. I also now knew he'd added another AP class. But boxing? When did he start boxing?

I flipped to the next page, which was just one day later,

and his opening line literally made me laugh out loud.

SEPTEMBER 10

AP IS SLOWLY KILLING ME.

I shook my head. *He's had the class all of one day and it's killing him. Unbelievable.* I continued reading.

EACH AP CHAPTER IS UP TO THIRTY PAGES, AND WE'RE EXPECTED TO MAKE AN OUTLINE FOR EACH ONE. I SPEND UP TO FOUR HOURS JUST ON AP, AND I HAVE ALL MY MAIN CLASSES TOO! SO THE HARDEST PART ABOUT AP IS BALANCING IT WITH OTHER CLASSES. MY OTHER CLASSES ARE USUALLY EASIER, SO THAT'S A RELIEF, BUT IT'S STILL A LOT TO TAKE IN. I JUST WANT TO PASS THESE CLASSES AND GET THEM OVER WITH. WE GOT A CALL FROM COACH ABOUT HOW ASH IS OUT OF INDOOR TRACK FOR THE SEASON DUE TO A STRESS FRACTURE. WILSON IS NOW SCREWED FOR INDOOR TRACK.

I paused before reading his next passage. Something wasn't right, but I couldn't quite figure it out.

I stared at the journal entry until it suddenly made sense—his penmanship had changed. Branson's normally perfect left-handed prose was gone, and in its place was a page filled with sloped writing. If I didn't know better, I would've thought Branson had broken his hand and written backhanded.

What the hell?

SEPTEMBER 11

TODAY IS 9/11, A DAY NO ONE WILL FORGET BECAUSE, LIKE A HOLIDAY, WE'RE REMINDED EVERY YEAR. WHY THIS DAY? WHY DON'T WE GET REMINDED EVERY YEAR ABOUT THE HOLOCAUST? NO, APPARENTLY KILLING JEWS IS NO BIG DEAL, BUT FLYING A PLANE INTO A COUPLE OF BUILDINGS IS. OUR COUNTRY IS TOO FOCUSED ON THIS ATTACK, SO IT'LL CONTINUE TO HAUNT PEOPLE. EVERY TIME WE TALK ABOUT IT, ALL IT DOES IS BRING UP BAD MEMORIES. AND THE IMAGES DON'T HELP EITHER: PEOPLE JUMPING FROM BUILDINGS, PILES OF ASHES WITH PEOPLE BURIED BENEATH THEM, PEOPLE IN SHOCK AND AWE ACROSS THE NATION. MAYBE WE DESERVED IT. MAYBE EVERYBODY HAS WHAT'S COMING TO THEM. DON'T GET ME WRONG, IT WAS A SAD AND MEMORABLE MOMENT FOR US HISTORY, BUT IS IT REALLY NECESSARY FOR US TO BE REMINDED OF THE HORRORS? I THINK THEY DO IT SO THE PEOPLE OF THE US WILL SUPPORT WHAT THE GOVERNMENT IS DOING, BECAUSE EVERYTHING THE GOVERNMENT DOES IS TO STOP TERRORISM, AND IF WE HAVE TO INVADE EVERY COUNTRY, THEN SO BE IT. THE GOVERNMENT DOESN'T WANT OUR PERMISSION, IT WANTS OUR SILENCE. THIS IS WHY 9/11 IS ALWAYS MENTIONED AND WILL ALWAYS BE REMEMBERED. IT'S PROPAGANDA AT ITS BEST. GOD BLESS THE UNITED STATES OF AMERICA.

Oh my God. I stood up and started pacing the room.

"That's not right." I walked to the corner of my office and ran my hands through my hair. "Oh no." I paced toward the other end of the room. "Okay," I exhaled. "Branson was only three when 9/11 happened. I remember it as if it were yesterday, but maybe his generation doesn't have that same connection to it."

I took a long, steady breath and returned to my desk, standing over his journal and staring at the entry. *This isn't the mind of a sane person. This is the journal entry I'd read in a newspaper article after someone did something horrific.*

I reached into my desk drawer and pulled out a silver tin that contained an X-Acto knife. Removing the safety cap, I carefully ran the blade down the spine of Branson's journal, extracting the single sheet and placing it in my desk drawer beneath the silver tin. I didn't care if he got graded down. Better that than have the journal entry circulate into the wrong hands.

I sat down and turned the page for the next journal entry. It was dated September 25, nearly two weeks later. I flipped around to see if Branson wrote an entry somewhere else, but the pages were empty. Reaching back into my desk drawer, I looked on the backside of his 9/11 entry, hoping another one was written there, but it was blank. *What?* I put it back in my desk drawer.

"Why is there a two-week break?" I skimmed the journal again, but there was a clear break in journal entries from 9/11 to 9/25. I looked around my office as if there were someone to answer my question, but I was alone. So I did what I always did and turned my attention back to my son's journal. The next entry was written in the same sloped writing as his 9/11 post.

SEPTEMBER 25

I'VE BEEN TEXTING MY FRIEND TREVOR EVERY DAY. I ENJOY HIS COMPANY, AND HE'S ONE OF THE ONLY TRUE FRIENDS I HAVE LEFT. LAST NIGHT I WATCHED THE PERKS OF BEING A WALLFLOWER. THAT MOVIE IS ONE I WILL NEVER GET TIRED OF BECAUSE IT RELATES

TO ME. LIKE CHARLIE. I'M TRYING TO FIND MY PLACE IN SCHOOL. THE ONLY DIFFERENCE IS THAT I HAVE A TWIN TO HELP ME OUT. I EVEN HAVE THAT INSPIRING ENGLISH TEACHER LIKE IN THE MOVIE. MY TEACHER USED TO GIVE ME BOOKS SOPHOMORE YEAR AND I WOULD FINISH THEM IN A DAY'S TIME DUE TO MY INTEREST IN THEM. UNLIKE THE MOVIE THOUGH, I HAVEN'T FOUND MY TWO FRIENDS TO CHANGE MY LIFE, BUT I HAVE FOUND ONE. HIS NAME IS TREVOR. ONE IS BETTER THAN NONE. I GUESS EVERY STORY DOESN'T WORK OUT FOR THE BEST.

My desk calendar indicated that we had just entered the second week of October, yet my son's last journal entry appeared two weeks ago. Another two-week absence. *What the hell?*

Trevor. I've got to find out who this kid is and what, if any, hold he has over my son.

I closed the journal and placed it back in Branson's backpack in the kitchen. When I returned to my office, the university software had finally loaded, but I still had unfinished business with Branson's bully to complete.

Before I entered my administrative password, I went to the staff portal and typed in Rachel's password. The IT department assigned everyone's password, from faculty to staff, and administrators were given a list of each one in their department. In the event we had to release someone of their job responsibilities, and I couldn't reach IT, I could disable staff's access to university records. In short, most people at the university knew they were fired before it happened because they could no longer access the university system.

Administrators were allowed to create their own

password, but the dean of the department had them on file. The university had to protect privacy at all costs, so I often reminded my staff to use an outside email, and not the university's, for personal correspondence. There were eyes on everything.

I scrolled through Rachel's files until I reached the database with the freshmen applicants for fall 2016. I pulled up my email to Fred Stanley and compared it with our online entry system that Rachel would've updated with my list. A check beside a candidate's name indicated they had been accepted as an early admission. Ashley Bailey's name remained unchecked, and her status was still a standard submission, not a legacy. I was sure that would change, but for now, it aligned with my story to Dean Bryant. I pulled up more legacy candidates who I hadn't chosen and changed their status to standard submission. Should more questions arise about my early admissions selections, this ensured a computer error was to blame.

When I logged off Rachel's account and entered my password, I was redirected to three different pages before I could access the administrative portal. I then scrolled through my files for the list of seniors at Wilson High School.

Trevor. Trevor. Trevor.

I had no last name, and I wasn't going to text Branson to ask for one. If this Trevor was, as Aaron feared, an imaginary friend, I had no way of knowing what I was up against or how to handle it. What I did know how to do— very well, in fact—was search an entire student body for a particular person. Or in this case a particular name.

I typed "Trevor" into the database and waited for the computer to filter through first, middle, and last names in a senior class of four hundred and eighty. Six potential BFFs for my son surfaced on my laptop, but only four had Trevor as their first name. While I knew my sons were often called Kovac by their friends, it didn't seem like Branson was referring to a kid's last name.

Trevor Thomas DiCamp

Trevor Marcus James

Trevor Lee Macon

Trevor Alan Steele

Ronald Todd Trevor

Warren Jon Trevor

I tapped my fingers against the keyboard. *Which one are you?* I copied the list of names and moved my cursor to the tab on my computer where I'd bookmarked Wilson High School. I typed in my parent password and entered the parent portal. The next step was a little tricky, because I had to figure out a way to cross-reference the kids in Branson's pre-calculus class with the list of Trevor names.

Think. Think. Think. There had to be a way. But the only person I knew who could figure how to do it was out eating ice cream.

I pulled up Branson's class schedule and saw he had pre-calculus forth block. His teacher was Mr. Batrow. I knew Jim; I could always call him and ask about this Trevor kid.

I shook my head at the thought. I knew there was no way Jim would break the confidentiality of his students, not for me or anyone. He was a by-the-books kind of teacher, which was why I chose him for Branson. He had his master's degree in mathematics and knew how to teach kids math in a way that they'd learn it for life.

I leaned back in my chair. Six Trevors were on one side of my screen and Branson's math class was on the other. In the middle was my access to every student at Wilson High School.

That's it!

I sat forward and scrolled back to my university log-in. Putting the list of Trevors in the database, I hit the tab that accessed transcripts.

Transcripts for each of the Trevors popped up beside their name. A wave of pride washed over me. "Bingo!" *I'm brilliant.*

I scanned the first Trevor and searched his list of classes for the fall semester. No calculus. No math at all. I minimized his transcript and went to the next one: Trevor Marcus James. He was in pre-calculus, with Jim Batrow as his teacher. I pointed toward the screen and followed my finger across to see what block Trevor James had pre-calculus. Fifth block.

I exhaled in a huff. *Okay, next one.*

I went through the entire list, but the only Trevor that had pre-calculus their senior year with Jim Batrow was Trevor Marcus James. And his class didn't align with Branson's.

I rubbed my temple. *That doesn't mean they aren't working together.* Branson wrote that Trevor was a kid in his math class. *Maybe he meant they both had the same teacher?*

"Hey, Ma, what's up?"

I shrieked.

Aaron laughed. "Didn't mean to scare you."

I shook my finger at him. "Don't do that!" He continued to laugh. I waved him over to the computer. "Look what I found."

"What am I looking at?"

"I found that Trevor Marcus James has pre-calculus with Mr. Bartow."

"Marcus? No, that kid's not Branson's friend."

"Why? And his name is Trevor."

"He's a cocky jock and he goes by Marcus, not Trevor. There's no way Branson would hang out with him."

"Are you sure?"

"I'm positive. The last time we talked to that kid, it was freshman year when we were on freshman football. He's not someone we would hang out with."

"And you don't think Branson would be working with him for calculus?"

"Ma, he wouldn't even make eye contact with that kid."

I sat back in my chair in defeat.

"What's wrong?"

I looked up at my son. "Well, that's the *only* Trevor in your entire graduating class who has pre-calculus this semester. And if you're telling me Branson wouldn't hang out with this kid...."

"Well, we'd better go talk to Branson."

I cringed. "He texted that he's staying overnight at this Trevor kid's house."

"Ma, we've got to find out where he is, because he's definitely not at Trevor's."

"And how do you suppose we do that?"

Aaron snapped his fingers. "Hey, use that app."

"What app?"

"The one you made us download because you were afraid we'd get kidnapped jogging." He rolled his eyes. "We're freaking almost eighteen, but glad you made us download the app."

"Oh, that's brilliant." I grabbed my iPhone and pulled up the Life360 app. A map of Casper appeared on the screen, along with four circles containing penny-sized pics of each of my kids. Jack's face was attached to mine because he didn't have a phone, and usually wherever he was, so was I. Finding Aaron, Branson, and Carson was as easy as pressing on their picture. I touched Aaron's picture and his location surfaced: 4505 Sunridge Ave. Carson's phone indicated she was at the same address, as did mine. We were all at home.

I touched Branson's picture. A message appeared on the screen: **Lost connection 9:15 p.m. Ask them to reconnect.**

I held my phone toward Aaron. "What does this mean?"

"It means Branson disconnected from the app."

"You can do that?"

Aaron grimaced. "Uh, yeah."

"Why would you do that?"

"Ma, we're almost eighteen."

I tossed my phone on my desk and crossed my arms over my chest. "Well that's just freaking brilliant. What's the point of an app if you're not going to use it?"

"Settle down." Aaron grabbed my phone off the desk. "Isn't there…?" He swiped his finger across my phone. "Yeah, here it is." He held the phone toward me. "There's a History button where you can check the history of where Branson's been and where he was last before he disconnected the app."

"Really?" I felt a wave of relief. "Where was he?"

Aaron held up the phone and then shook his head.

"What?"

"The last time he was connected, he was at 260 North Central Ave."

I shook my head. "I have *no idea* where that is."

"Ma, it's in Felony Flats."

I jumped out of my chair. "What! What's he doing there?"

Aaron gripped my shoulder and handed me my phone. "Relax. He's not at Trevor's. He's at Dakota's."

CHAPTER 21

BRANSON

"*DUDE,* wake up."

I barely opened my eyes and rolled to my right. "What the hell are you doing here?"

Trevor was dressed in his normal attire of a gray T-shirt and baggy jeans. I stood up and quietly ushered him into the kitchen so he wouldn't wake Dakota.

"Dude, your mom's been texting you all night. She needs you home. She called me to come get you."

I held up my hand. "Stay here." I snuck back into Dakota's room and grabbed my cell phone. It was three in the morning, and the brightness of the screen lit up the room.

I ducked back into the kitchen as I saw a string of recent messages waited for me. I ran my hand through my hair. "Oh, shit."

"Yeah, you need to get home. You're in deep shit."

"Man, thanks a lot." I nodded toward Trevor. "I've gotta tell Dakota I'm leaving."

"Make it fast."

I went back into Dakota's room and grabbed my T-shirt off the edge of the bed, gently touching her shoulder. She turned and smiled with her eyes closed.

"Hey, I'm going to head home."

She opened her eyes. "Why?"

"My mom found out I'm not at Trevor's."

Dakota blinked and rubbed her eyes. "Oh no. Is she mad?"

I shrugged. "I don't know. I'll find out. Just go back to sleep."

I kissed the top of her head and pulled the blanket back up around her. Finding my shoes under the bed, I headed toward the kitchen.

"What are you doing?"

Trevor had a beer in each hand.

"Dude, you gotta put those back."

"Oh, come on. Dakota's mom won't notice. She had like a thirty-six pack."

"No, that's not cool."

"Dude, let's just drink it. It's only one. She won't notice anyway."

I shook my head. "I'll drop you off and you can drink the beer." But by the time we reached the bottom of Dakota's stairs, I had already chugged half of the cold, hard-to-stomach malt liquor.

"How'd you get here?" I asked Trevor.

"I drove my car."

"I didn't know you had a car. Why am I driving you around all the time?"

Trevor gave me his standard shit-eating grin. "It saves me gas money."

"So, dude, where's your car?" I busted out laughing, thinking of the cheesy movie line.

Trevor laughed. "It's right over here." He nodded toward a pimped-out black Subaru Impresa with a decent-sized spoiler and chrome hubcaps. The car cost more than the entire apartment complex in Felony Flats.

Trevor reached under the front tire and grabbed a magnetic hide-a-key.

"Dude, why don't you have a key chain?"

"What, so I can have a lanyard out all the time and look like every other jock on campus? No thanks." He handed me the key. "I just chugged this entire beer. You gotta drive."

I drank the rest of my beer and then tossed the can in front of the apartment complex. It blended in with the dozen others littering the yard. I slid into the leather interior, and the car purred when I started the engine.

The dashboard glowed three fifteen in the morning. I was tired and just wanted to get home and back to bed.

"Dude, I want to go fast. Go up to Wyoming Boulevard and hit it."

I shook my head. "I don't want to get pulled over."

"Dude, it's my car. I'll pay for the ticket."

I shrugged. "All right. It's your car and your money." I turned onto Wyoming Boulevard and hit the gas pedal. The needle on the speedometer quickly passed sixty-five, the speed limit on Wyoming Boulevard. The highway markers flew by in a blur.

Trevor turned up the music, and the subwoofers in the back I hadn't seen before blared and made the entire car vibrate to the beat of dubstep. A smile stretched across my face as Trevor rolled down the window and screamed. We looked at each other and smiled.

We passed a side road where a church stood, and the silhouette of a car caught my peripheral vision.

"Oh crap." My heart skipped a beat. I looked at the speedometer and it was nearing ninety. My foot hit the brake instantly, slowing us down. *Fuck. Fuck. Fuck. Fuck.*

"Hey, why'd you slow down?"

"Dude, shut the hell up and turn off the music," I said through gritted teeth.

Red and blue lights filled my rearview mirror. "Fuck." I pulled to the side of the road. "I told you," I said to Trevor.

"Shut up. It was fun and you know it."

I cut the engine and rolled down my window. The officer walked toward the car, his hand on his sidearm, and a cold sweat came over me as I watched him approach. The closer he got, the faster my heart beat. It felt like I'd just sprinted a four-hundred.

He leaned his head into my window. "Do you know how fast you were going?"

"No, sir." I shook my head.

"If I had seen another car, I would've thought you were drag racing. You almost hit a hundred. Can I see your license and registration?"

My eyes started watering with the sudden realization that I had downed a beer and I was driving someone else's car. "Officer, I just want to let you know that the registration isn't under my name. It's under my buddy's name, Trevor." I pointed toward the passenger side, not breaking eye contact with the officer. "I was driving him home. He had a couple of beers."

The officer looked past me to the passenger seat. A look of confusion appeared on his face. "Where's your buddy? Hidden in the trunk?"

I turned to my right. Trevor wasn't there. It felt like someone pulled a plug in my body and drained all my blood.

"What the hell?" I looked back at the officer. "I swear he was just there."

"Son, there's nobody in the car. Would you mind stepping out of the vehicle for me?"

My whole body trembled and my fingers fumbled with the seat belt. *Where'd he go?*

I stepped out of my car cautiously like this may be a joke and Trevor was hiding. But all I saw was the police car with its lights blowing up the side of the road. There was a chill to the air that bit through me and I couldn't stop shaking.

The cop stood with his arms on his hips and a concerned look on his face.

I've got to get my shit together.

"All right, I'd like you to take nine heel-to-toe steps along this line." The officer pointed his flashlight toward the solid white stripe that ran the length of Wyoming Boulevard.

I had to piss, and I knew if I didn't, I'd have jumpy legs

for sure. "I've really gotta take a leak."

"Make it fast." He cocked his head toward the sagebrush that bordered the side of the road.

The moon cast light while I urinated on what looked to be former grass. *Where'd he go? I can't believe Trevor would leave me like that. It's fucked up. Doesn't matter now, because I'm the one who's gotta walk the line. Fucking asshole.*

When I returned, I looked at the officer. "Nine heel-to-toe steps on this line?" I repeated. *I'm not going down as the joke of the senior class because I couldn't walk a straight line after one beer.*

I carefully took even heel-to-toe steps, not losing my balance, even when he stopped me on step seven.

"Okay, turn around and repeat it going the opposite direction."

"But I haven't taken nine steps yet." *Yeah, Johnny Law, I'm operating on all cylinders.*

"Yes, please repeat the process going the opposite direction."

I turned on the heel of my Nike and began the heel-to-toe walk while staring into the lights of an oncoming car. It slowed down.

Great. Probably some lookie-loo.

When the car pulled over behind the officer's, my stomach dropped. *Is that Dakota?*

The officer approached the car with his flashlight aimed at her Jetta and his hand on his sidearm.

Dakota stepped out of her car. "Hello, Officer," she said cheerfully.

One of the guys I'd seen hanging out below her apartment climbed out on the passenger side. *What the hell? Is that Scotty?*

"I think there's been a little bit of a mix-up," Dakota said.

Mix-up? What is she doing?

"Yeah, I loaned my buddy Branson here my car," Scott said to the officer.

I stared at the car on the side of the road and suddenly realized it wasn't mine. Worse yet, I had no idea whose car it was or how I'd ended up with it. It was like waking up from a dream—only this was a nightmare.

Oh fuck.

"What's your name?" the officer asked the guy standing way too close to my girlfriend.

"Scott Nelson." The twentysomething-year-old with a sleeve of tattoos shook the officer's hand. "I should've driven Branson home myself, but it was late and I was tired."

"Your friend claims he was driving Trevor home and that it was registered in his name?" The officer kept his hand on his firearm.

Scott threw his head back and laughed. "Well, that's Branson. Always messing up people's names. Didn't he call you Cheyenne for the longest time?" He turned to Dakota, who smiled.

"Yes he did," she squealed.

I smiled. It was true. I knew her family derived from the Dakota tribe, which I think originated out of Cheyenne. I could never remember. But when we were first dating, I'd call her Cheyenne, not Dakota.

"Branson does that all the time. My brother is Trevor. I'm Scott." The dude looked at me and smiled. "Scotty, not Trevor, you goof."

The entire world felt like it was spinning.

"So this is your car?" The officer looked at Scott, who nodded. "Can you provide proof of insurance and registration?"

Scott nodded toward his car. "It's in the glove box."

The officer escorted Scott to his car and told Dakota to stay where she was. He was outnumbered. It had to be nearing four in the morning, and I had no memory of how I'd ended up in this dude's car on the side of Wyoming Boulevard.

The flashlight shone on the paperwork and then Scott's wallet. They must have lined up, because the officer then approached me. "I'd like you to take a preliminary alcohol screening test. It's a portable breath test to determine the presence of alcohol."

A cold chill crept down my neck and made me shudder.

"Officer, isn't that a voluntary test?" Scott asked.

I looked at the officer, who reluctantly nodded. "Your friend said his buddy had a beer, but there was no one else in the car with him. I'd like to determine how much alcohol, if any, he's ingested."

"My brother, Trevor, was drinking tonight, and I think Branson just got confused. It seems like he was passing the field sobriety test, and the PAS test is voluntary," Scott said.

I glanced at this dude who didn't look like he could

string together a cohesive sentence, let alone talk the same language of the officer, but fuck if he wasn't, and taking the man to task to boot.

"The test is voluntary," the officer said, "but your friend was driving close to ninety miles per hour when I pulled him over, and he appeared to be weaving."

"Weaving," I said wryly. "I don't even know how to crochet."

Dakota giggled, Scott laughed, and even the officer started smiling.

I started to regain my footing and my mind. "Officer, I didn't realize I was driving so fast. I was just trying to get home." Suddenly the texts from my mom flashed in whatever part of my mind wasn't damaged. "I fell asleep on the couch at my girlfriend's house, and I knew from all the texts my mom sent that she was worried." I reached into my jeans pocket and withdrew my phone. "I was already past curfew and I…." I shook my head. "I should've been more responsible." I purposefully sidestepped the entire issue of beer because I honestly didn't even remember drinking.

What the fuck happened?

"If you drive him home, I won't cite your friend for driving past curfew." The officer looked at Dakota.

"Thank you," she said.

"And it's probably not wise to ever loan your car to a teenager after curfew," the officer told Scott.

He nodded. "Understood. Thank you."

I glanced at the officer and expected a verbal beatdown. Instead, the look in his eyes reminded me of Clive. "Get home, son, and get some sleep."

I swallowed hard and nodded. "I will. Thank you." As I walked toward Dakota's car, heat crept up my neck. I couldn't look at her.

"I don't know what happened," I said to the ground with my hand on the passenger door window.

"It's okay." She paused. "Branson." I glanced up, and a gentle, loving smile greeted me from across the roof of her car. "It's okay. We'll figure it out later."

I barely nodded.

The car ride to my house was quiet. She placed her hand on my knee. "I'm not mad."

I puffed out a mouthful of air. "Well, you're probably the only person. That guy Scott looked like he was going to rip my head off."

She shook her head. "He was just concerned. He's not mad either."

"I really don't know what happened." I sounded like a pathetic idiot, but the last thing I remembered was falling asleep next to Dakota.

"No one's mad," she said.

"Why?" I looked at her. "I'd be pissed."

She softly chuckled. "It's not your fault. You weren't being malicious to hurt me or Scott. I think you just got confused when you needed to go home and took Scott's car instead of mine."

I had to laugh. "Yeah, because they look *so* much alike."

Dakota's giggle was really high-pitched and girly. "Okay, they're not alike, but his car was parked beside mine, and I told you about the hide-a-key. Plus you know I have a hide-a-key on my car." She shrugged. "It was an honest mistake."

I don't deserve you.

She drove slower than the posted speed to my Eastside neighborhood, pulling into my driveway a few minutes later. "You're home safe. Get some rest." She leaned over and kissed my cheek. "Go to bed. We'll talk tomorrow."

I held onto her tightly, like it might have been my last time.

"Branson," she said in my ear. "Don't stress. Everything's alright."

I wasn't into baseball, but it didn't take a diehard fan to realize I had two strikes against me. Strike one, blacking out and coming to in the school's restroom with bloody knuckles. Strike two, coming to on the side of the road with a stranger's car and no clue how I got there.

If fear had a feeling, it was like diving into String Lake, where the water was so dark it was hard to find the way back up. I didn't know if I was sinking or swimming toward the surface.

What's happening to me?

I climbed out of her car and walked toward my house in complete shame and total disbelief.

Strike three and I'm out.

CHAPTER 22

TARA

I couldn't sleep. Even though I knew Branson was at Dakota's house, that he had lied, but that I should've been relieved he wasn't at Trevor's house, whoever he was, none of those revelations made my restless mind relax. His journal entries alone had me fearing for my son's sanity. Worry had a vise grip on my brain and filled my every waking thought.

How is my son? Where is my son? What is he hearing? What is he seeing? What is he thinking? How can I help him?

I grabbed my iPhone and scrolled until I found the music app, paging down until I located a long, lost favorite. The string of the guitar was a salve.

I tapped my foot on the stack of decorative silver and cream-colored pillows at the end of my bed. The southern jam rock of the Allman Brothers Band had a smooth sound that went down easy.

"Somebody's Calling Your Name," was filled with

heartbreaking lyrics that fit my mood. Somebody's waiting for you. *Does my son know I'm waiting? And that I'd always be here?*

I walked toward the kitchen, palmed the wall for the light and turned on the overhead. A pile of unopened mail scattered on the kitchen table. An ivory-colored envelope that looked collegiate caught my attention, but when I fished it out, I quickly realized it wasn't from an Ivy League university.

First, it was addressed to the parent of Branson Kovac. And anyone worth their salt in academia knew better than to mess with the educational privacy rights of a student. FERPA ensured that a student, and only a student, would receive the letter that either accepted, rejected, or waitlisted them into college. Now, whether their nosy mother opened said letter was completely a separate matter.

The second telltale sign was that the return address bore no name, simply an address. *Gotta be medical.* With HIPAA regulations on privacy, physicians didn't even stamp their envelopes with their name anymore, lest someone file an invasion of privacy lawsuit.

I slid my finger through the back flap of the envelope.

October 1, 2015

Dr. Tyler Washburn

Referral: Branson Kovac

DOB: 03/12/1998

Branson is a 17-year-old who presents with both auditory and visual hallucinations. I would like to have him evaluated neurologically with a sleep-deprived EEG to rule out organicity. Branson is currently taking Paxil, and I will suggest he start Geodon as soon as possible at our next appointment.

Thank you for your help.

Sincerely,

Richard Cordova, M.D.
Child/Adolescent Psychiatrist

Awesome. Branson's EEG was next up on the playlist of hits that kept coming our way.

I closed my eyes and grabbed another piece of mail, fingering the envelope. It was thick, small, and quality parchment, like linen. *Let me guess,* military?

I opened my eyes. *Close.*

United States Senate

The return address appeared in an Old English font that looked like one of our forefathers penned it himself. *What would Branson think of this? Seriously, why is my*

Holocaust-loving, 9/11-misguided, anti-government kid even considering a career in the military?

The letter from the Senate was addressed to him, but I opened it anyway. When it came to my son's privacy, I broke every rule.

```
William Scott Bailey, Jr.
Senator of the United States
Wyoming
```

The father of Branson's bully had his title blocked, cursive, front and center. *Isn't that just swell?* The letter was dated, aligned and just freaking perfect. It made my stomach literally turn—or it could have been the remnants from Big A's dinner. It was hard to tell.

```
October 3, 2015

Dear Branson,

Thank you for completing the necessary
paperwork for a congressional nomination
to the United States Naval Academy. My
selection committee is looking forward to
an interview with you. Following is the
requisite information:

Date: Wednesday, November 11, 2015
```

Place: Dick Cheney Federal Building, Room 5555, 100 East B Street, Casper, WY

Interview Time: 3:35 p.m. - 3:50 p.m.

If you need any additional information, please contact Arnie Gray in my Cheyenne office at 307-555-1212.

Sincerely,

William Scott Bailey, Jr.
United States Senator

There is no way in hell Branson can continue this charade. It was one thing when we thought it was depression. It was worse when we thought it may be PTSD. But now?

I lowered my head on the table and rocked it back and forth to the rhythm of Greg Allman echoing the refrain. I wanted to get up and dance in the dark, but I didn't. Instead, I bounced my leg on the chair and looked at the kitchen floor as I sang very loudly and very off-key.

"Why are you up so early?"

I jumped and whipped my head in Carson's direction, quickly turning off my iPhone.

"You trying to get your hands on my blueberry muffins? They be mine." She struck a gangster pose, but it was more like squatting while she held up peace signs. She looked so innocent, so free, so unencumbered by life.

I used to be like that.

Suddenly the tears I had been trying to keep at bay unleashed. I lowered my head and let it pour.

"Oh, Mummy. Why are you crying?" She came up and wrapped her long, slender arms around me.

I leaned into my daughter and pushed the letter out in front of me.

"What happened?"

I shrugged. "Just more appointments for Branson. More doctors. More uncertainty. Less hope."

"That's just life," she said without any pity or sadness in her voice. She moved my messy hair off my face. "Mummy, you know there's never any certainty. No clear path that leads to your final destination."

Her logic was so rational I couldn't help but laugh and look up at her. "Who are you?"

"I'm a poet and didn't even know it." She pulled away from me and started to move her shoulders up and down. "Just doing my shoulder dance, trying to make you laugh."

"Well you did, and you're a sweet daughter." I glanced at the kitchen window. The faint light of the moon, or perhaps an early sun, shone through the pane. "Why are you up?"

"It's five. I always get up at five to start getting ready for school." She leaned her head toward me. "I need a ride, by the way."

I laughed. "Yeah, got that. I'm your ride. I haven't forgotten." I smiled at her. "Granted, I've had a lot on my mind, but getting you to school isn't something I'd forget."

"All these rough patches you're going through right now are all the years you're going to learn the most about yourself.

During the happy times, you don't learn anything."

I shook my head. "Seriously, where do you get this stuff? Is this from your science class on genetics and how to parent your emotionally wrecked mother?" I tried to muster a laugh, but it wasn't there.

"I just read a lot of books," she said, resuming her shoulder dance. "And I'm good at advice, really. That's my thing."

"So what advice would you give me now?" I held up a halting hand before she answered. "First, you should probably know that Aaron thinks Branson has an imaginary friend. Second, this imaginary friend, *Trevor*, who Branson has possibly created, has become his alibi for staying overnight at Dakota's. Oh," I said with eyes widened and hand still held up, "he's moved from hearing voices to seeing things." I grabbed the letter off the kitchen table. "So the good doctor," I continued, shaking it like a pom-pom, "wants to rule out if Branson has a brain tumor or something that's causing these visual and auditory hallucinations. But"—I placed the letter back on the table in defeat—"in the meantime, they want to start him on an *antipsychotic* medication to stop the hallucinations. And somehow"—I picked up Senator Bailey's letter—"Branson is still moving through the ranks in his quest to join the Navy when really he shouldn't be anywhere near an aircraft carrier, destroyer, or submarine. Not with the way he feels about our government." I rolled my eyes and tossed it on the table. "In a nutshell, that's life at our house."

"That is a lot to figure out at five in the morning."

"Yeah, not helping there, peanut," I said.

"I'd say... hmmm." She put her hands in her pajama pockets and started walking the length of the kitchen. "Imaginary friend." She paced back and forth. "Hearing voices. Seeing things. Lying to Mom." She turned on her bare foot. "Instead of observing things behind closed doors, why don't you go talk to him? As much as he's *not* going to want to talk to you *or anyone* at this point, it's better if you reach out to him. Because I think he's trying to reach out to you, but he's too afraid to go the extra mile."

"What makes you think that? How do you know he's trying to reach out?" I sat on the edge of the kitchen chair while my daughter paced.

"Everyone who's going through something tries to reach out, even if they don't do it consciously. Like they'll tell you their favorite movie and it could be about mental illness."

"Like *The Perks of Being a Wallflower*?" I asked.

She paused and looked at me, "Yes, which is rare that there's a movie about mental illness, but still, that's just an example and *Perks* is a good one. It'd just be one way of reaching out."

I leaned toward my daughter and thought about joining her pacing. She seemed to be coming up with gems by wearing a path on my old linoleum. "So how else do you think Branson has reached out?" I asked.

"Um, by maybe acting out? Maybe lying? Because eventually everyone knows they'll get caught, especially with you as their mother."

I half-laughed. "What does that mean?"

"Well, in your job, you see kids who don't have any influence or structure on them or in their lives. So you automatically assume we could end up like that if you don't keep an eye on us. I don't mean to be offensive, but you told me about meth addicts when I was five and saw a needle on the street when we were walking." She stopped pacing. "We've known since forever what to watch out for, what to be scared of, and what not to do. And sometimes kids just want to just say no and lash out because it's suffocating when you have all these rules and barriers you have to follow."

I sat back. "That makes total sense, but...." I could hear the rationalization forming on my lips. "Branson isn't lashing out because he's mad at me. He's got a mental illness."

"I don't think he's necessarily mad at you. I think he's mad at the world, he's lashing out at the world and society. Don't take it personally if he lashes out at you, or the government." She shook her head at me. "You said government, right?"

I nodded.

"Yeah, I don't think he means any of what he's saying. He's lashing out at everyone."

"Has he lashed out to you?"

"Uh, yeah."

I almost sprang out of my seat. "How? When?"

"It's no big deal." Carson shrugged her bony shoulders. "I'm an easy target because I'm his little sister and I probably annoy him. And I speak my mind a lot, even when it's not very nice."

"What did he do?"

"It was after school. I don't remember what I said, something about anger management and that he needed it."

"O-kay. And then what happened?"

"He got in my face, and when I showed him I wasn't scared, he looked for the next thing to scare me with, so he squeezed my water bottle that was on the table beside me. He squeezed it until it exploded." She rolled her eyes. "It shocked me more than it scared me, and that gave him the reaction he was looking for. Then he just went to the backyard and sulked. I knew then that something was wrong, but I also knew if I engaged him, that would just make things worse." She sat down beside me. "Sometimes it's better to leave things unanswered."

"So I don't hold him accountable about lying and where he spent the night?" I couldn't believe I was asking my daughter for parenting instructions.

"I think it's better to just listen than to ask. If he finds out you knew, he'll think you're invading his personal space and he'll get mad. Then he'll shut down because he'll be embarrassed."

I nodded. "Yeah, I could see that happening." I twirled the doctor's and Senator Bailey's letters on the table like a pinwheel. "How is it that you know so much about this and how to handle it? Because I'm at a complete loss."

"It's got to be harder for a mom, because that's your son and you feel like it's your fault."

I stared at the spinning letters. The words blurred until they no longer looked like words.

As a mom to four children, I wasn't supposed to have a favorite. I was supposed to love all my children equally. But when Branson was born, he was the smaller twin, the one struggling to suck, swallow, and breathe. He was underweight, jaundiced, and apneic. Every minute of his premature life was a struggle. The priest arrived with holy water and a rosary, ready to perform last rites, but I pointed to the door of the neonatal intensive care unit and told him where he could go. I wouldn't allow death near my son.

Instead, I placed my hand in Branson's incubator to save him, to protect him, to do whatever a mother of a few hours did for her child. The NICU nurse told me I was nothing more than a blurry image to my son and not to expect much of a reaction, if any. That Branson probably wouldn't make it through the night.

Her voice, like the priest, was white noise. I pushed them away and placed my hand gently on my son's wispy blond hair. Faint hazel eyes looked up at me, and my breath caught. Staring directly into my soul, he knew. He knew I was his mother. That I would never leave him, or give up on him. He knew I loved him more than I had ever loved another being. So little, he was my gentle giant, my warrior. I was his, and he was mine.

Of all my children, Branson got me. *I miss him. I want my son back. The one I knew. And the one who knew me better than any of my other children.* My body ached for him. There were no words, no salve that would make the pain go away. It was an ever-present shadow that followed me.

"Oh, Mummy, why are you crying again?"

I shook my head and stopped spinning the papers to look up at her. "You have an old, beautiful soul."

She gently smiled.

"I've wondered if this is my fault. If there was something I could've done or should've done. Or still need to do," I said.

"Well, I'm his sister, and I'm his friend, and all friends want to do is help so we don't feel guilty for what's happening because we didn't have him inside of us." She rubbed her stomach. "Growing inside of us. We don't have that connection, so it's just easier to look at their point of view because the emotional connection is different."

I stared into her emerald eyes that were so different than Branson's. "I just want to fix him and have my son back."

"You can't fix everyone. You can only help mend. Or help improve upon the situation."

"I'm trying." I sounded as defeated as I felt.

"When Aaron and I found out Branson was hearing things, we didn't try to fix him. We just tried to make him laugh and improve on the dark situation by making things a little brighter."

"How'd you do that?"

"We were downstairs, but I don't remember the specifics. All I remember is that we were pretty crude."

"About what?"

"We were just all downstairs making fun of Branson."

"Nuh-uh." I leaned forward. "What'd you say? How did he respond?"

"Oh you know, we made school shooting jokes, as awful as that sounds. But we were like 'Don't wear that black hoodie. I know it was you. Don't gun me down, bro.' And Branson would just laugh and be like 'Yeah, that's exactly what I'm gonna do. Better watch out. I'll be on *Criminal Minds* soon. That'll be me.' It was just fun, and Branson laughed with us and enjoyed the company of not making it dark."

I sat back, stunned. "You actually made jokes about his mental illness? And he was okay with it?"

"Don't get defensive." Carson sat down beside me. "What you don't realize is that it made us all feel better."

"I'm not defensive. I just don't think it's funny to make fun of someone's disability. And mental illness is a disability. It's not his fault."

"Mom, we weren't sticking him out and putting him in the spotlight. We were all together making fun of it, and he was part of it. If he wasn't, we wouldn't have done it. Comedy is just a coping mechanism at this point." She took a long, steady breath. "I mean, how else are we supposed to react when we find out our brother is gone and he's not the same?"

It was twice in the same night where one of my children admitted they had lost something too. That Branson was not the brother they remembered and loved. That they were hurting as much as I was.

"So by joking, it helped you connect," I said.

"Uh-huh."

"I don't know if I could joke about it."

"You don't necessarily have to joke about it, but you've got to be open to accepting it. I overheard you and Aaron talk about schizophrenia and that Branson may have it."

I nodded. "We tried to talk while you were with Jack at the jukebox. I didn't want to burden you with it. But"—I held up my finger—"Branson *hasn't* been diagnosed with schizophrenia."

"He doesn't have to be diagnosed. I know he has it."

"As much as I value your insight and your help, and I do," I said with my hands extended toward hers, "there's no way you know for certain if Branson has schizophrenia."

"You don't have to be diagnosed to know there's a problem. I'm not going to attack you right now. All I'm going to say is you're in denial." She abruptly stood and started to walk away.

"Are you kidding me?" I stood up and met my daughter face-to-face. "You can't throw down that accusation and walk away." *Unless you're more like your father than I know.*

"Hearing voices. Seeing things. Blacking out. Imaginary friends," she listed, going toe-to-toe with me. "What part of this isn't schizophrenia? It's not like minor depression or teenage angst. It's schizophrenia, and it's not going to go away. It's going to get worse until we treat it."

I hit my breaking point. "First you suggest I don't take it personally and that I should make a big joke out of it instead like you and Aaron do. And then in the next breath, you say I need to have Branson treated, and that it'll only get worse before it gets better. So what is it, Carson? Fun or life-threatening?"

My tone was snarky, rude, and completely out of control. *What am I doing?* But I already knew the answer. When it came to Branson, there was no limit to where I'd go to protect him. No matter how much I wanted to handle this differently, I didn't know how.

"You're not getting my points," Carson said softly. "I'm saying you do need to have Branson treated because it won't go away. But instead of it being a life sentence for him, *lighten up.* He doesn't need you to look at him with disappointment and disapproval. He's already getting that from his peers and teachers."

I took a tentative step toward her, and she walked into my outstretched arms. "I'm sorry." I exhaled the hot breath that was fueled by anger, hurt, and resentment. I challenged everyone, including my other children, because no one knew Branson the way I did. He was my baby. My son. And I couldn't fix him. I couldn't seem to get him back. All I wanted was for my son to return.

Branson. The hurt cut deep and wide and overshadowed reason and logic. I was alienating everyone close to me to save the one person who didn't seem like he wanted to be saved.

Carson leaned her head against me—willingly, kindly, and without any intention of hurting me or her brother.

My voice shook and tears fell on her beautiful wavy hair. "Oh, my little girl. I'm so sorry. I shouldn't be talking to you about this. I'm the parent. You're the child. I just haven't said a word about this to anyone. You and Aaron are the *only* ones who know about it because…."

"You don't want people to think of him differently."

The fight that raged inside me suddenly surrendered. "Exactly." My heart rate slowed and my breathing evened out. "That's exactly it. I don't want anyone to think of my son differently, or to look at him strangely, or to talk behind his back, or"—I thought of Ben's 'schizo' comment—"call him names."

"Mom, I get it." She pulled away enough to look at me. "I haven't told any of my friends either because it's none of their business. But I'm your daughter and Branson's sister. This *is* my business. I'm in the same situation you are. I understand. That's why we have our jokes to break the ice, to lighten the load. I'm not criticizing you or your parenting, I just want you to understand what's happening."

"I know. I do. I just get…."

"Crazy?" She flashed me a wild smile.

"Yeah. I get crazy when it comes to Branson and protecting him. I've kept so much in for so long that I forget I'm not alone in this and that my other children are living through it too." I rolled my eyes. "That is *crazy.*"

She hugged me tightly. "Mummy, it's okay."

"It's not, but I'm trying to get a better handle on it. Thank you for being the adult when I wasn't." I kissed the top of her head. "I'll be honest, I'm not sure how much levity I can bring to this, but I can try."

Carson smiled. "The next time you see Branson, just be there. Don't try to evaluate it or fix it or overthink things. Just be there for him."

I thought of his incubator and staying by his side throughout the night. "I can do that." I gently pulled away from her. "And I can definitely do one of your blueberry muffins right now."

I started toward the kitchen with Carson laughing on my heels when the front door abruptly opened. Bandit came barking around the corner, and Carson and I turned toward the foyer.

Branson stood motionless in the doorway, faint hazel eyes locked onto mine.

He needs me. He's afraid. He's expecting me to yell.

Instead, I smiled at my beautiful blond-haired warrior. "Late night, huh?" I said. "Us too. Come have a muffin with your sister and me."

CHAPTER 23

BRANSON

"I don't know what happened," I said to Dr. Cordova.

My mom sat beside me on the couch in his office. When I walked into the house this morning and told her how I ended up on the side of the highway in someone else's car with no knowledge of how I got there, she didn't lecture, yell, or cry. *Nothing will shut a parent down more than finding out your son is a certified psychopath.* She'd grabbed her car keys and we'd headed straight to Dr. Cordova's office.

"One minute I was asleep at my girlfriend's house, and the next thing I know I was on the side of the road with someone else's car, a cop thinking I was drunk, and my girlfriend and this dude bailing me out." I didn't even look at my mom. "I swear I'm not lying. I don't remember how I got into the car or nothing."

I was waiting for my mom to correct my grammar, but she didn't. She just sat motionless. She only said three words to me when I confessed what happened: "I love you."

How anyone could love me at that point was beyond me, but I'd take it.

"What you experienced is called a fugue state." Dr. Cordova didn't mince words, just laying it all out there immediately.

"What's that?" I asked, leaning forward on the couch.

"A fugue state is like a blackout. A person functions, but has no memory of what happens or is happening."

"So getting into someone else's car and driving without any conscious memory of it is completely normal?"

The panic in my mom's voice made me sad. She was scared, and I understood. So was I. I didn't understand what was happening to me, and I was afraid my chances of getting better had passed. I was crazy, and I'd always be crazy.

"There's nothing normal about a fugue state, but it is a symptom of his illness. This is the second occurrence where Branson has lost track of time." Dr. Cordova flipped through my file that was starting to look more like a novel. "He first reported blacking out at school and coming to in the boys' restroom." He looked at me.

"Yeah, but that was, like, maybe five minutes that I don't remember. This was like a lot longer." I ran my fingers through my unwashed hair. It felt sticky and gross, and I was sure it smelled just as bad. "I don't even know when I left Dakota's house, or how I got the car or anything."

Dr. Cordova nodded. "Dissociative fugue states can range from hours to days, with periods of unplanned travel and wandering involved."

"You're kidding, right?" I said.

He shook his head. "No, I'm not."

I didn't know why I'd even asked. The man was as serious as a heart attack. No bedside humor, strictly fact. "So what do we do? Because I don't want that to happen *ever* again."

"I had discussed with your parents about starting you on an antipsychotic medication. The next step was discussing medication options with you. You aren't currently taking any psychotropic drugs, like heroin, cocaine, meth—"

"No." I blurted, and again I expected my mom to jump my shit, but she was practically mute beside me.

"What about marijuana?" he asked.

I looked up at the doctor. "Yeah, but I haven't smoked pot in a while." I elbowed my mom. "I told you I've smoked pot."

She nodded.

"Okay, just so you know, with your kind of ailment, alcohol and pot could exacerbate it, particularly pot," Dr. Cordova said. "High levels of alcohol can also affect it. The pot can really mess with your prescriptions."

"No more pot." I laughed, and surprisingly my mom did too. I reached for her hand and held it. "I'm sorry," I said under my breath.

She shook her head. "It's not your fault."

Yeah, that's what Dakota said. So who do I blame, then? It's my body. It's my mental health.

"What are some of the concerns you have?" Dr. Cordova directed the question to my mom.

"I don't know how to help him." Her voice was so shallow and low. It made me want to hold her and tell her

I was okay and that I'd be all right. That I'd get my shit together and never be a problem again.

"There's a support group. The National Alliance for Mentally Ill, or NAMI. It's inexpensive to join, and there's a Wyoming chapter."

I didn't think it was the answer my mom was expecting to hear, because she barely registered a response. I felt the couch shake slightly, and when I looked at her, she was crying. I squeezed her hand.

"Oh, Mom."

She shook her head. "I'm okay." She leaned forward on the couch. "Okay. So this is new ground. And I guess what I don't understand is how do you know if this is real?"

"Real?" Dr. Cordova repeated.

"I'm sorry. I know this seems insensitive, or perhaps completely inane, but how do you know if what Branson is saying is real? That he's not just making it up to get out of trouble?"

"Ask Branson. Have him answer," Dr. Cordova replied.

"I wouldn't make it up," I said quickly.

"Okay, but how do *you* know, from a medical standpoint, if it's real?" my mom pressed the doctor for an answer that was more concrete than the one he was giving her.

Way to go, Mom.

"When what is real?" Dr. Cordova asked.

He either wasn't getting it, or he was refusing to answer.

"His diagnosis. I don't even know what it is," she said. "I'm still…."

"There are a lot of illnesses, like bipolar disorder and

schizophrenia, that become clearer in adulthood but are less clear in adolescents," he said.

You could have heard a pin drop from how quiet it was in the room. Both my mom and I were riveted to what he had to say, because honestly, it was the most the guy had given either of us about what was causing me to black out and end up in strange places.

"But some of the symptoms Branson has are much more on the schizophrenia spectrum. Hearing multiple voices, the kind of thoughts that become very intrusive, wanting him to do things, almost like a command hallucination—it's not typical of people with a mood disorder. Usually if it's something like depression, the hallucinations would only be singular, not multiple, it would be limited to mainly putting you down or calling you names, everything that's more consistent with saying you're a bad person and you need to die. With mania, you can get some of that, but you don't have manic symptoms. You don't have the rapid speech, the grandiosity, hyper energy, overly cocky, not needing sleep." He took a long pause. "Branson's symptoms are more typical of schizophrenia."

Schizophrenia? That can't be right, can it? I didn't look at my mom. I didn't want to see her reaction.

"My suggestion is to start Branson on a low dose of Geodon," he said. "He's been having more symptoms than he originally reported. I don't know if he's shared that with you?"

Thanks, Doc.

"No, he hasn't," my mom said and then turned to me.

"What other symptoms?"

"More intrusive thoughts." My tone was clipped and short. *She doesn't need to know every detail of my morbid life.*

"I want to start him on sixty milligrams," Dr. Cordova said.

"How often do I have to take this?" I asked. "Like for four weeks?"

"Every day. We'll get to the length of time in a moment." *Well fucking awesome.*

"Sixty milligrams is still a low dose, so we'll have room to go. The target is not to create side effects but try to control the intrusive thoughts," Dr. Cordova explained.

"The side effects are important to me, because if I gain any more weight, I won't be cool with that," I said.

The doctor nodded. "Weight gain is one of the potential side effects of Geodon."

"Is there something else I can take? Any other options? Because I've already gained ten pounds from the antidepressant *you* prescribed when you gave me the wrong diagnosis." My anger was uncontrollable. "So if you're going to give me more medication, you better make sure it won't affect my athletic performance and make me gain more weight."

The doctor crossed his legs. "I understand your concerns. I did not prescribe the antidepressant you're currently on, though I have kept you on it because you responded well to it and it's helped alleviate your depressive symptoms. But with your illness, often when the depression lifts, the psychosis becomes stronger. You've experienced more auditory and visual hallucinations and now more fugue states."

Just make sure not to mess up this time. I'm not going to gain weight every other week or I won't stay on this shit.

The doctor uncrossed his legs and looked at my mom. "Branson already has a lot of things going for him." He then volleyed his attention to me. "You have good social skills. You've been successful. You're smart. You haven't ventured into alcohol." He paused.

And we all laughed.

"Okay, with the exception of your fugue states where you may or may not have drank, normally you're not venturing into alcohol," he amended, then leaned back in his chair. "Those are all positive qualities. The people with schizophrenia who struggle the most are the ones who are premorbid early on. They start out as kind of a loner, they don't take care of their hygiene, and they're very socially awkward and withdrawn. That's one of the things you don't have. And the other thing that hasn't happened, which is extremely huge, is that you haven't been put into a hospital for it."

Hospital? Oh fuck no.

"At some point you might," he hedged, "but hopefully not." He paused. "Particularly if you stay on top of things."

I barely said, "Okay," and my mom practically screamed, "We'll stay on top of it."

"I've had some kids where we've gotten things going pretty well early, and as far as I know they've never seen the inside of a hospital, nor do most people ever know they have the illness."

If no one ever had to know I have this....

"The hospitalization, would it happen because he went off his medication, or the symptoms got worse?" my mom asked.

"If it ever got so bad that Branson wasn't sure he could keep himself from hurting somebody or hurting himself, or just that his illness got so much in the way that he couldn't function," he replied.

I took a deep breath. *I've gotta keep this shit in check.*

"You seem so calm with this diagnosis," my mom said to me. "It doesn't scare you, Branson?"

It terrifies me. I shrugged. "No."

"As a mom, it's...."

"It's one of those illnesses that, when people hear the name, it's considered a serious psychiatric illness, but so are severe depression and manic or bipolar depression."

"It's just so misunderstood," my mom said, as if she had grasped what we'd just been handed when I knew damn well she hadn't.

"It is misunderstood," Dr. Cordova agreed. "And part of that is because historically, there's not a clear understanding of the illness." He looked toward me. "You ended up with yours sort of late in adolescence, and that's about the time frame that many can start getting their symptoms into adulthood. The thing that predicts the worst outcome of schizophrenia is not staying on top of symptoms and not being compliant with medication."

He took a long pause and held eye contact with me. I figured he was trying to unnerve me, but at that point, nothing spooked me anymore.

"Sometimes what happens is you'll get on the medication and you'll think, 'I'm doing so great' because you've gotten rid of the symptoms, and then you'll just stop taking your meds. But the symptoms could sneak up on you, or come back really fast—we just don't know. You may go off the meds for a while and it may not be a big deal. But you don't want to ever go off your medication without the aid of your psychiatrist. I would suggest we go a good full year without symptoms, and I don't think any psychiatrist would disagree, before we think we could go with a lower dosage." He crossed his arms over his chest. "Sometimes you may need more, but the odds are you're probably going to have to be on meds most of your life."

And there it was. My death sentence. I wasn't just crazy, I was confined to a life of medication, shrinks and, by the looks of it, the pity of my own mom.

"You want the meds to work without causing problems," Dr. Cordova said.

"Are you all right with that?" my mom asked.

As if I have a choice.

"Yeah, I'm fine."

CHAPTER 24

BRANSON

HALLOWEEN. *Great time to dress up as someone you're not and party with a bunch of people you don't know.*

I glanced in the full-length mirror in my mom's room, repositioning the police hat so it would fit more squarely on my head. My shaggy hair seemed to stick out on the sides, no matter the adjustment. I tucked the thin, shitty navy-colored costume shirt into the matching pants and ta-da, I was a cheap cop or bachelorette party stripper. It depended on how I wanted to look at things, and since Dr. Cordova put me on crazy pills, I was seeing things a little more clearly.

"Aaron, are you about ready? The girls are almost here."

Of course, there was no reply. He was probably working on his hair, though I didn't know why since his hair was going to be covered with a firefighter's helmet. I shook my head and pulled the aviators from the front pocket of my shirt, sliding them over my eyes.

Damn, I look hot. Maybe Aaron was right when he said

taking care of myself paid off.

Tonight's going to be perfect. I'm feeling great, and I get to grind against Dakota all night in her slutty police uniform. Halloween is the best.

I was still admiring myself in the mirror when Bandit started barking. "Looks like the girls are here." I hurried to the door and swung it open.

"Officer Dakota, reporting for bootie!"

My girlfriend was stunning. Her long black hair fell down to her exposed breasts that were playing peekaboo from her naughty police uniform, her long, slender legs capped off by boots that she'd borrowed from my mom. A pair of handcuffs were strapped to her narrow waist, and if at all possible, her aviators looked even better than mine. I saw my reflection in the tinted mirrors and smiled.

"Can't wait to use those handcuffs tonight." I smirked.

"You wish." She placed her hands on her hips and looked sassy as hell.

Behind Dakota, Chelsea was dressed in a fireman's outfit that barely fit her more athletic body.

"Goddamn, girl! You are looking suh-weet!"

I turned in the direction of Aaron's loud voice and started laughing. He was wearing a pair of baggy black jeans held up by thick, red suspenders. To complete the look, my dorky brother had smeared something all over his face and bare chest. A fireman's hat sat lopsided on his round, melon-sized head.

"What the hell are you wearing?" I stared at him.

"Charcoal, bruh."

I rolled my eyes. "What...?" I didn't even know what else to say I was laughing so hard.

Chelsea wrapped her arm around him. "Ah, don't tease Aaron. I think it's cute."

My mom suddenly appeared in the front room, standing off to the side and seeming hesitant. I looked down at her hands and noticed her cell phone clenched tightly in her fist.

"Hey, guys, photo time," I announced.

She looked at me and softly smiled. Three weeks ago, I was driving during a blackout in a stolen car, but now she seemed to be smiling a lot more. Maybe it was Halloween, or maybe it was the meds. I didn't know for sure, but it was good to see her smiling regardless.

The four of us lined up in front of this mammoth-like table that was tougher than stone and had been my French grandfather's. The legs on the wooden table were thick, dark, and etched with carvings that made it look like it belonged in a haunted house. But my mom loved the old piece of furniture, so we pretended to like it too.

My mom held out her cell phone and smiled along with us. I put my arm around Dakota's waist, and right before the flash went off on my mom's cell, I whispered in her ear, "I'm the trick, and you're my treat."

***

The four of us approached the alley in downtown Casper as if we were actual policemen and firefighters. Aaron tried to show off his muscles by pushing into a large green dumpster tagged with white graffiti, but it barely moved an inch. We all laughed and he patted it with his hand. "Okay, well it's fine where it's at."

"You're an idiot," I said.

Dakota pointed toward a steel spiral staircase that seemed to reach toward the sky. "Everyone takes their senior photos on it."

I nodded. "Yeah, I could see that."

In the distance, the lights in the alley were nonexistent and the businesses vacant.

"Nice neighborhood," I said to Aaron.

He shrugged. "Justin said it was the cheapest place to rent at the last minute."

"You guys are worrying about nothing," Dakota said, taking the lead. "It'll be fine."

Chelsea lingered behind Aaron. I stepped up beside Dakota and tilted my aviators at Dakota. "I'll protect you, ma'am."

"Oh, what would I do without you, Officer?" She winked.

The warehouse we were looking for wasn't easy to see, but it was easy to detect, the building vibrating from the bass of the music that blared from within. I strutted toward the back door and rapped my knuckles on the steel.

The door opened, and Justin appeared dressed as a hippie with round glasses, bell-bottoms, a tie-dyed shirt, and a headband wrapped around his stringy blond hair.

I shook hands with the known stoner and long-distance runner on my indoor track team. "Justin, thanks for the invite, man!"

Once he released my hand, he extended his arm toward the open warehouse that was alive with music and grinding high schoolers. "Happy Halloween! Let's party!"

Dakota and I instantly went to the dance circle in the middle of the warehouse and started to grind. Her butt pressed against my pelvis, I grabbed her waist and started to move back and forth to the beat.

In the distance, I spotted Aaron and Chelsea engaged in what seemed like an argument. *Already?* I leaned forward to whisper to Dakota but had to yell to be heard above the music. "Trouble in paradise." I nodded toward my brother and his firefighting date.

Dakota rolled her shoulders. "That's one fire he can't put out."

I laughed. "Very true."

I glanced around the warehouse. Justin had put on this party at the last minute and had done it right. Orange and black strobe lights circled the empty space and made it seem like a haunted house. A large black *cauldron* with what had to be dry ice blew smoke into the air. People dipped clear plastic cups into the cloudy vat and drew out a red liquid. I wasn't sure what they were drinking, only that they seemed happier afterward.

I glanced at the speakers that were almost as tall as me and did a double take.

It can't be. I squinted. *Trevor?*

He caught a glimpse of me and waved me over.

I turned to Dakota. "Hey, I'm going to go talk to my friend."

She nodded and headed in the direction of Aaron and Chelsea, who seemed to have already made up, as I worked my way toward the men's room where Trevor stood. He pushed the door open and I followed him inside. Even on Halloween, Trevor wore a gray T-shirt and baggy jeans.

"Glad you dressed up," I teased at the urinal beside him.

"Got to look good for the ladies. I don't need a costume for that," he said with a grin.

"Then why were you dancing all alone?" I zipped up my fly and bumped him on the shoulder on my way to the sink.

"Hey, watch out!"

"Oh, sorry about that. I was joking around."

"Speaking of joking around," Trevor said, joining me at the sink, "I heard Ashley saying some shit about you."

"Really?" Heat spread throughout my body like someone had lit a match against my skin. My face felt like it was on fire. "What the fuck did I do?"

"She keeps saying you're trying to hit on her to prove you're not gay."

I punched the cinder block wall hard. It felt good to strike something. "Why is she doing this shit? I've never done anything to her." My anger was rising quickly.

"I don't know, man. It's just what I heard. She says *a lot* of shit about you."

I clenched my fist and slammed it down on the sink. It stung, but I hit it again. "What a bitch."

"You gotta stop taking that shit. You've gotta stand up for yourself." Trevor's voice was harsh and aggressive.

I glared at him, and he crossed his arms over his thick chest.

Trevor was built. I wasn't nearly as big as he was. "What can I do?" I asked.

"Send a message."

"And how do you suppose I do that?" I was clearly irritated with Trevor, and he knew it.

"I saw her car parked up in the alley."

"You want me to vandalize her car?" Now I sounded hysterical.

"No, no. I want *us* to vandalize it."

I shook my head. "Nope, not a chance. Listen, I'm not 100 percent clear what happened at Dakota's house, but what I *do* know is that I came to in someone else's car on the side of the road *alone* with a cop. So no, I'm not vandalizing anything—with you or anyone." *That was hell. There's nothing worse than coming out of a blackout, or fugue state as my lovely doctor called it, in front of a cop. No thank you.*

Trevor leaned against the bathroom wall. "Okay, that's fair. I guess she'll just keep talking shit about you."

I rolled my eyes and started to walk out of the bathroom. "See you, Trevor."

"Oh, I plan on it, Branson."

CHAPTER 25

BRANSON

"BRANSON, I think we need to discuss these congressional interviews." Her voice entered my bedroom before she did. I was sitting in my gaming chair, tucked into it like I always was when I was playing. "Why are the lights off?" I heard my mom palm the wall in my room for the light switch.

"Mom, don't!" My tone was a bit harsher than I would have liked, but I was playing a post-apocalyptic game that challenged me to survive in the harsh wastelands of America, and I played it better in the dark.

She fumbled her way over to my unmade bed and sat on the edge. "Bran, if you're still really serious about these interviews, then you need a suit."

I nodded. I had a bomb strapped around my neck, and if I got around any radio frequency, I would die.

"I'm still not sure this is the best direction," she said.

The more she kept prattling on at me, the more I kept

walking into radio waves and splattering like a fly on the wall.

"Mom, I don't need a suit. I'll just borrow one of Aaron's."

I think she nodded; my peripheral vision saw her head do something. "Okay, that'll save money. Will you try one on later?"

I knew if I agreed, it would get her out of my room and back to my game. "Sure. Yeah. I'll do it."

But she stayed on the edge of my bed. *What now?* I paused my game and turned around in my chair.

"I'll try on Aaron's suit."

That time I saw her nod.

"What?" I said. "Are you okay?" I couldn't tell, but it looked like maybe she was crying.

She shook her head and cleared her throat. "I'm...." She cleared her throat again. "These interviews." She raised her shoulders. "Why is it important to you?"

"I just want to see how far I can go in the process."

She didn't say anything for what seemed like a really long time, and I just wanted to get back to my game, but I knew if I didn't wait it out, she'd never leave.

Finally she reached over and gently brushed my hair off my face. "Then we'll get you ready for the interviews." She stood up and kissed the top of my head. "Love you."

I nodded. "Love you too."

She left and I returned to a deserted casino that looked like something out of a horror movie. The hallways were dark, the scene was macabre, and I knew danger lurked around every corner. I grabbed a .357 revolver and had to find the key to unlock the bomb that was fastened around my neck. It was the only way to escape this hellhole. I walked down a long corridor that looked like something out of *The Shining* and ended at a room. Opening the door, I aimed my revolver at a dusty movie projector and it suddenly started to roll tape.

The grainy image that projected on the movie screen in the casino was blank. *This is some freaky shit.* I hurried out of the projector room and turned another corner into an abandoned bar. Broken whiskey bottles littered the floor. I had to be careful not to step on the glass and alert the security holograms that still protected the casino. *That's all I need is to get shot while I'm strapped with a bomb around my neck.*

The key had to be in the casino, and if it wasn't in the bar or the projector room, it had to be on the dance floor where the vault was hidden.

I was heading toward the ballroom when Aaron came into my room.

"Mom says you need to try on one of my suits."

"What the hell?" I was one key away from escape and battling the boss that put the bomb collar around my neck when Aaron started snapping at me. I waved away his annoying hand.

"Come on, Branson. Put the game down for two minutes and try on the suit."

A bunch of security holograms were protecting the stage. *I wish I had the same security protecting me and my bedroom.*

"Dude, come on," he said and playfully nudged my shoulder.

I grunted and paused my game. "Turn on the light." Now I meant for my tone to be harsh.

The overhead light was blinding, and I had to blink a few times before I slipped off my elastic-waist athletic shorts and grabbed the slacks from Aaron. When I put my legs into the pants, it was a snug fit across my thighs. *Jesus, what the hell? Am I getting fatter?* I twisted around in them while pulling them up, but I was unable to get the pants past my hips. I couldn't get them to zip, let alone button.

For a moment, I stared down at my body in complete disbelief. My six-pack abs had been replaced by the beginning of a baby gut. My thighs and ass must have grown too, because everything was tight.

I looked up at Aaron. "I can't get them up all the way." Tears stung my eyes.

Aaron stepped toward me. "It's all right, bro." His voice was reassuring when his face looked as shocked as mine. "We'll just get you new pants."

"It's that goddamn medication. I'm gaining weight. I've never gained weight before." Heat coursed through my veins. I tore the pants off and kicked them away from me before picking up my gym shorts and putting them back on.

"Branson, it's no big deal. It's just a pair of pants, and these are from like freshman year."

I nodded. I knew my brother meant well and that he was worried, but the medication was causing me to gain weight.

And that messed with my head more than anything.

I wiped my eyes and shook it off. "I'm okay. I just want to go back to my game."

"Dude, it's okay. Don't do anything stupid."

"I won't. I just want to chill."

"All right." Aaron picked up the pants and turned off the light on his way out of my room.

Grabbing my controller, I went back to killing the monsters. I was about to Google where the key was hidden when my mom stood in the doorway to my room.

"So how'd the suit go?" Her voice was singsongy and light like a bird that I wanted to smash against the window.

"Shut the fuck up, Mom! Get out! Go away!"

She stumbled out of the doorway, startled, scared, and afraid.

"I'm sorry," I called out after her. "Mom."

She stood in the basement living room that separated my room and Aaron's. Her green eyes were wide, and her pale skin looked even paler. She stared at me like I was someone she had never seen before.

"I didn't mean it," I said, leaning over in my chair.

She barely nodded, like one of the zombies in my game that move but don't really seem to know what they're doing. Her actions, along with her voice, seemed dead. "It's okay."

No it's not. But instead, I looked away from her and stared at the empty vault on my television screen. The key wasn't inside the ballroom vault. It seemed like I would always be searching for the key to unlock the bomb that was tied around my neck. I couldn't find the damn key.

I'll be tied to this ticking bomb forever.

CHAPTER 26

TARA

SIX weeks had passed and I was back in Dr. Cordova's office. I knew why I was there. The letter was on the couch beside me, but I wasn't ready to deal with it. And he didn't seem to be in any hurry.

"When Branson was little, I used to sing to him at bedtime. It was our routine." I looked from my hands in my lap up to Dr. Cordova. His nod prodded me to continue. "I sang to both of the boys. I sang the Barney song to Aaron."

I chuckled, but it sounded as fake as it felt.

"With Branson, our song was different." Suddenly, it hurt to breathe. Every cell in my body ached for that moment again, to reclaim my son and protect him from whatever went wrong. Tears fell down my cheeks and onto my lap. I didn't bother to wipe them away. Why? There'd only be more.

"With Branson, our song was 'You Are My Sunshine.'"

I closed my eyes and saw my little blond-haired, hazel-eyed boy staring up at me. My shoulders shook and I pinched my nose before wiping snot on my jeans. I didn't care what Cordova or anyone thought of me. I didn't care who saw what a mess I was or how they judged me. I only wanted my sunshine back. I wanted that sweet little boy's face to look up at me with wonder and excitement, not fear and distrust.

"What did I do wrong? Was it something in my pregnancy?" My leg bounced nervously on the couch. "Did I hurt him? Was there something I should've done?" I couldn't control the hurt that poured out of me. "Please tell me what I can do. How can I fix him? What do I need to do to make him whole again?"

Dr. Cordova's voice was steady. "Nothing. There's nothing you could've done, and there's nothing you didn't do. Schizoaffective disorder isn't something that could have been prevented."

I placed my hands over my ears. "No, he doesn't have that. He doesn't. No. Please don't say that." Even though I went to the pharmacy religiously and picked up medication to treat the disorder, I still hadn't reconciled the illness with my son.

I felt his hand on my knee. "Tara, look at me."

I shook my head. "No. I can't. My son is okay. Branson is fine. He's just..." *Scared. Frightened. Lost. Angry.* I opened my mouth, but the only sound that came out was the wounded cry of a mother for her child. I grabbed his hand and held it tightly. "Please. We have to fix him. There's got to be something."

"There is." He didn't let go of my hand. "We've started a treatment plan. Branson is responding well. He's still taking his meds?"

I nodded. "I got one of those pill boxes like you suggested, the one with the days of the week so he won't lose track."

"That's great."

I shook my head. "No it's not, but it's all I can do. It's all I know how to do."

"When a parent finds out their child has a mental illness, there's a period of mourning."

"What?" My vision was blurry, but now my hearing seemed to be cloudy too. "Mourning? He's not dead."

"You mourn the child you lost, and the dreams you had for him."

"No, no." I pulled my hand away and held up a finger at him. "No. Branson's not lost. He's still there. And so are all his dreams." I thought about the congressional interviews that were lined up. The interviews I knew I had to cancel, but hadn't.

"He'll be in the Navy," I said in the face of overwhelming reason to the contrary. "He wants this. He's ready for this. He'll be fine. I'll find a way to get him into the Navy." I wiped my eyes and quickly regained my composure. "Hell, I literally wrote the book on getting kids into school. I've got this. Besides," I continued, crossing my arms over my chest, "he still has his congressional interviews. We haven't canceled them. He has just as good a chance as anyone else."

Doctor Cordova sat back in his chair. "Branson won't

pass the medical exam."

"You don't know that." I leveled him with a look. "You don't know *dick* about academia."

"Tara, even if you don't tell the Navy what's going on, they'll draw blood and they *will* discover the medication he's on and what it's used to treat. And if by some grace of God he passes that, he won't pass the psych eval."

"You don't know that. You think you do, but you don't. By your own admission, my son has had these symptoms since the eighth grade. The *eighth grade*." My tone bit with an anger so strong, it practically came out of my mouth and mauled the doctor. "Branson's done a bang-up job fooling everyone into thinking he's"—I held my fingers up in air quotes—"'normal.'" I lowered my hands into my lap. "So yeah, he'll pass the psych eval just fine. Just fine. Don't you worry. My son's navy-bound. *Anchors aweigh*."

Dr. Cordova said nothing, and it only fueled my rage.

"You don't want to cure my son, you just want to pump him full of medication so you can go back to your life until you have to deal with him again in a month when his prescription runs out. You're an ass."

"I understand you're upset."

"Oh do you? Well bravo." I slow-clapped. "Good diagnosis, Doctor."

"I understand you want to blame someone."

I tightened my hand into a fist and shook it at him. "Yes, I want someone to blame. I want someone to hurt as badly as I do. I want my son back!" I lowered my head. The pain felt like it was going to rip me in half. "I just want him back. I want Branson, not this zombie you've created with all these drugs." Although that was far from the truth. I had noticed a change in Branson since he started his medication, but he wasn't zombie-like. He was simply more mellow, less irritated. Unless I was interrupting his video games and asking him to try on a suit. Then all bets were off.

The truth of how I felt, nestled beneath all my anger, finally came out in a whisper. "I want his dreams to still be alive. I don't want to be the one who takes them away."

"You didn't take them away. Branson still has dreams, they're just different now. They're more realistic to his situation. He's highly functional, and there are sitting court judges and hospital presidents who have diagnosed schizoaffective disorder. They've been able to live very productive, full lives."

"They just can't navigate a submarine, fly a plane, or see combat duty." My voice cut with cynicism.

A soft smile crossed his face. "That's right."

"Well it's bullshit, and it's not fair."

"No, it's not. That's why there's a period of mourning."

"Why Branson? Why him?" My body shook, and I lost any ground I had in my fight against the doctor. "Why Branson? He's always been my sweet, soft, kindhearted, shy little boy. Since the moment he was born, he's been my quiet warrior."

Dr. Cordova leaned forward. "Tara, he's still fighting. He's still your warrior. I haven't seen a young man work this hard to treat his illness."

"No! There shouldn't be any illness to fight. He's been fine *his whole life*. He's been fine."

Dr. Cordova shook his head. "He hasn't. He's just been good at masking his symptoms."

"So he's been hurting this whole time and I didn't know?"

"No one knew. Not even Branson. He wasn't sure what it was. His symptoms presented early in his adolescence and progressively worsened. To your son's credit, he learned to live with it."

"I don't know if that makes it better or worse."

Dr. Cordova nodded. "None of this is easy."

I finally picked up the letter beside me. "Yup, and getting these results." I slowly shook my head. "Not what I was hoping for."

"The EEG report?"

I nodded.

"It shows the sleep-deprived EEG performed on Branson was normal. There weren't any potentially epileptogenic discharges or seizures present," he said.

Again, I nodded.

"You were hoping for a different outcome?"

"I was hoping for a brain tumor."

He tried not to smile, but failed. "That's understandable. There's always an adjustment period with mental illness."

"Adjustment period. Mourning period. My God."

Please just rewind the clock and let me stop this before it starts. Before medication, before counseling, before EEGs, before blackouts, hallucinations, static, and everything that made my son look like he was haunted when he should be happy. I'll take us away to a place where mental illness would never touch him.

"It's never going to be over, is it?" I asked.

"Your son's mental illness is a condition he'll have most of his life."

I lowered my head and cried until I didn't think I could cry anymore. I kept it together at work, at home, and in what existed of my personal life. But in this office, alone with the good doctor, there was no one to save face for.

I looked up at him. "Please make it stop hurting."

"I wish I could."

CHAPTER 27

BRANSON

AN envelope was stuck in my track locker.

"Branson" was written in red pen.

Hmmm.

I looked around the locker room. No one else was in there, but that wasn't much of a surprise since it was third block. I was supposed to be aiding in the office, but I left. Told old lady Tuttle I had a bad stomach. I might have farted before I spoke to her. Nothing got a kid excused faster than a good case of the gas.

I opened the envelope and unfolded the typewritten form letter.

First, I want to congratulate you for being among the few athletes who have qualified for the Wyoming State Indoor Track Meet. Well done! The competition was fierce. Secondly, I want to convey that the State Indoor Track Meet is three grueling days of intense competition. It's not intended for the weak of mind or body. It is befitting of only the most mentally fit minds and the most physically tough. You must push yourself to the limit for each and every day of the competition.

If you want to be a state champion, only you can make that happen. You must choose to be a state champion through your performance during the next three days. As a team, we can win overall, but individually, only you can run the distance to make that happen. If you choose to be a state champion, then this choice will be shown in your actions on and off the track. Good luck!

Beneath the form letter that Coach sent out every year at the start of the State Indoor Track Meet was a personalized note in purple ink.

Branson,

You've worked hard this season. Go get the thing you want, a medal in the 300s.

Coach

I nodded. *All right, all right, all right.*
I was feeling good. Dr. Cordova was right, and the meds

had been working, but Coach nailed it. State track was a choice. And I chose to stop taking my meds. The weight had obviously been catching up, and I had seen a decrease in my time on the track.

Besides, what's the harm of a few missed days, maybe a couple weeks, anyway?

The static hadn't nearly been as loud, and the shadow people had remained on the edge. I knew they were still there, but they hadn't attacked anyone for no good reason. In fact, I hadn't seen one of them randomly slice someone in a really long time. I only had state track and the congressional interviews left to complete. Then I'd get back on my meds.

Things are pretty good.

I grabbed my track bag and headed for the bus.

"Hey, wait up!"

I turned around and saw Trevor exiting the bathroom.

"Dude! Good to see you." I walked toward him, grabbed his arm and pulled him in for a bro hug. "It's been like a month or so."

"Tick tock goes the clock," he said.

I shook my head. "Whatever. Where you been?"

"Oh yeah, I was just visiting my hometown and my family. But I'm back now."

* * *

We unloaded the bus in Sheridan. It was a beautiful day, and I'd be stuck inside.

Hopefully my dad would forget that state track was happening in his hometown. The last thing I needed was for him to show up. My nerves were already jumpy.

State track meet. The big show.

But indoor track meets had to be the worst, because the indoor facility smelled of rubber and sweat. Warm air filled the arena, making it stuffy and hard to breathe.

The dank smell wasn't helping my mood, which went further south when Coach told me some college recruiter was there to watch me. *Fucking Coach thinks I'm actually going to give up the Navy for this shit? Joke.*

Besides, I'd only qualified for one event: the 300-meter hurdles. So I only had one chance to show my all. *Fuck, I hate stress.*

I decided to chill by our camp, which was a makeshift cluster of track bags, nutrition drinks, and water bottles. The overhead announcer blared that one of our teammates was about to run.

"You gonna go cheer him on?" Trevor asked.

I shrugged. "Why not."

Most of the team was already up at the gates to watch Nick run. He was a good guy, and I wanted to support him, so I headed down to the gates, pushing my way through the crowd of people. Nick was going to the start line in the first lane. I elbowed my way through and stood next to two figures I hadn't recognized. When the starting gun went off, so did my lungs.

"Let's go, Nick! Don't let them catch you!"

I was so immersed in the cheering that I didn't realize

I was yelling right in front of him. Not that it would have mattered.

"Hey, that's my fucking ear, you retard!" Jesse turned on the heel of his spiked shoes and shoved me.

Shocked, I stepped back. Jesse was taller than me, stronger than me, and uglier than me. He was also two times my size and wore Wilson colors identical to mine, but that didn't seem to matter, because he shoved me a second time, even harder. I took another step back, but he didn't stop.

The guy was after me, and hard. Jesse wrapped his hand around my throat and pushed me against the wall in the gym-like building I was stuck in for the next three days.

My body flooded with emotion. I was pissed off, confused, and slowly losing my breath. For a minute I thought maybe it was a joke, but when his hand tightened around my neck, I realized this motherfucker was for real.

Instinct kicked in and I brought my elbow down on his bicep, trying to break free. When that didn't work, I swiped my spiked foot down on his thigh all the way to his calf. He screamed, releasing his grip on me as blood streamed down his leg and he stumbled away. Before he had a chance to recover, I grabbed him by the bicep, pulling him toward me and using the momentum to get behind him. I wrapped my arm around his throat and brought him down hard onto his butt, squeezing tighter around his throat, flexing my bicep to cut off his airway. In shock and pure panic, he stumbled back, forcing me to take three steps back, tripping over a track bag. But it didn't matter—I still had him, and I wasn't about to let go.

I knelt over him with his life in my hands and whispered in his ear, just faintly enough for him to hear me, "Tick tock goes the clock."

He looked up at me as I smiled and laughed. "Tick tock goes *your* clock. Tick tock goes *your* clock."

His face drained of color, and I knew with one swift twist I could easily take what was left of him. I started to hear voices telling me to do it.

"Fucking do it. He just tried to kill you."

The static grew stronger.

"He deserves it. An eye for an eye."

Each voice grew louder, dominating my thoughts, propelling my actions. I had no choice but to obey.

"Branson! Stop it! He's not breathing anymore!" Aaron's voice came from somewhere behind me.

Then everything went black.

CHAPTER 28

TARA

I leaned my head away from my computer terminal and called from my office to Rachel and Ben, "Is the university web advisor down?"

"Mine's working," Rachel said.

"Me too," Ben added.

"Mine's not loading." I clicked the Refresh button, but that did nothing to get the university software to load. *I hate missing time in the office to attend stupid seminars.*

"Try the internet," Ben suggested.

I clicked onto another tab and Internet Explorer launched immediately. "That's odd," I said. "Yeah, the internet's working."

"Maybe there's a glitch in the administrative network software," Rachel offered.

I nodded. "Yeah, maybe."

I checked my university email, but I couldn't access it either. My stomach took a sudden drop. *Oh no.* I tried to log into the staff portal using Rachel's password and my computer was denied access.

My adrenaline kicked into high gear. *This isn't good.*

I casually glanced past my computer screen to the foyer where Rachel's and Ben's desks were positioned. Nothing was out of the ordinary. I didn't know if I expected a security guard to suddenly appear, march in and escort me off property, but I had definitely been denied access to the administrative and staff portal along with university email.

Why now?

I glanced at my desk calendar and flipped through the gilded edges. I had been at the three-day professional development seminar Dean Bryant made me attend. The awareness sank into my skin. *He wanted me out of the office. Bastard.*

I leaned away from my computer. "So I meant to ask how things went while I was at that professional development seminar," I called out to Rachel and Ben.

I glanced in their direction.

Rachel looked up from her computer and rolled her eyes. "Dean Bryant had more questions about the early admissions list."

I feigned an exasperated eye roll in return while thinking I was going to puke. "He's like a dog with a bone," I said, hoping it would be just enough to prod her further.

Rachel nodded. "It wouldn't have been so bad, but he had Senator Bailey and his wife with him."

"Ex-wife," Ben quickly interjected.

What the hell?

I rolled my chair away from my desk just enough to seem interested but not enough to seem like I cared. "Senator Bailey was with Dean Bryant?" I scoffed. "Huh. VIP in our office."

Rachel's eyes widened. "Did you know his ex-wife is Ecuadorian?"

I could practically taste bile in my throat. *Oh shit.* I rolled my neck like I was bored, when in reality I was trying to break the tension that had seized me. But my neck wouldn't crack; it was wound too tight.

"I *do* remember his ex-wife is Ecuadorian." *I just forgot that it made their daughter half-Ecuadorian.* So not only did I reject a legacy, but also a woman and an Ecuadorian. In stomping on the university's affirmative action plan, I hit the trifecta and rejected a double-minority. *Brilliant!* I may not have wanted Ashley Bailey on campus, but by changing her admission status and rejecting her application, I had practically set back equal rights and civil rights faster than a right-wing racist in a time machine.

I covered my mouth with my hand. *Oh my God.*

"Tara, you okay?" Rachel asked.

I nodded, trying to keep my breakfast at bay. I removed my hand and waved away the bitter taste that lingered on my breath. "Just thinking of all the work I have to do to play catch-up. Being away from the office for three days." I rolled my eyes again. "It's…" *Enough time for Dean Bryant to have IT do their homework.* I scooted my chair over to my desk. "I guess it's back to work!" I said in the most unusual, high-pitched singsong voice.

Rachel and Ben both looked at me and laughed. "Okay, boss."

By now the IT department had identified that my access code had changed Ashley Bailey's admission status. And I was fairly certain they had traced my home IP address to the changes I made to other legacy candidates when I used Rachel's password from my home computer. It was only a matter of time before I was called into Dean Bryant's office. *Crap.* I needed to check the fall list of admissions to see how badly I'd screwed up, but I couldn't even retrieve it to review.

I tapped my Manolos on the plastic floor protector beneath me when I accidentally kicked my Burberry briefcase.

I snapped. *That's it.*

I pulled my briefcase to my lap and pulled out the file folder with the email to Fred Stanley. *Fucking Fred. If he had protected Branson, I wouldn't have had to go after the bully myself.*

I skimmed the list, but it didn't get me any closer to how many candidates I'd tampered with. It only listed who I'd randomly selected when I chose candidates based off my "go fish" process of picking file folders versus my actual five-step process. I had been mad, angry, and ready to settle a score, so I didn't know who'd ended up in the reject pile alongside Ashley Bailey. I didn't know who deserved to be admitted and hadn't.

Deserved. There's a contradiction. If people truly got what they deserved.... My mind started playing a wicked game of revenge fantasy when my desk phone chimed. It was the direct line to Dean Bryant.

And here it comes.

"This is Tara," I picked up before the third ring, university standard.

"Tara, I was hoping you'd have a moment to come to my office. There's a pressing issue that needs to be addressed."

"Absolutely. Is now a good time?"

I had obviously taken him off guard, as he paused and then said, "Yes, that would work. Give me twenty minutes?"

Twenty minutes to get human resources to your office to witness my termination? Sure. "How about thirty?" I said with a playful tone, clearly taking him for a loop.

"Perfect."

I hung up the phone, grabbed a thumb drive from the inside pocket of my briefcase and downloaded every file I had on my hard drive that I could still access. I didn't know if I'd ever need what I was copying, but at that point, I was operating on sheer instinct. Then I checked to make sure no one was looking before discreetly placing the thumb drive in my bra.

I knew security would check my briefcase and all university files would be confiscated, so I emptied my briefcase of every work file and neatly placed them on the corner of my desk. I highly doubted they'd check my physical body. If they did, I'd feign stupidity of some sort. Or perhaps, I shrugged, insanity. *Why the hell not? My son's been diagnosed with schizophrenia. Perhaps he inherited it from me.*

I glanced at the silver-framed pictures on my desk, looking for Branson, but first I had to admire a baby picture of chubby Jack. A toddler picture of Carson in pigtails. And then my boys. The final frame on my desk held a picture of Aaron, Branson, and me on their first day of kindergarten. Ed encouraged me to join the picture because after seven years with the university, I had been promoted to the director of admissions. The three of us stood next to the school bus dressed in new clothes, and each of us held new backpacks and a briefcase. Bright eyes and fresh faces, we were all excited about the upcoming year. It was the start of something new.

I picked up the picture and leaned back in my chair. It was the most current picture I had of the three of us. *My God, where have I been?*

I glanced around the office. My gym bag on the floor beside the door contained everything I needed to shower and dress before work. I didn't need to close the door to my office to know an extra Lord and Taylor suit hung on the back. On top of the walnut file cabinet, an espresso maker was plugged in and ready to brew a perfect cup of my favorite roast. Inside the file cabinet, an extra set of makeup, a straightener, and hair dryer were neatly tucked inside. My office was my home away from home.

Where have I been? I've been here. For the last twenty years, I've made the university more of a home than my own.

I carefully placed the frames in my briefcase and unplugged my phone charger. I didn't want the humiliation of sorting through my office with a security guard standing beside me, so I packed what belonged to me and left the university purchases, like the espresso maker, exactly where they were.

I scanned the bookshelf. There wasn't any book on the admissions process that equaled mine, nor any book that actually told the truth, including mine. In the world of academia, it wasn't just about affirmative action that opened doors. Nor was there a magic five-step process that ensured a perfect candidate. The dirty little secret of the admissions process was that it boiled down to public perception. By tampering with the list of admission candidates, I not only misrepresented facts, I undermined my image. That could easily be rectified by terminating my employment. But by rejecting the senator's daughter, I undermined the university's brand, and there was no greater sin in academia than to threaten a college's brand and, in turn, its ranking.

I had crossed a line that there was no coming back from.

Sliding my chair under my desk, I turned off my computer and placed my phone on night mode. I grabbed my suit and gym bag, walked into the foyer and said goodbye to Rachel and Ben. Then I headed to Dean Bryant's office without looking back.

I was escorted into his office, where Ryan, a representative from human resources, sat nervously in one of the upright chairs beside Shawn's desk. I was on the hiring committee that interviewed Ryan. I smiled in his direction and his face relaxed.

A member of the university board of directors, some gray-haired bitty whose name I always forgot, sat cross-legged and stoic in another chair. She never liked me, and the feeling was mutual.

Shawn stood behind his desk, his blond hair was perfectly in place, along with his pressed blue shirt, red tie, and navy slacks. His green eyes were sincere, and it was clear he was not happy about what he had to do.

So before he uttered a word, I did.

"I understand human resources is here to document the last date of my employment, notify payroll so a final check can be issued, notify IT to remove my access to email, company networks, and applications." I paused and held up my hand. "Wait, that's already been done," I said with a lightness in my voice that made Shawn slightly smile.

I lowered my hand. "What's left is for Ryan to discuss Cobra insurance options and ensure the rightful return of all company-issued equipment and badges." I unclipped my university photo ID and placed it on Shawn's desk. "Thank you." Tears filled my eyes and emotion caught in my throat. "You believed in me and my abilities long before anyone else." I swallowed hard and quickly flicked away a tear.

"You taught me how to be a good instructor in the classroom. You told me that if I knew how to teach and connect with young minds, I'd know how to identify a good candidate, because they were more than just their application packet." My shoulders began to shake as the last two decades of my life came to an abrupt end. I quickly regained my composure and looked at my mentor and colleague. "When I was writing my book, I really wasn't sure if my five-step process would work." I laughed halfheartedly. "But you were convinced I was on to something, and then you opened the door for me to practice my process. I wouldn't have had nearly the success I have if it weren't for you."

I didn't break eye contact with him, and he didn't once look away. "It has been a great honor working under your tutelage and direction," I finished.

"If it was such a 'great honor,' as you claim, to work at the university," the board member said, "then why did you sabotage the application process for the daughter of one of Wyoming State University's most distinguished alumni?"

Because the little bitch bullied my son and no one ever held her accountable. But I knew it was better to neither confirm nor deny my involvement, so I simply maintained my focus on my dean. "Thank you again for everything." My hand went to my chest. "I will truly miss working with you."

A tear rolled down my cheek, but I quickly wiped it away. It took everything not to break down and tell him what had been going on. That my son was mentally ill. That I had made poor choices. That I screwed up. I had to leave before I completely melted into a puddle of tears, but I knew my termination was far from over.

I extended a shaky hand toward Shawn, and he shook it without question. His face was filled with doubt, but he was too much a professional and too kind a gentleman to push when he clearly knew I was not going to delve into the why of my actions. It simply was. I had made choices that placed us both in an untenable situation, and no reasoning would change that.

I turned on the spiked heel of my Manolos that I wanted to stick straight up the spindly ass of the board member, but instead, I kindly smiled toward Ryan. "I'm sure you have a lot of paperwork you need to go over with me."

He nodded and stood. "We can use the private conference room."

***

As security walked me to my car, I realized I wouldn't be sitting in the university parking lot watching the autumn sunset before I headed home. Sunset was still a few hours away, so I'd have time to find a new place to enjoy my nightly routine.

Maybe that was for the best. I couldn't remember the last time I watched a sunset with my kids.

CHAPTER 29

TARA

I was almost in my driveway when my cell phone rang. I knew news of my termination would travel fast, but the university guttersnipes who liked to take potshots were unusually fast.

Let me think. It has to be someone in admin. They always hear gossip first. Or maybe one of the English department snobs. They love to feast on fresh carcass.

I hit the clicker to my garage door and watched it rise before me. My cell phone continued to ring and ring and ring. *Leave me alone.* A chime sounded when a call rolled into voice mail. I grabbed my things and bumped the car door shut with my hip, then walked into the house.

Aaron and Branson were at state track in Sheridan and would be gone for the next three days. Maybe I'd take Carson and Jack to Sheridan. Why not? Nothing keeping us from a road trip.

I walked into the kitchen from the garage when my cell

phone rang again. "For the love of all things holy." I glanced at the screen. "Ed?" I looked up at my kitchen ceiling and noticed a crack that ran the length of it. *Awesome.* "What does *he* want?"

I blew out a mouthful of air, set my things on the counter, and slid my thumb across the screen. "This is Tara."

"Tara, it's Ed."

I nodded.

"Tara?"

"Yes, Ed. Hello. What's up?"

"Nothing much. I just wanted to call. Branson blacked out again."

My knees weakened and I reached for the countertop to steady myself. "What?"

"Yeah, I guess he was dehydrated again."

Again? He wasn't dehydrated the first time. I shook my head. "What happened?"

"I don't know. I got a call at work from Aaron. It's like ninety degrees in those indoor tracks, and he probably didn't drink enough water."

I nodded as my mind tried to play catch-up with what my ex-husband was saying.

"Where is he? Where is Branson?"

"He's just chilling here at my house. I brought him here. He's on his bed in his room. Oh, and get this. I guess he fought a kid too."

"What?" My voice rose along with my heart rate.

My ex seemed to think that was funny because he laughed. "Oh relax. Branson was just sticking up for himself. About time. That damn Jesse kid was always bullying him."

"Is he in trouble?"

"I couldn't tell you. I just picked him up after Aaron called that he blacked out. I didn't ask any questions."

Of course you didn't. "How's Aaron?"

"He just called me to say he finished his events. He got eighth in pole vault, and PR'd by a foot."

"He didn't go with you?"

"Nah, I forced him to stay there. I told him this was an important date and he shouldn't miss it because his brother didn't drink enough damn water."

I shook my head. *Unbelievable.* "Is Branson out of the meet? State, I mean?"

"Well he already missed his *one* event," he sniped, the disdain clear, "so yeah, there goes our full ride to college."

"Who gives a damn about the money, Ed? He just blacked out. You told me some kid was bullying him, he got into a fight, and he blacked out. What do you think that is, Ed? A lack of water? This isn't about water!"

"I gotta go."

"No. I'm on my way to Sheridan."

"Don't bother. I'll meet you halfway and bring the boys home."

I grabbed my car keys and purse. "Ed, I'm in the car. I'm heading to Sheridan, and we'll take it from there. Branson may need to go to the hospital and there's one in town."

"For God's sake, Tara, don't come up here. Just trust me for once."

Yeah, because our son blacked out because he's dehydrated. "I'm on my way."

"All right, whatever. I could've driven him home," he huffed.

I waited for him to disconnect the call so he maintained the one thing he valued most: control.

Whatever. Sonuvabitch.

The next call I made was to my retired neighbor, Helen, to pick up Carson and Jack from school and watch them until I returned home. Overnight, if need be. I wasn't sure what condition Branson would be in when I reached him.

CHAPTER 30

TREVOR

FINALLY *he let me in.*

I looked at the end of the bed and saw Branson sitting on the edge. His hands were in his lap, and he had a horrified look on his face.

"What have you done?" His voice was that of a man betrayed.

"Don't worry. I got this," I said to Branson. My other half. My weaker self.

"You can't be making me do this. Let me back in."

"No can do. I kind of like it out here." I leaned back on the bed and crossed my arms behind my head. "I'm willing to do things you'd never let me do."

"Who are you talking to in there?" Ed's voice came from the hallway.

I picked up the cell phone off the nightstand and put it to my ear. "Just a friend," I said when Ed poked his intruding face into the room. "Seeing how they did at their events."

"Okay. Your mom's on her way to pick you up."

I nodded. *That should be fun.*

When Tara walked into the room, her green eyes looked like she'd been crying.

"Mom." Branson stood up to meet her. "I'm sorry."

But she couldn't hear him, let alone see him.

I stayed flat on my back and let her approach me.

"Hello, Mother."

What resembled a laugh rose from her throat. "You've never called me that before."

Okay, maybe a little too Psycho. "I guess I hit my head too hard."

She rushed to my side and placed her hand on my forehead. "Is there a bump? Or a bruise?" She felt my head for injuries, her hand warm, her touch gentle.

For a second, I turned off and Branson turned on. Tears ran down his face. I watched from the outside, desperately wanting control again.

She wiped his tears and kissed his forehead. "Are you all right?"

He shook his head. "No."

"What can I do?" she asked.

"I need my medication."

CHAPTER 31

TREVOR

"PILLS weren't part of the plan," I told him.

"There is no plan." Branson opened the one thing that could shut me down forever. It was labeled with every day of the week.

"Come on, what are you, fifty and popping pills? Next you'll need a blue capsule to make your dick hard," I said.

He scooped two pills in his hand and popped them in my mouth. I tried not to swallow, but Branson was getting stronger.

"Hey, we're heading to the track party if you want to come." Aaron appeared in the mirror beside us.

I nodded. "Oh yeah, let's party it up." If there was one thing that would keep me around, it would be getting high and drunk. And I was still in charge.

I tossed Aaron the keys. "You drive."

The party was being held at some kid named Jacob's house. An Eastside home that made Branson's look like a shithole. It would help my cause. Nothing like being in a mansion off *Cribs* to make you feel like you have so little.

I walked in behind Aaron, who was sporting a T-shirt that was one size too small and American Eagle jeans that sat so low his plaid boxers showed.

He always thought he was better than Branson. Always.

I turned to Branson. "Why would you even *want* to hang out with him?"

"He's my twin, my brother. I love him to death."

"Whatever. He's still a douche." I cocked my head toward Aaron, who looked back at me.

"Who's a douche?" he asked.

"Jesse." I looked across the room at the cocksucker I'd almost killed and grinned, making eye contact with him. *That's right motherfucker. I'm back.*

"Hey, we're not starting that shit tonight," Aaron said. Always the diplomat, the peacekeeper. The bore.

I slipped away from Aaron and headed toward the backyard where the alcohol was. Anything that someone could grab from their parents' fridge, minibar, or buy from their older siblings was laid on a patio table beside a stack of red plastic cups.

I grabbed a bottle of Captain Morgan and chugged half of it. It tasted like shit and burned my throat, but it would get me fucked-up drunk and quick.

"Dude, are you even tasting it?" one of the shot putters asked.

I shrugged. "Taste? The faster you get it down, the quicker it does the job."

I felt a hand on my back. "Hey, babe."

Dakota. Great. What does she want?

I cocked my head in her direction. "What's up?"

She shook her head. "Uh, nothing. What's up with you?"

"Just drinking like an Indian on payday," I laughed.

Shock filled her face before she turned and walked away.

"Dude, isn't your girl Native?" the shot putter asked.

I shrugged. "Don't know. Don't care."

I shoved a bottle of beer in the pocket of my loose-fitting cargo shorts and put a bottle of vodka in the front pocket of my hoodie. I was well on my way to maintaining control of Branson, who stood beside me glassy-eyed and confused. Medication and booze were not a good combination.

"Hey, you need to take a break."

I spun on my heel and found Aaron in my face.

"Take a break?" I shook my head. "Hell no."

"Dude, I'm going to drive you home right now if you don't knock it off. We're here to have fun, not ruin our fucking lives."

"Just fuck off." I turned to walk away when Aaron grabbed me by the shoulder.

Shouldn't have done that.

I went in for the tackle but stumbled and fell in slower than anticipated. Aaron reached around and grabbed me by the neck, pulling me forward using his momentum and sweeping my feet out from under me. I fell to the ground hard.

Shocked, I stared up at both Aaron and Branson. "What the fuck?"

They stared at me in disgust.

Dakota appeared beside them. "Let's just go home," she said softly.

"Fuck you, rez trash," I said to the Native American who Branson adored and I despised.

Dakota's dark eyes filled with sorrow that cut through the alcohol fog and medication that blurred my vision and slurred my speech. Even though I was losing my hold on Branson, I made sure everyone in that party heard my parting remarks before I passed out.

"You're all dead to me."

CHAPTER 32

TREVOR

WHEN I woke up, I wasn't in Tara's *Better Homes and Gardens* house or Ed's bachelor pad. I looked around at the mauve-colored walls with paintings of flowers and landscapes, then glanced out the one window before settling on the narrow bed with adjustable side rails and scratchy sheets.

I was in some fucking hospital.

What the hell am I doing here?

Branson's identical half walked in with his arms crossed and stood in the corner of the bleak room.

Aaron. I gritted my teeth to shut Branson down. *There's no time for sentimentality. Your brother is not your friend. He tried to kill you last night.*

"What's up?" I said.

Aaron stayed silent.

"Really? We're going to do this?" I shook my head. *See, Branson, what did I tell you? He's not your ally.* "I don't need you here, and I'd rather you just leave."

"I'm not going to leave until you do." Aaron took a step out of his corner. "I know you're not Branson. My brother would never flip out on me like that, and the brother I know cares about his girlfriend. He's not an ass to her."

Maybe I pushed it too far last night. What would Branson do? But suddenly Branson was quiet. "I'm sorry, bro. I guess I let the alcohol get to me."

For a moment, I watched Aaron consider my response. I looked like his twin brother. I sounded like his twin brother. For all he knew, I *was* his twin brother.

"No, I'm not buying it," Aaron said at last.

Well I suppose I could always let the shadow people convince you. "Look, I understand you're skeptical. I would be too. But I'm back on my medication, and I was just letting off some steam last night."

"I called Mom last night. She checked your meds. That's why you ended up here. She called Dr. Cordova when you were behind on your pills by three weeks."

"You saw me take my pills last night. I swear to God I'm on my meds."

"I saw you take one pill. And no, you didn't take your meds during state. So shut the hell up or I'll keep you here a week straight while they pump you full of medication," he seethed.

"You can't and you won't." I rose out of bed, ready to attack this prick, when Dr. Cordova walked through the door. The anger dropped from my face, and a soft, pleasing, Branson-like look took its place. "Hey, Doc.

What's up?" I smiled in his direction.

He nodded, then turned to Aaron. "I'm sorry to cut your time short, but I need to have a session with Branson."

I stared at Aaron from behind Dr. Cordova and smirked. "I win," I mouthed. *And I always will.*

Aaron begrudgingly left, and Dr. Cordova pulled up a chair beside my bed and hit me right away with a handful of asinine questions.

"So it looks like you've been off your antipsychotic medication for about two, two and a half weeks?" He looked up from his file.

I hopped out of bed, grabbed a chair and sat beside him. I was not about to have my therapy session in bed. That was way too weird.

"I dropped back on my dosage so I could perform well at track," I told him.

He nodded. "Dropped back? The Geodon were still in your bottle."

"Yeah, but I was still taking the Paxil, so it wasn't like I was *completely* off my medication."

Again, he nodded.

"Do you have trouble knowing who Branson is?" he asked.

I looked at him like he was nuts. "No." *I know exactly who Branson is, and he ain't coming back.*

"Are you Branson?" he asked.

I stared right at him and smiled. I couldn't help myself. "Yes."

He didn't react.

"Are you a moody person?"

"Not normally, unless I get asked a lot of questions." I smiled again for good measure.

"Do you often feel empty inside?"

For some reason, that question made Branson surface. "Yes." His voice was much shallower than mine, yet it seemed to hold more power. It was hard to describe, only that it made Dr. Cordova stop writing and look up from his notepad.

"What happens when you feel empty inside, Branson?"

Tears ran down his face. *I can answer this.* But Branson's voice rose above mine. "I stop taking my medication."

"And when you stop, what happens?"

I've got this. But again Branson spoke. "He appears."

Dr. Cordova nodded. "Who is he?"

I shook his head hard.

"It's okay," Dr. Cordova urged.

It's a lie. Branson, if you tell who I am, he'll separate us forever.

"Who is he? Does he have a name?"

"At first I didn't give him a name because it would make him real."

Shut up! Shut the fuck up!

Branson covered my ears with his hands.

Dr. Cordova leaned forward and touched my knee. I wanted to whack it away, but Branson was too busy shutting me out.

"It's okay," Dr. Cordova repeated.

Branson shook his head. "He won't go away. He won't

go away."

Branson lifted his hands off my ears just long enough to hear Dr. Cordova. "Medication will help alleviate the visual hallucinations. When did you give him a name?"

Branson shook his head. "I don't remember."

"But giving him a name, that made him real?"

Branson slowly nodded. I could feel myself losing control.

"What does he look like?" Dr. Cordova asked.

Branson sat forward like the question interested him. I took great pride in that. I was, after all, his best friend. Really his only friend. "At first, he looked like an assassin."

Dr. Cordova tilted his head.

"You know, like Bourne Identity," Branson said, and I smiled. *That's right, Branson. I'm a badass.*

Branson shook his head hard and it hurt, like he was trying to erase me. Like I was an Etch-A-Sketch and could just be erased. Like I had never mattered.

You need me, Branson. I'm all you have.

But Branson closed his eyes tight until it got so dark that I couldn't see him and he couldn't see me.

"Branson?"

When Branson opened his eyes, I was still there, but my vision was hazy.

"Are you okay?" Dr. Cordova asked.

No, I'm not okay. But Branson nodded.

"So why an assassin?" Dr. Cordova prodded.

"My mind had to make sense of my actions," Branson said as clearly as he had spoken in a very long time.

Let me back in, Branson. I'm here to help.

"What actions would those be?"

"All the fucked-up shit the shadow people did," Branson replied.

"Is it one person or multiple?"

"One person."

"I'm not sure I understand the shadow people."

"It started off as shadow people," Branson said and then suddenly shook his head.

"Branson?"

"That's not right."

It's okay. Branson. You don't need to tell him. You've said enough.

"What's not right?" Dr. Cordova asked.

Branson, details aren't important. Just answer the fucking questions and let's get back to our life.

"It *didn't* start off as shadow people," Branson corrected.

"Okay." Dr. Cordova flipped a new page in his notepad.

Oh great. Here's another hour we'll never get back. Fucking Branson. What the hell?

"Can you recall the first time you *consciously* remember seeing something?" Dr. Cordova asked.

Branson closed his eyes, and I could tell he was trying to remember when it first started. That was a long time ago.

"In the eighth grade," Branson said with his eyes still closed. "I was using the restroom at school, and I thought I heard the door open. I'm still not sure if it did or not. But I finished using the restroom and opened the door, and there was a black shape outside."

Suddenly I felt his heart rate accelerate at the memory. *You don't need to relive this, Branson. You've got me now.* But Branson's eyes remained closed, and he continued to recite the nightmare to Dr. Cordova.

"It freaked me out. It was like this big thing touching the ceiling. It was all dark. Oh God, I don't even know how big it was, but it scared me." Branson opened his eyes and they were misty. The memory scared Branson.

I'm here for you. I'm your protector. You don't need to be afraid when I'm around.

"That must have been awful. Did you tell anyone?"

Branson shook his head. "I went back into the stall and curled up in a ball, trying to hide my feet so it wouldn't see me. And finally, after a couple of minutes, I figured if it was there, it would've gotten me by that point. So I opened the door and it wasn't there anymore."

"How old were you?"

Branson shrugged. "I don't know. Eighth grade, so like twelve, maybe thirteen."

"And then the shadow people appeared?"

"Actually, it was these blurry little images that did things. Like all these shadows that merged into one person that did something. I never really saw one person, just a shadow of a person. Does that make sense?" Branson looked at Dr. Cordova, and I could tell it made perfect sense to him.

Shut up, Branson. This is our shit. We don't need to tell him our secrets.

But he did. It was like once he started talking, he couldn't stop. Either that or it was the medication they kept pumping him full of. *Fucking hospitals.*

"And the shadow people grew into this assassin?" Dr. Cordova asked.

Branson laughed. He hadn't done that in a really long time. "I don't know if he *grew* into an assassin, but I had to build a character in my mind of someone I don't want there, but has to be there to explain all the fucked-up shit I do."

"And what is it this person you created does?"

"I had to create a character who would execute what I needed them to do," Branson said, and even I heard him repeat himself.

Dude, you're sounding like a Rainman. "One minute to Wapner. One minute to Wapner."

"And what is it you have this person do?"

Branson may have repeated himself before, but he was pretty loud when he leaned forward and looked right at Dr. Cordova. "Defend me."

"And who is your defender, Branson?"

Don't say it, Branson.

"What's his name?"

Don't open your fucking mouth.

Branson heard me and smiled like I had when I looked at Aaron before Dr. Cordova kicked him out of our room.

You need me.

"Trevor," Branson said strongly, loudly, and with clear conviction. "His name is Trevor. And I want him gone."

CHAPTER 33

TARA

BRANSON was in a psychiatric critical care unit. "He just needs a little pharmaceutical help from a licensed professional," I told Ed, my children, and even Clive, his counselor. I began to believe that in a matter of days, Branson's brain would clear up and he'd be back on track, making new goals.

On the way home from the hospital, I phoned Senator Bailey's office and canceled Branson's congressional interview for the naval academy, explaining that Branson had a physical setback at state track that landed him in the hospital. I hadn't lied, but I stretched the truth. Branson didn't land in the hospital until a few days after state track. Even though he had resumed his medication when I brought him home from his father's house, the effects of missing so many doses quickly caught up with him. When Aaron called from the end-of-the-year track party and I counted Branson's pills, I knew the next call was to Dr. Cordova. He suggested we check Branson into the psychiatric care unit.

"Let's have him evaluated and see where he's at," he'd said.

So I left my son for a few days of treatment. *He just needs a little pharmaceutical help.* I repeated the mantra every five minutes as a salve to ease the pain that stabbed at me and made it hard to function.

My mind kept wandering back to Branson looking up at me in his father's house. Tears in his eyes, pleading for help. *He just needs his meds.*

The only way I knew how to get through this without the numbing distraction of work, which I no longer had, was to do the next best thing: bake. I wasn't a great cook, but I could bake.

I dusted off my cookbooks and went to task in the kitchen.

Before long, I'd placed a tray of warm, fresh-out-of-the-oven blueberry muffins on the kitchen table. A copy of the Wilson High School newspaper was tossed beside Aaron's backpack. I sat down with a cup of coffee and looked at the front page. Senior class photos of the homecoming court were featured front and center. I glanced at the row of potential king and queen candidates and gasped.

"Ashley Bailey?"

"Yeah, I want her to win." Aaron walked in and grabbed a blueberry muffin off the tray.

"*Why* would you want *her* to win?" I looked at my son while he practically inhaled the muffin in one bite.

"Ashley's the nicest girl in the school, and she's beautiful."

I think my jaw dropped; for certain my stomach did. "I can't believe you'd want that skanky little girl to win when she's made your brother's life a living nightmare."

A puzzled look crossed Aaron's face.

"Is it the blueberry muffins, because I'm still kind of new to the whole baking thing," I said.

"No, they're perfect."

"Then why the look?"

"Why the hell would you think Ashley made Branson's life a nightmare? She's the nicest person Branson and I have ever met."

I feigned a laugh. "Well I guess she may have been nice to you, but Little Miss Senator's Daughter was going around bullying Branson and spreading gay rumors about him."

"Uh, no she wasn't." He reached for another muffin. "She would *never* say anything like that in her entire life, and if she did, I'd know about it. The girl barely says 'Jesus Christ,' and that's the worst swear she says."

I shook my head. "Aaron, I'm not talking about swearing. I'm talking about slander and spreading vicious, malicious lies about your brother's sexuality and basically bullying him."

"I don't know what you're talking about," he said, heading toward the refrigerator and grabbing the gallon of milk.

I walked to the cupboard and handed Aaron a glass, lest he drink straight from the jug. "Well I'm not proud of this, but I read all about it in your brother's English journal. Ashley Bailey made Branson's life a living hell."

"Ma, I don't know what he wrote down, but it's not true. I'm always with Branson. Besides, they don't even have any classes together."

I leaned against the kitchen counter. The heat from the dishwasher radiated against my back. "They've got to be in a class together, because Branson made some comment about her driving or something? Anyway"—I grabbed the dishtowel off the kitchen counter and folded it—"he got in trouble and had to serve detention for his comment and missed track. She's not nice."

"Ma, Branson was in detention for screwing off in anatomy. He was messing with the chemicals when they were doing a lab."

"So he wasn't sent to detention over something he said about Ashley's driving?" I placed the towel neatly on the counter.

"If there are any comments going around, it's from Branson about Ashley. He's always messing with her." Aaron held up his hand. "In a joking way though. If anything, Branson's kind of flirtatious with her."

If I wasn't already leaning against something, I would've dropped like a fly. "What? You mean he *likes* her?" I felt light-headed. "Then why would he write in his journal that he doesn't and that she was spreading rumors about him being gay?"

"Ma, he's obviously not been in his right mind when he was writing that."

I covered my mouth with my hand. *Oh my God.*

"What's going on?"

I shook my head.

"What did you do?"

I dropped my hand and looked at my son. "I completely torpedoed my career because I believed everything I read in his journal."

"Why would you do that?" The mixture of anger and sadness in his voice was palpable.

I understood. It made no sense to my son why I would forfeit my job, our financial security, and my reputation. It made no sense until I looked into his beautiful hazel eyes and explained.

"I had to protect him."

CHAPTER 34

TARA

"HOW are you?" Dr. Cordova scooted his chair toward the couch, something he'd never done before.

The air left my lungs as I looked at him. "What's wrong?"

His lips pursed together like he was considering how to phrase his next sentence—again, something he'd never done. "Branson suffered a psychotic break."

I shook my head. "No, he just got off his medication for a while. He just got off track."

He said nothing.

I looked into his gray-blue eyes. I didn't know this man very well, but I knew he had never lied to me before. Covering my mouth with my hands, I cried into them as I rocked back and forth, but nothing comforted the loss that tore through me. Branson wasn't going to come home today or tomorrow. The Branson I knew wasn't ever going to come back home. I was completely shattered, and there was no way to put the pieces back together.

I lowered my head and wept.

"Tara?"

I looked up at him.

"I'd like to discuss some treatment options with you."

I nodded, then shook my head. "Actually, could you first explain to me more about a psychotic break? I know I should know more about it, but I don't." Internally I knew. I knew the moment I saw Branson at Ed's house. I knew the way a mother knows when something's wrong with her child before he even utters a word. It was my mind that couldn't seem to make sense of what my soul already had.

He tilted his head. "Once a person has a psychotic break, they never fully recover to their functional level from before."

My body trembled. "Oh my God. I should've made sure he was taking his medicine. I checked his daily pill holder, but each day was always empty."

"He was probably putting the pills back in the bottle."

"I should've made sure. Oh my God." I wiped my eyes, but the tears streamed down my face faster than I could wipe them away. "This is my fault."

He shook his head. "Staying on top of symptoms and being compliant with medication are key with this illness."

"Branson was feeling better. He seemed better."

He nodded. "And he had state track and didn't want the weight gain, so he stopped taking his medication."

I closed my eyes, mentally berating myself. *Why didn't I check the bottle?* I opened my eyes and looked at the doctor. "So when he stopped taking his pills, that's what caused the psychotic break?"

"His symptoms progressed quickly. We never know from case to case how going off the meds will affect someone. For Branson, his psychotic break means he went from seeing shadowy figures and hearing things to actually believing his friend, Trevor, was real."

It felt like someone had walked across my grave. "He's not real?"

A grim look crossed Dr. Cordova's face. "No, Trevor is a delusion. He's as real to Branson as you are to him. However, when Branson's illness is being treated, Trevor no longer appears. When he's off his medication, Trevor comes back."

"So... it's like he snapped? Like what we read about in the newspaper when a gunman goes on a shooting spree?" *Oh my God.*

"Contrary to what is often written in the news, people who suffer from a mental illness that has psychotic symptoms, like schizophrenia, don't snap, but they do have drops, with some drops being greater than others. Mental illness is greatly misunderstood in our society."

Wounded cries rose from my throat. The cries of a mother for her child when he's lost and she can't find him. I just wanted to get to him, hold him and make him better. Society may not ever understand my child, but I would.

"Can I see him?"

His face revealed his answer before he did. "It's best if Branson has this time to focus on his recovery and getting back on track with his medication."

"You said it'd just be a few days. It's been three already."

He nodded. "Branson hasn't fully recovered. Trevor is still trying to function for him."

"He has a split personality? Like Sybil?"

"No, he doesn't have *dissociative identity disorder*. Schizophrenia and dissociative identity disorder, or DID, are often confused. However, schizophrenia and DID are two *entirely* different disorders." Dr. Cordova must have sensed I needed more information because he continued. "There are various aspects that make up a person's identity. With DID, each of these aspects is separated so profoundly from the others that they appear to have multiple personalities. DID isn't a thought disorder, but schizophrenia is. I understand how it's easy to confuse the two."

"But I still don't understand." If my tone didn't convince him, my words would. "By its very name, schizophrenia means 'split mind.' Isn't a *split mind* an apt description for multiple personality disorder or DID?"

Dr. Cordova's face never seemed to falter from neutral. "The mind splitting that the name 'schizophrenia' refers to has nothing to do with personality splitting. It refers to the fractures in *cognitive* functioning. To simplify it, think of schizophrenia as a thought disorder," he said, and it started to make more sense. But I still had more questions than answers.

"Okay, then explain Trevor. If he isn't a separate personality, then what is he?" By that point, Dr. Cordova knew I was nothing if not persistent. I wouldn't leave his office until I understood, or at the very least had a better handle on my son's mental illness. Or thought disorder.

"Unlike a separate personality, schizophrenia is the breaking or splitting of the mind's capacity to function. Trevor is a form of protection. He's a delusion, a form of his psychosis that allowed Branson to function," he said.

"So Trevor isn't some alternate personality?" I asked.

"Not at all. Trevor is a *delusion*, and even though this delusion felt real to Branson, delusions are irrational and they aren't real. It's important to understand, Tara, that during a psychotic break, it's harder for Branson to distinguish actual reality from this altered reality that his brain tells him exists. Often people with schizophrenia— or in Branson's case, schizoaffective disorder, to take into account the depressive component of his illness—will go off their treatment protocol because a hallucination may tell them to do so, which—"

"Is that what happened to Branson? Trevor told him to go off his meds and he did?"

"Yes, but with the right dosage of medication and therapy, the delusions dissipate."

Medicine, dosage, delusions. My mind was in overdrive. Nothing made sense anymore. "Do you think the schizophrenia or schizoaffective disorder or whatever could have come on because he was being bullied, and that's why Trevor showed up?" My son was in a wing of the hospital somewhere in this maze, and I just wanted to get to him.

"I know he wasn't being bullied by this girl. I know that now," I admitted. "But I wondered if maybe he just hit his saturation point with this Jesse kid."

I wiped my nose on the back of my hand. Dr. Cordova handed me a box of tissues, and I grabbed one to blow my nose.

"That's what they called it with me when I was in a domestic situation. I hit my 'saturation point.' And he was being bullied at the track meeting." I raised my shoulders "Maybe he just hit his breaking point and that's why he got violent. That's why Trevor appeared."

Dr. Cordova didn't have Branson's file on his lap or a legal pad. A pen wasn't at the ready. Everything about this session was different. As the silence dragged between us, I filled it with more rambling.

"Granted, this kid drew first blood, but maybe his schizophrenia, it just seemed like it became a coping mechanism, you know? From what he experienced in our home and then with this kid at track."

Dr. Cordova waited until I was finished with my farfetched explanation for Trevor and my son's mental illness. But in the last three minutes, I had used the word "schizophrenia" without a bittersweet taste lingering in my mouth like I had to puke. Progress took many different forms.

"Just so you know," he said gently, "it's unlikely that bullying can cause schizophrenia. It's more possible that a person is predisposed to that direction anyway, and the bullying just kind of added to it. There's really no data to show a connection unless there's massive head trauma." He paused. "Did Branson ever experience any head trauma during your marriage to his father?"

"No."

"Did he ever work with anyone on the bullying issue?"

I shook my head. "I don't know how much bullying he actually experienced."

The doctor looked at me.

"I just discovered that Branson's English journal, the one I've been reading… well, nothing he wrote was actually true."

Dr. Cordova slowly nodded. "When a person loses contact with external reality, it usually takes the form of hallucinations, delusions, or disordered thinking. It makes perfect sense that Branson's journal wasn't an accurate account of his activities."

I was sinking fast. "Please, let me see him." My entire body trembled. "Just let me see my son."

"He's not in any condition to see you." He was not going to waver on the issue. "My goal is to get him ready to come home for a few days."

"A few days?" I shook my head. I could no longer hear that my son wasn't okay and that I couldn't take him home with me. "No, that's my baby. You can't take him away from me."

"Tara, what Branson needs is to be in a longer-term treatment center where he can deal with some of the residual anger he has and get back to a stronger functioning level. If he comes home now, or even in a few days, but doesn't continue the treatment, he'll have another break and the drop will be even greater."

I leaned forward and cried. "I just never knew." I sobbed. "I had no idea. I want my son back. Please bring him back to me."

"I'm trying."

CHAPTER 35

BRANSON

"THAT'S funny." I began to laugh and couldn't seem to stop.

"What's so funny?"

I turned around in my chair and saw Dr. Cordova enter the room. I whipped my head back around and realized no one was there.

"Who were you talking to?" he asked.

I shrugged and pretended like it didn't happen.

"Branson?" Dr. Cordova pulled up a chair beside mine.

The sun was full and bright in the Wyoming sky, and I was stuck inside. Worse, the sun was melting what was left of the first good snowfall of the season. *Ski season. I just need to be outside.*

"Who were you talking to?" he repeated.

I moved my gaze from the sun to the people on the sidewalk below my window. Everyone was hurrying somewhere, but the slushy pavement was slowing them down.

"No one." I watched a woman grab her son by the arm and scold him for doing something. *Probably just being a boy.*

"When I came in, you were laughing and said, 'That's funny.'"

I nodded.

"Was it Trevor?" Dr. Cordova tried to make eye contact with me, but I dodged his stare.

"Yup." I exhaled.

"He's still around?"

"Apparently." I gripped my hands into one fist.

"Did you see him?"

I paused. "No. I think I was just talking to him."

"Okay, well that's progress."

I nodded.

"We're still working on finding the right dosage."

"It's just upsetting," I said, breaking the silence, breaking the hold Trevor had on me. "The only person I could talk to isn't even here. He's gone. He wasn't even real. Fuck. What now?"

"That's a valid question," Dr. Cordova replied. "Trevor is a symptom of your illness. Once we have your illness under control again, the feeling of loss won't be as significant."

I looked at the doctor carefully. He seemed to know his shit.

"So let's talk about Jesse and what happened at the track meet." Dr. Cordova flipped a page in his notepad.

I don't know what he does with all his notes, but the guy sure takes a lot of them. "I wanted to hurt him because he was choking me, trying to prove to everyone that he was the strongest."

Dr. Cordova nodded. "From what your brother's said, he's also bullied you before."

"Yeah, the guy's a major prick."

"And the voices?"

"They got really strong that day."

"Stronger than before?"

"Stronger than I've ever heard them."

"What do you remember the voices saying?"

"'Kill him,' or something like that. They were really mad at Jesse. If I'm really angry, I'll start to distinguish sounds."

"And when you distinguish sounds, what do you hear?"

"Them just telling me to do things. It sounds like my self-conscious, like I'm talking to myself, but I know I'm not."

"How do you know you're not?"

"Just kind of a feeling, because I know I wouldn't harm someone."

"But you did. You choked someone until he passed out."

"Well the kid fucking deserved it," I snapped back.

"Maybe so," Dr. Cordova said. "He's got his own history with bullying, but what you did…."

"I don't see it as wrong."

"Let me ask you something, Branson. Why don't you see choking someone as wrong?"

"Because I didn't choke him. Trevor did."

"Trevor isn't real."

I looked out the window at the sun beginning to drop in

the sky. "I know Trevor isn't real. But...."

"But what, Branson?"

I gripped the chair and leaned forward. "I don't like to think I could hurt someone like that. Not even some douchebag like Jesse. It scares the fuck out of me that I could do that, okay?" I sat back in my chair.

"You have an illness."

"An illness doesn't make it right. And I've always been able to keep it in check before. I've *never* had to worry about it before."

"Worry about what?"

"The voices and stuff. You know, I've had it for so long I've just kind of got used to it. But then the voices became more distinguished."

"Like how?"

"One day I was just sitting in class. I was in anatomy and the static got louder, and then it started to clear up."

"And that was unusual?"

"Yeah. Before, it was always a bunch of people mumbling. It wasn't clear. And usually I couldn't hear the static when I was in a classroom or around a lot of people."

Dr. Cordova nodded and wrote something on his notepad. "When the static cleared up, what did you hear?"

"Uh, just telling me to hurt people. Like anyone I saw, anyone who pissed me off. It ranges. The static would suddenly get louder and would give me direction on how to do it, how to hurt them. It started to get bad when I started to want to do it. When I felt compelled to do it."

"How would you stop yourself from acting on it?" Dr. Cordova wasn't taking notes anymore.

"I would just, uh… I don't know. I just didn't." I paused. "Actually, that's when I called my mom and told her I was hearing voices. I felt like she would be a good person to talk to because she wouldn't freak out."

Dr. Cordova slightly smiled. Not like a shit-eating grin, more of a "you did the right thing" kind of smile that a guy gives another guy.

I thought of my mom, but then I had to push her out of my head. I missed her and my twin brother, but I couldn't think of them or I'd never make it through this hellhole.

"That's when your mom got you in to see the counselor at school?"

I shook my head. "Blacking out at high school and punching the bathroom wall got me in to see Clive, who got me to that lady doctor I saw once who put me on Paxil. And then after I talked to her, I must've freaked her out because I never saw her again."

Dr. Cordova chuckled. "You didn't freak her out, but she did make a referral."

I rolled my eyes. "Whatever. I'm here now." I looked back out the window. A school bus was dropping kids off. It was mid-November, and the snow berm on the side of the road hadn't reached the heights it would by the end of winter. When Aaron and I used to ride the bus, we loved jumping off the steps and onto the berms. We'd come home wet and full of dirty snow. Made our mom mad, but we didn't care—it was fun as hell.

"With your illness, symptoms range and can manifest quickly. Your symptoms escalated from fugue states and static and shadow people to Trevor."

I grimaced. "Actually…."

"Was there something else?"

I nodded. "There was this one animal hallucination." I looked at him. "I guess that's what it would be called, a hallucination."

The doctor quickly licked his thumb and turned a page in his notepad. "I don't remember anything about an animal."

"Yeah, it was fucking trippy. I heard something coming down the stairs, and then I saw this little dark thing on all fours charging toward my chair where I was sitting playing video games. It scared the shit out of me." My heart rate increased just remembering it. "I realized it wasn't there and continued playing video games, but it freaked me out."

"This animal, did it appear before Trevor did?"

I nodded. "Yeah, like weeks, maybe a month or so? It was bad."

"Did you tell anyone?"

I shook my head.

"It's important to your future emotional health to share these things with your therapist or psychiatrist. It's as important as keeping on task with your medication," he said.

"That's why I told you."

He nodded. "And that's good. I don't care how mentally healthy or smart someone is, with this illness, staying on top of the symptoms and medication is the only way to manage it."

All the fight in me left then. It was no longer a death sentence. He was extending me a hand to pull me out of the hole.

CHAPTER 36

BRANSON

"HEY, thanks for picking me up." I looked at my twin brother and smiled. I wasn't sure what a better sight was: him or the snow-covered mountain behind him.

"Yup, no problem." He grabbed my duffel bag. "Mom wanted to, but I told her I'd make less fuss."

I laughed. "Well, thanks."

"So you're home for how long?" Aaron said.

"Long enough to get my skis into that powder." I nodded toward Casper Mountain.

"For sure." Aaron opened the trunk to our car and dropped my bag inside. "So seriously, you're home for a while, right?"

"A week furlough before I'm shipped off."

"That sounds like you're heading to basic training."

I laughed as I climbed into the passenger seat. "Kind of is, bro, only for the mentally insane."

Aaron strapped on his seat belt. Actually, we did it in

unison. We usually always did everything in tandem. I missed that in the hospital. I missed laughing at the same Vines and YouTube videos. I missed seeing him in the hallways in high school. As much as I hated high school, I missed my brother.

He caught me staring at him and he grinned.

"Why the hell do they need you back again?" he asked. "Wasn't a week long enough?"

"I guess some mental cases are tougher than others."

He turned out of the hospital parking garage and onto Second Street. I rolled down the window and let the cold November air hit me in the face.

"What are they gonna do? They already know you're crazy," he said.

"Just intense counseling to deal with some past anger issues that'll help make the shadow people and static stop. Or," I said, hearing Dr. Cordova in my head and thankfully no one else, "keep them from reappearing, at least."

"Well, that's not too bad." Aaron turned onto Wyoming Boulevard and headed toward our neighborhood. "How long will you be gone?"

I stared at the snow berms along the side of the road that looked like they had doubled in size. Seven days and so much seemed like it had changed.

"Branson?"

"Sorry. It's a twenty-eight-day treatment center."

"Twenty-eight days? Dude, you'll miss Christmas."

I shook my head. "No, actually I'll be home just in time for Santa."

"Well that's cool. So what about school? And the Navy?"

"I'm going to take the GED." I turned away from the window and lightly punched Aaron in the forearm. "And what the hell do you mean about the Navy? You're the one who told Mom the Navy doesn't want basket cases."

"What?" His hazel eyes widened. "I never said that."

"Bullshit." I always knew when Aaron was lying. His eyes gave him away, and his voice got high-pitched like a little girl. "Carson told me when Mom brought her to the hospital. I was worried about telling you that Mom had to cancel my congressional interviews. Carson said she heard you talk to Mom when I started getting letters from the Navy. That's when she told me you said the Navy doesn't take kids who are basket cases."

Aaron started laughing. "Okay, maybe I said *something* like that."

I chuckled.

"But come on, bro, you had just blacked out at school and come to with bloody knuckles. You were crazy to think the navy would take you."

I tilted my head toward him.

He raised an eyebrow. "Did you *actually* think the navy would take you?"

I shrugged. "I wanted to see how far I could get in the process."

Aaron shook his head and drove past our high school. Suddenly it seemed much smaller to me.

"Then why did you tell on yourself?" he asked. "To Mom, about the voices and stuff."

"I didn't want to risk other people's lives."

For a moment, my brother looked at me and I looked at him. "I'm sorry you had to withdraw your application to the Navy," he said finally.

"I didn't want someone else to not get considered when I knew I wouldn't get past the psych eval. Me withdrawing gave someone else a chance."

"You're a straight-up gangster," Aaron said.

I laughed. "You're an idiot."

"So how are you and Dakota? You patch things up?"

A good, warm feeling filled me at the thought of my girl. "Yeah."

"You guys still together?"

"Yup. She came and saw me in the hospital. I was able to, you know, explain to her what was going on."

"That's cool."

I laughed. "No, bro, it wasn't. Having to tell my girlfriend I have schizophrenia isn't something I ever thought I'd have to do."

"Yeah, but dude, it's Dakota. She's so chill."

"I know, but I was pretty mean to her."

Aaron turned his focus away from the road for a moment. "No, it was that prick Trevor. It wasn't you."

I rolled my eyes. "We're kind of one and the same."

"I understand that, but anyone who knows you knows you weren't in your right mind."

I patted him on the shoulder. "Thanks, bro."

"I'm your twin. I knew you'd never do and say what you were doing." He turned into our subdivision. "You and

Dakota going to the homecoming dance?"

"That's the plan," I said as he pulled up in front of our house. "You taking Chelsea?"

"Nah, I broke up with her." He cut the engine.

I looked at the "Welcome Home" banner made out of construction paper. *Carson and Jack.* My chest swelled. It was draped across the front door, and snow had collected on the triangle-shaped pennant. The letters "me" in "Home" sagged. Still, it was cute as hell.

"I don't know who I'm taking to the dance," Aaron said. "I'm just kind of winging it."

The front door opened and my mom stood behind the glass dormer. I stared at her, and again there was a tug in my chest.

"Me too."

CHAPTER 37

TARA

I stood on the perimeter of the gym, watching everyone else dance. Tapping my feet, I felt like Scarlett O'Hara when she attended a fundraising gala but couldn't dance because she was in mourning.

"I just want to dance," Scarlett had said as she collected coats and watched the evening unfold without her.

I understood. Mourning fit. Aaron and Branson were attending what would be their last high school dance together. Aaron would have others, but Branson wouldn't. I hadn't reconciled that yet. And maybe I didn't need to.

At the last minute, the boys asked me to chaperone. Chaperones weren't encouraged to dance, which I discovered when I showed up and was pointed toward the back of the gymnasium and told to be an "adult presence" in the room. Ironically, since I was no longer employed by the university, I wasn't as concerned about my "adult presence."

I had dug through the back of my closet and pulled out

a fun and flirty black taffeta pleated skirt. It had extra body and volume that would kick up on the dance floor—if I ever got on the dance floor. I teamed it with a charcoal-colored cashmere sweater, black tights, and chunky heeled patent leather Mary Janes that gave me an extra three inches. I was party ready.

The gym was alive with swing music. Better yet, my son was home. My Branson was home. I wanted to dance because I felt like I was floating on air. Everywhere I looked, everything around me sparkled and shone.

The theme of the night was Paris, and it felt like I'd been transported to another country. For certain it didn't feel like we were in Casper, Wyoming.

Strands of lights were strung across the ceiling, transforming the gym into a starry night that even Van Gogh would have been lost in. Themes of France and French impressionist-inspired art filled the room. It was an eclectic assortment that blended together oddly well with the country western music.

I had lost Branson and Dakota and Aaron and his date in the crowd from the moment we arrived. I didn't even bother to look for them anymore; they were having fun, and that was all that mattered. For this one night, everything in my life was good—maybe even perfect. So I tapped my feet and swayed to the music.

When the first slow song of the evening began, it practically cleared the gymnasium floor, teens scattering.

I turned to the other parent beside me. "Don't they know these are the best songs?"

She smiled. "Youth. It's wasted."

I was about to say something else to her when she nodded toward someone approaching. I turned in that direction.

He bowed slightly before me. "May I have this dance?" he asked.

I nodded because he literally took my breath away, then followed him onto the dance floor as Hunter Hayes sang "Wanted."

"Mom," Branson said as I placed my hand in his. "Let me lead."

I smiled. "What about Dakota?"

He blushed. "Actually, she's the one who suggested it."

I laughed as my tall, graceful son moved us around the dance floor like a king among men. It felt as though my feet never touched the ground.

When Scarlett ignores what others think and does what feels right for her, dancing the Virginia Reel with Rhett Butler, she says, "Tonight I'm going to dance and dance." When my seventeen-year-old didn't care what his classmates thought, I felt like the luckiest girl in the room. And we danced.

Tears streamed down my face. I didn't want the dance to end—ever. I didn't want that moment with my lucid, happy son to vanish.

"Mom."

I could hear the tone shift in his voice.

"Don't," I said, stopping him.

"You lost your job."

"But I didn't lose you."

"Mom."

"Branson, jobs are replaceable. Children aren't." I flicked away a tear. "Please, just dance with me. We haven't danced enough in our family."

He smiled, and in that smile, I felt something I hadn't in a long time: hope.

CHAPTER 38

TARA

IN my bedroom there was a vanity that would rival any period piece on Downton Abbey. While it wasn't huge, it had a grand, eye-catching presence. It dated back to the early 1800s, something I bought at an estate sale. But unlike most furniture of that era, instead of the dark, foreboding mahogany, my vanity was a rich, creamy walnut the color of butterscotch. Three drawers ran down the left side of the piece, where I stored my silk scarves and wool winter hats, just like Granny. But the bottom drawer wasn't neatly arranged or strategically on display. It held trinkets my children had made that I would never part with.

I pulled on the hand-carved decorative knob and opened the drawer. All my inspiration, all my motivation, everything that used to keep me going when I wanted to quit work on my master's degree, when I wanted to stop writing the college handbook, when I wanted to toss in the towel and pick up waitressing again was in that drawer. Dust lined the lip of the drawer because I rarely, if ever, dug through its contents. I earned my master's degree, I wrote the book that landed on the *New York Times* bestseller list, and I never looked at another server tray again. But in achieving all that success, I lost sight of what motivated me. What gave me purpose and direction when my life had little to none.

I opened the rainbow-striped box that held my life, and tears collected in the corner of my eyes. My throat swelled and no matter how hard I swallowed, I knew the last decade I had missed would come crashing down on me.

I gently removed the silver chain that rested on top of the handmade cards and valentines. A long, thin chain with two intertwining silver hearts, a birthday gift from Aaron and Branson that I never wore because it was cheap costume jewelry that wouldn't possibly fit in with any of my designer suits.

I lowered my head and cried. *I'm so sorry. I've had my priorities all wrong.* Hot tears of shame and regret ran down my face and smeared my makeup. A large ruby-like ring was beside the necklace, and I placed it on my finger. Another gift. I wiped my eyes, unlatched the necklace's clasp and secured it around my neck, then glanced in the vanity mirror.

Two silver hearts laid perfectly against my ivory silk blouse. Even if it didn't, I wouldn't have cared.

I held out my hand and smiled.

"I know how much you like red, Momma," Branson had said when he proudly presented it to me. It was the size of a golf ball and sat on my hand like a beacon for the world to see. My son's heart on my hand.

My chest shook and I couldn't stop crying. *Come on, Tara. Get it together. You can do this. He's counting on you.*

"Mom?"

His voice came from the doorway to my room. I discreetly wiped my eyes, closed the drawer, and rose to meet my son.

"You ready?" he said.

I wanted to shake my head. *No. I'm not ready. I'll never be ready.* I tried to quiet the inferno in my chest, but it was like trying to stop a volcano about to erupt.

I walked toward my beautiful son and gently touched his cheek. "I'm not sure I know how to do this," I confessed, the tears still falling.

"Well, that makes two of us. But I...." A flicker of concern flashed across his face before he looked down at the carpet in my room.

I reached for his hand and was about to say something when he burst out laughing.

Startled, I jumped. "What?"

"That is a gawd-awful ring."

Now when my chest shook, it was with laughter. "This?" I held my hand out on display. "This bling is some swaggy shit, dog."

Branson shook his head. "Please stop. You are—"

"I'm a gangsta straight out of Casper." I stole a move from my daughter and started to bounce my shoulders up and down. "Know what this is?"

Branson slowly shook his head. "No idea."

"It's my shoulder dance to make you laugh."

He reached up and gently cupped my shoulders to stop the rhythm. "I'm going to be okay."

I leaned my head against his, and his hands dropped from my shoulders and wrapped around my back. My boy was hugging me.

"I love you, Mom."

"Oh, Branson, I love you more than you will ever know."

Please don't go. Stay here. I'll take care of you. I'll make you better.

Heat coursed through my body like a rash that couldn't get out. I was so empty I didn't think I could hurt any more, but the pain still cut through me swifter and faster than before.

I'll be better with your medication. I promise. I'll be a better mom. Don't leave. But I silenced my selfish thoughts. Branson needed my support, not my voice weighing him down. He had a lifetime of voices doing that; I wasn't going to be one more.

I gently pulled away from my son and held his hands in mine. "Since that day you called me and told me about the voices, the static, I've done everything to avoid getting to this point." I took a slow, steady breath. "I think I always knew there would come a time when you would have to go somewhere... for treatment." I swallowed hard. "And I've just had a hard time letting go."

"Mom, you're the only one I trusted to tell," he said. His hazel eyes were soft and full of life.

"I know. And that couldn't have been easy for you."

"It's easier now."

I softly smiled. "I know you'll be away for a while. And if you need more time, take it. Take as long as you need," I said, and meant it. "I'm not going anywhere. I'll be right here wearing my ruby dazzler." I squeezed his hand and he smiled. "Just come back to me, Branson."

"I will."

CHAPTER 39

BRANSON

I walked to the garage with Aaron, and he put my suitcase in the trunk of our mom's car. "No matter what happens, I'll always love you," he said, closing the trunk.

"I know."

"Seriously." He stared at me. "Get better, because I want my twin 100 percent for college or I'll have to room with some crazy person." He smiled, and it was like looking at a positive reflection of myself on better days.

Aaron pulled me into a hug, holding me tight for what seemed like a really long time before he let go. Tears filled his eyes. "Love you, bro."

"I love you too."

Carson was next, still dressed in her pajamas. She wrapped her arms around me. "Get better," she told me.

"Will do."

Little Jack handed me a Pokémon card. "This is my only Charmander card."

"Oh, buddy, you don't have to give me your only Charmander card."

Jack pursed his lips together. "No, it's okay. Charmanders have fire power. This will help you recover."

My throat tightened. "That's probably the nicest thing anyone has ever done for me."

Jack raised his shoulders. "I love you, Branson. You're my big brother."

I bent down and scooped him up in my arms. "I'm sorry I was rough with you and called you names. I was...." I thought of what Dr. Cordova often said. "I have an illness, but now I'm taking my medication."

Jack's arms squeezed my neck and tickled me. I laughed and so did he. "I know," he said. "I take my Scooby-Doo vitamins every day."

I set him down and put my Charmander card in my back pocket as Carson took Jack inside the house.

Dakota stood off to the side. My beautiful girlfriend.

"Don't hide over there," I said.

"I'm not hiding." She giggled and walked into my outstretched arms.

"I'm coming back. It's not like I'm going overseas or off to war or something. I'm not going to be gone forever."

"Shut the hell up!" She swatted my chest. "I know that."

I kissed the top of her head. "I can have visitors." I lowered my voice. "And I think they allow conjugal visits."

She shook her head. "Shh! Your mom's right over there."

I smiled. "Yeah, I'd better get going." I kissed her gently, softly, lovingly. "I love you, Dakota."

She nodded with tears in her eyes. "Love you too."

I looked over at Aaron. "Keep an eye on her."

"Of course."

I glanced across the garage at my mom. In her eyes, I saw that no matter what I did or who I was, it wouldn't matter to her. For a moment, I wanted to reach out and hug her again. Instead I said, "Ready?"

She nodded with a smile.

As she pulled out of the driveway, Dakota and Aaron followed the car out and stood on the snowy sidewalk beside our house. I glanced in the side-view mirror. Everything I loved, I was leaving behind. I wanted to be with them, but I knew I wasn't like them. Not yet. Probably not ever.

I had to let go of them as much as they had to let go of me.

I had to let go so I could come back.

And more than anything, I wanted to come back.

EPILOGUE

BRANSON

I turned on the audio recording app, tucked my cell phone into my pocket, and made my way to his office.

Dr. Cordova was in his high-back chair with a legal pad on his knee and pen in his hand.

"Branson, hello. How was your day?"

I sat down on the couch. It wasn't very comfortable, but it wasn't a hospital room, so I was grateful. "Good."

"So we made a switch about a month ago. How is the medication doing?"

"It's going really, really well." It felt like a swarm of butterflies took flight in my stomach. I hadn't felt this good in a really long time.

"How is it going well?"

"Um, it's been working the same as the last medication you had me on in the treatment center, but without all the side effects. I'm not bloated. I lost a lot, and I mean a *lot* of weight. I think my mood's increased a lot too. I think

I'm happier."

"You were discharged from the treatment center almost three months ago?" He flipped through my file that was beneath his legal pad.

"Yeah, that sounds about right."

"That's right. We found the medication had lost some of its effectiveness. Sometimes medications can plateau, which is why we made the switch last month."

I nodded.

"So you're on the new dosage twice a day, every day. What time are you taking your pills?"

"Once in the morning and once at night right before I go to bed." I thought about the two pill containers that lined my bathroom. If I happened to miss the daily pill trackers, there was no missing the bottles next to my body spray and deodorant.

"How are the symptoms?"

"Really well," I said.

"No trouble?" Dr. Cordova looked at me skeptically.

"If I don't take the medication, I can't sleep very well, but if I do, I fall asleep right away." "Do you forget to take it often?" His voice sparked with interest.

"I forgot it yesterday, but that was the only time."

"So your moods, how would you describe them?"

"Happy." I nodded. "Yeah, happy."

"So how are things going *today*?"

"Do you mean is Trevor here?" I looked at Dr. Cordova, who smiled.

"Is he? Is Trevor joining us today?" he asked.

I looked around his office and shook my head. "Nope."

"How does that make you feel?"

"Good." I paused. "Relieved, actually."

"How about your intrusive thoughts?"

"Um… not as frequent."

"How often?"

"Maybe about once every week."

"And how intense are they?"

"Same. Kind of just intense."

"How long does it last?"

"Uh, it varies. From around a couple minutes to like an hour sometimes. It all depends."

He wrote something on his notepad. "So how do you deal with it?"

"I usually distract myself."

"Does that work?"

"Usually."

"Does it?"

"I just kind of deal with it or ignore it." That didn't seem to please Dr. Cordova. I leaned forward on the couch. "The thing I've learned about *schizophrenia is that it never truly goes away. There are just varying degrees of the illness. Unless you placed me in a catatonic state, the static is still there. It just isn't as loud.*"

"And how often do you experience the hallucinations?" he asked.

"Those haven't happened ever since we got rid of Trevor."

"Really?" His voice rose in apparent interest. Everything

else was standard protocol, but when I broke from what he was expecting to hear, I actually got a reaction. I heard it in the lilt of his voice, like he was some damn cheerleader rallying against my delusions.

Poor Trevor. It's not his fault.

I smiled. "Yeah, it's been great."

"Any paranoia?"

"Not that I know of." I paused and then started to laugh.

"What's so funny?"

"Well... okay, Doc, every time we meet, you ask about my paranoia. But really? If I was paranoid, would I really be the one to know? Would I be the best one to ask?"

He shook his head. "Branson." He flipped another page in his notepad. "Any suicidal thinking?"

I shook my head.

"Any homicidal thoughts?"

"No."

"So these intrusive thoughts, they're what exactly?"

"Well, I guess they would be homicidal." I said it without any shame attached or guilt. It was part of my illness, and I was treating my illness.

"And they tell you to hurt people."

"Uh-huh."

"Have you ever been inclined to do it?"

I shook my head. *Not since Jesse.* "Uh, no. I would never act on those thoughts, no."

"How is your attention span?"

"Uh, it's good." I shrugged. "I don't know. What do you think?" I looked at the clock. "We've been going for what, about twenty minutes?"

"You're doing fine. I just mean at work and in your personal life."

"Fine."

"Have the intrusive thoughts ever happened again when you're in class? I know in our last session, you mentioned you were an early admission into Wyoming State University. I bet that made your mom proud."

I forced a smile. "Yeah, Mom didn't know I had actually applied early or to WSU. It wasn't part of her *plan* for Aaron or me." I laughed. "The funny thing is I kind of don't even remember applying." I shrugged. "It worked out in my favor when the new admissions director reevaluated the list of early admission candidates and I got in, because honestly?" I shook my head. "With my grades and attendance at Wilson, I don't think I would've gotten in anywhere else."

"I thought you mentioned that you were already taking college classes?"

"I am. There're some college credits I can earn now, so I'm doing it. I finished my GED, so now I'm taking classes at WSU."

"Okay, that's right. Well, how are your intrusive thoughts when you're in class?"

"They used to be really bad. Like when I took the ACT the second time, it started to happen. But it usually doesn't happen in class."

"How did you do on the ACT?"

"I got the same exact score."

We both laughed.

"What was the score?" he asked.

I rolled my eyes. "Twenty-six."

"What was your GPA in high school?"

"Really? Let's not go there. We're having a good session."

He threw his head back and laughed. "Oh, Branson. So why were you taking the ACT again?"

"I wanted at least one more point on my ACT to get a higher tier of my scholarship."

"Any more tests coming up?"

"Yeah."

"Are you going to take it again?"

"No," I chuckled. "I kind of took it as a sign that I wasn't supposed to take it again."

We both laughed.

"Are you this happy most of the time?"

"Yeah. Usually." I leaned back and felt my cell phone in the pocket of my jeans. It was still recording. "Yeah. I am."

"How about your thinking? Is it always logical, or do you find it jumping around a lot?"

"It's usually logical. I don't find myself jumping around."

"Still no alcohol or drugs." He posed it more as a statement than a question.

"None."

"Okay, just so you know, with your kind of ailment, alcohol and pot could exacerbate it."

"Yes." I nodded. "I remember."

He made a few notes, then glanced at the clock. "I think we may need to up the dosage on your antipsychotic medicine," he said toward the conclusion of our session.

"Uh, how much are we talking?"

"Another twenty milligrams."

"Uh, okay, sure."

He must have heard the hesitancy in my voice, because he quickly explained his reasoning. "I'm trying to get you to where the intrusive thoughts aren't bothersome."

"Okay."

"There are people with heavy hallucinations who are on much higher doses. You're still on a healthy dose, and the little bump will minimize the intrusive thoughts."

"Okeydokey."

"Everything good with you and your family?" he asked.

"Yeah, everything's going well."

"All right. Any plans for spring break?"

"Thought I'd go hang out with an old friend."

"That sounds fun." Dr. Cordova cupped his knees with his hands when he stood. "Okay, Branson, I'll see you again in a month."

I stood and shook his hand. "See you then, Doc."

I walked to the front of the office and made my next appointment, tucking the reminder card into my pocket beside my cell phone. After I climbed in my car and had driven far enough away from the doctor's office, I pulled out my cell phone and stopped the recording.

"Thanks, Branson," I said.

He looked at me from the passenger seat. *Trevor?*

"Tick tock. You just bought me another month of freedom."

ACKNOWLEDGMENTS

I always knew *A Divided Mind* would require a publisher who would read my manuscript and be as passionate about it as I was.

Olivia Ventura, my romance editor with Hot Tree Publishing, was the first reader in the industry who messaged me, "This book needs to be published," and then together with publisher, Becky Johnson, ensured that it happened.

I fumbled my way through my first call with Becky Johnson about *A Divided Mind*. My work with Hot Tree Publishing was nothing short of wonderful, so when Becky told me of the new imprint, Tangled Tree, I knew the publisher I long imagined and prayed for had materialized.

Becky, thank you. Thank you for not judging me, my son, or the work. Thank you for letting me into your publishing family with open arms. You have fulfilled a promise I made to my son, and for that, I am forever grateful.

Kristin Scearce, I was fearful when I saw the many red edits and comments, only to find that you understood this story, my voice, and worked hard to maintain both. Thank you. I look forward to your editing finesse with the sequel!

Jas Ward with Ink-N-Flow Management Group, you made the process of rebranding me and my work fun! Thank you for adding humor to my life and always being available to field my crazy questions. #INFTeamBilliter

I was newly remarried when I began writing this story. To my groom, Ron Gullberg, thank you for understanding that the only way I was going to work through what was happening was by writing through it. I often forget we're married because it's so easy with you. I love you to the moon and back. #BilliterGullberg #Always

And finally to my children…

Austin Thomas, thank you for helping to shape this work with your humor and compassion. I know this wasn't easy for you. Thank you for opening your heart and sharing it with me.

Ciara Thomas, sometimes I wonder who parents who! Thank you for grounding me during this writing process and then nailing the tagline!

Super Cooper, you make parenting effortless. I love your giggle and funny jokes. Thank you for sharing me with your brothers and sister.

ABOUT M. BILLITER

M. Billiter is an award-winning author, cancer survivor, and college writing instructor best known for her emotional honesty. She doesn't write about well-adjusted people, but rather the wounds in life. M. Billiter writes with clarity and raw emotion to explore difficult subjects and issues close to her heart.

WWW.MBILLITER.COM

WWW.FACEBOOK.COM/MBILLITERAUTHOR

ABOUT THE PUBLISHER

As Hot Tree Publishing's first imprint branch, Tangled Tree Publishing aims to bring darker, twisted, more tangled reads to its readers. Established in 2015, we have seen rousing success as a rising publishing house in the industry motivated by our enthusiasm and keen eye for talent. Driving us is our passion for the written word of all genres, but with Tangled Tree Publishing, we're embarking on a whole new adventure with words of mystery, suspense, crime, and thrillers.

WWW.HOTTREEPUBLISHING.COM

WWW.FACEBOOK.COM/TANGLEDTREEPUBLISHING